"We should be going back." She had meant to speak firmly, but her words came out in a quiver that ended abruptly as Hawkley gathered her into his arms.

Rosamund felt as though this was where she had longed to be all her life. Here there was no sense of lack, or homesickness, or loneliness. Here was security and excitement and the joyous realization that she had come home.

And then he kissed her, and all these thoughts shivered away. Rosamund felt herself lifted out of time and place to a universe where no one existed but the two of them.

For a moment the magic held. Then one of the grays flung up its head and snorted, and like a thunderclap, reality returned. To his horror Hawkley realized that he was kissing Rosamund. He was kissing her in the open road as if she were some common serving wench.

And this was the woman he had promised to safeguard!

Also by Rebecca Ward
Published by Fawcett Books:

FAIR FORTUNE
LORD LONGSHANKS
LADY IN SILVER
CINDERELLA'S STEPMOTHER
ENCHANTED RENDEZVOUS
MADAM MYSTERY
GRAND DECEPTION

THE WILD ROSE

Rebecca Ward

FAWCETT CREST • NEW YORK

Sale of this book without a front cover may be unauthorized. If this book is coverless, it may have been reported to the publisher as "unsold or destroyed" and neither the author nor the publisher may have received payment for it.

A Fawcett Crest Book
Published by Ballantine Books
Copyright © 1993 by Maureen Wartski

All rights reserved under International and Pan-American Copyright Conventions. Published in the United States by Ballantine Books, a division of Random House, Inc., New York, and simultaneously in Canada by Random House of Canada Limited, Toronto.

Library of Congress Catalog Card Number: 92-97065

ISBN 0-449-22164-4

Manufactured in the United States of America

First Edition: March 1993

For Ruth and Ed Booth, on their 50th wedding anniversary.

Chapter One

While trundling up the stairs en route to his tea, the Viscount Craye nearly collided with the Duchess of Broon and her eight-year-old daughter. With what he considered remarkable aplomb he regained his composure and bowed.

His greeting was met with a poisonous glare. Startled, the viscount blinked, regrouped, and tried again. "Er . . . how is Your Grace this afternoon?" he inquired.

The lady vouchsafed no answer as she sailed past him, but her daughter stuck out her tongue and made a hideous face before following her mother down the stairs.

Much shaken, the viscount proceeded to the first-floor yellow saloon. Here he found his wife prostrate on the orange Chinese daybed while his mother-in-law, Lady Orme, stood by exhorting her dearest Cassandra to remain calm.

"Good Gad, ma'am," the viscount said, gasping. "What's to do here?"

The viscountess was unable to reply, but her mother sighed deeply. "Nothing short of disaster, Craye," she intoned. "Little did I know when Orme quit this vale of tears, compelling me to seek the protection of my son-in-law, that I should be subject to such a terrible scene. To behold a guest—and she the wife of a peer—insulted under the roof of my own daughter is too much."

"Y-y'mean, someone insulted the duchess?" The viscount's small, nearsighted eyes widened at the thought. "Who?"

His viscountess raised her golden head, ornamented with ribbons that exactly matched her becoming primrose-colored muslin day dress, and wailed, "Who *else*?"

"I am afraid Cassandra means me," a clear voice explained.

A tall young woman had walked briskly into the room. "I'm sorry the duchess was angry," she went on, "but I couldn't be a party to an injustice."

The viscountess once more collapsed onto the daybed. Her lord and master goggled nervously at his younger sister. "*What* injustice?" he demanded. "Explain yourself, Rosa."

Before Miss St. Helm could reply, Lady Orme interposed, "Ask your sister if she did not take it upon herself to reprimand dear little Charlotte."

"I did. She is an unspeakable brat. Bevan, Charlotte found Penelope Weaver playing in the back garden. She shouted at Penelope and tore off the head of her doll. And when the poor child went to defend her property, Charlotte pushed her down and kicked her."

Lady Orme looked down her high-bridged nose. "My dear Rosamund," she said, sniffing, "the child of a gatekeeper cannot be compared to the scion of a ducal house. Moreover,

2

the guttersnipe actually dared to raise her hand to Charlotte."

"So would you if someone tore off your child's head." An appreciative spark lit Rosamund's dark blue eyes. "Penelope landed a facer on the brat, who bellowed as if she were being scalped. Charlotte accused Penelope of starting the brangling, but fortunately I was walking in the garden and saw what really happened."

The viscountess sat bolt upright on the daybed and addressed her sister-in-law in throbbing tones. "Was it *necessary* to lead the child into the house by the ear? The duchess is one of the most well-connected women in society. I have tried for *months* to have Her Grace visit us here in Kent. Now I am persuaded that she will never set foot in this house again."

"You may well be fortunate." Rosamund walked over to the table, which was set for tea, and poured herself a cup. "The duchess reminds me of a Scottish fur trader we knew at Port Arthur, Robbie McKenzie by name. He was pompous, arrogant, and quite vicious when crossed. Papa said he would never turn his back on Robbie, and he was right."

The viscountess lost her temper and shrieked, "How *can* you compare the duchess to a *fur trader*?"

Rosamund felt a twinge of remorse. She knew that since their father's death over a year ago, she had been a sore trial to Bevan and his wife. She was fond of her fussy, stodgy brother and really did not mean to antagonize him or his wife, but unfortunately she seemed to be constantly falling afoul of the endless rules that regulated their lives.

She attempted to explain. "I feel that a person's character is more important than his rank. Let me ask you this: Could you honestly trust the duchess—or Charlotte?"

Recalling his encounter with the child on the stairs, the

viscount felt a rush of fellow feeling for his sister. "Something in that," he conceded. Then, catching Lady Orme's baleful eye, he quailed visibly and subsided.

"That," Lady Orme said waspishly, "is the sort of talk that will not *do* in polite circles." Sinking into a gold damask chair, she unfurled an ivory and lace fan, which she commenced to wave languidly in the air. "You have hardly had a conventional upbringing, my dear Rosamund, but surely you must see that what was suitable in the wilds of Canada is not acceptable here."

"Is it acceptable to bully people who cannot defend themselves?" The afternoon caught the blue lights in Rosamund's black hair as she set down her teacup and turned to face Lady Orme. "If there is no fair play here in England, ma'am, I prefer the 'wilds of Canada.' "

The viscount scowled. All too well could he recognize the influence of their late father.

Jeremy, Lord St. Helm, had not been content to be younger brother to a viscount. He had wanted adventure and "experiences." In true cockle-brained fashion he had decided to leave his comfortable estate and living and travel to Canada with his wife and small daughter so as to acquaint himself firsthand with his investments in the Hudson Bay Company.

Lord Jeremy, Lady Mary, and ten-year-old Rosamund had taken ship at Liverpool and with their entourage traveled to the New World. Once there they had traveled fifty-two miles up the west coast of Hudson Bay and settled there for many years.

A timid youth, Bevan had never wanted to go to Canada. The thought of living in primitive conditions and rubbing elbows with Canadians, fur-trading Scots, wild Indians, an American or two, and other unspeakable folk was enough to bring on the hives. He had been profoundly grateful that his education had been considered important enough for him to remain in England and reside with his bachelor uncle, the then current Viscount Craye.

Life had gone on like this for nine years. Then Lady Mary had succumbed to diptheria, and that same year the viscount had been killed in a hunting accident. Jeremy St. Helm had perforce returned to England with his motherless daughter and assumed the title.

Bevan cringed at the memory, for his late father had made an execrable viscount. He had no sense of his own consequence and was always shocking people by talking about the dignity of the common man. Then, a year and some months ago, he'd had a severe set-to with the Marchioness Malquith about the social order, succumbed to an apoplexy, and had been gathered to his fathers.

Bevan, who worried about almost everything, took seriously the responsibility of succeeding to the title. He had also hoped to restore some luster to the family name. But how, he asked himself, could he do so with his sister living under his roof? When he recalled Rosamund's confrontation with the duchess, it was all he could do to keep from having apoplexy himself.

"Good Gad, Rosa," he growled, "you can't go on in this way. You ain't attained your majority, and since you're in my care, you must stop acting in that hurly-burly way." Then, encountering his sister's steady gaze, he faltered, cleared his throat, and looked uncertainly at his wife.

The viscountess hastened to pick up the cudgels. "Bevan is right, Rosa. You are in England now, and when in Rome, et cetera." She paused to add in a coaxing voice, "I am persuaded that you could be *most* popular if you chose. Lady Selfield was saying, just the other day, that she would be *delighted* if you would call on her and her daughter."

Rosamund, who considered Lady Selfield a mean, hypocritical woman and her daughter the worst gossipmonger she had ever met, remained eloquently mute.

"And then, you ride *so* well," the viscountess continued. "Turn that talent to advantage and accept the invitation to Lady Natherby's outing. There will be a ride in the woods and a picnic luncheon for the ladies while the gentlemen ride to hounds."

"You forget," Lady Orme pointed out acidly, "that Rosa does not care for fox hunting."

"It is because I saw so many wild creatures in the forests around York Factory," Rosamund explained. Her eyes sparkled with enthusiasm as she recalled those cool, dark forests. "Silver foxes, pine martens, and wolves—all of them free and so magnificent and so proud! I wish you could have seen them. Then you would understand why I hate to think of a terrified fox running for his life with a pack of hounds at his heels."

"Oh, rubbish, Rosa," the viscount exclaimed petulantly. "Good Gad, the pater made money from the Hudson Bay Company, which dealt in furs. I tell you plain, I don't understand you."

Neither did she understand Bevan. Unhappily Rosamund looked at her family and saw incomprehension, distaste, and distrust in the three pairs of eyes that were regarding her fixedly. Not for the first time that day, she felt a wave of homesickness tinged with claustrophobia.

"Perhaps a change of scene will help," the viscountess was suggesting. "We were in mourning for your papa last year, but this spring will be different and we hope to reside in London for at least part of the season. Rosa will find the cotillion balls and turtle suppers and musical assemblies *most* diverting."

Visibly wincing at the thought, Rosamund said, "It may be that I won't go to London at all. I've had an invitation to visit a friend."

In the surprised silence that followed this announcement, Lady Orme reflected that any acquaintance of Rosamund's was sure to be socially unacceptable.

Not for the first time, she regretted the fact that her pretty daughter, a diamond of the first water and the toast of her season, had married Craye. Not that the man himself was in any way objectionable—he had a considerable fortune, a time-honored title, and had the added attraction of being pleasantly stupid and easily led—but his sister was quite another story.

A handsome girl, my lady thought, with that wealth of black hair and those almost violet eyes, but handsome was as handsome does, and Rosamund's views were keeping her on the shelf. She had already refused offers from several gentlemen, including the most eligible Marquess of Bradmere. Since she was twenty-four and past her prime marrying years, Bevan might have her on his hands for a long time—perhaps forever.

The thought of having to deal with Miss St. Helm each day of her life made Lady Orme's tones more vinegary than usual. "And from whom did the invitation come, pray?" she asked.

"From Amber House in Sussex. You see—"

She was interrupted by the viscountess clapping her hands. "But how *wonderful*. I did not know you were acquainted with Lady Amber."

"Good family." The viscount approved. "I know Lord Amber slightly m'self because his property abuts that of a schoolfriend of mine, the new Earl of Hawkley." He glanced at his wife and mother-in-law and continued with studied nonchalance, "Julian Dane was a few years behind me at Eton."

The viscountess smiled reminiscently. "I collect meeting the earl—he had not yet succeeded to the title then—on the occasion of our wedding. A tall gentleman, with broad shoulders and chestnut hair and the *most* speaking dark eyes—" She caught her mother's eye and added hastily, "That is to say, *I* did not remark him, but all the other ladies present cast sheep's eyes at him. Do you remember him, Rosa? But no—You had the grippe the week Bevan and I were married."

"I'd have asked Hawkley to visit us," the viscount said, "but he's been busy since his father died. Got his properties to see to, and hunting and shooting and his horses, naturally. Always was a top sawyer, Julian. I'll call on him when I escort Rosa to Amber's."

"That would not be possible," Rosamund said. "Lord and Lady Amber no longer own the property. Their house was sold to pay Lord Amber's gaming debts. But," Rosamund added helpfully, "I'm sure that Lucy will be glad to have you visit her."

The viscountess frowned. "Really, Rosa, you are being *most* vexing. Who is Lucy?"

"I am telling this badly," Rosamund admitted. "Let me try again. Lucy is Mrs. Sample, an American lady who lived near us at Port Arthur. She—she nursed Mama when she became so ill."

Rosamund's expressive eyes grew shadowed; her clear voice faltered into silence. After a moment she continued, "I was sick of the putrid throat myself, and Lucy came to stay with us and nurse me after Mama died. She was so kind! Later, she and her husband—he was a very successful fur trapper and trader—decided to come to England with their

8

daughter, Anemone, and they established a business in Norfolk. We have written to each other many times, but I have not seen the Samples for years."

Lady Orme dropped her fan. "Rosamund, you cannot be thinking of visiting a—a colonial. We are at war with America. Think what people would say if you were found consorting with the enemy!"

Rosamund stared hard at the cream-colored wall behind my lady's head. She drew several deep breaths—a calming trick she had learned from Tall Reed, a wise old Mohawk she had known in Canada—and managed to reply quite civilly.

"I can assure you, ma'am, that Lucy is completely loyal to the crown." Seeing that Lady Orme remained unconvinced, Rosamund added, "She is a widow, now. Mr. Sample passed away last year and left her with a great deal of money. That is how she came to buy Amber House."

She looked at her brother, saw that he was about to make some further objection, and rose from her chair. "As Cassandra says, I'm certain that I will be the better for a change of scene. I will write to Lucy at once."

No one spoke as Rosamund left the room. The yellow saloon remained deathly silent until her footsteps had died away. Then the viscountess clenched her small fists and drummed them on the daybed. "No," she wailed. "No, no, *no*!"

The viscount gave a strangled groan. "My sister's going to visit an American who smells of the shop. Oh, by Gad, if word of this gets out, we'll be the laughingstock of our set."

"Cannot you reason with her?" demanded his mother-in-law. "Calm yourself, Cassandra, I beg . . . Hysterics bring on wrinkles, and that would never do. Craye, I demand you take action. You are the head of the family and Rosamund is dependent on you."

"No, she ain't. She don't have full control of her fortune yet, but the pater left her with a comfortable allowance. And you know well enough, ma'am," the viscount added dispiritedly, "that my sister does what she likes."

Social disgrace loomed on the horizon. The viscountess winced as if she could already hear the poisonous whispers and rumors flying among her circle. The viscount cringed, envisioning the contempt of his friends. A man who could not control his sister's madcap ways would have little respect from his peers. He began to pace the room.

"She is bound to disgrace herself in Sussex," Lady Orme fumed. "If only Orme were alive! *He* would not allow this wicked girl to ruin our good name."

The viscount paused in his pacing to object to this. "That's doing it too brown, ma'am. Rosa ain't wicked, she's just—"

"She is wild to a fault. No, Craye, I refuse to wrap plain facts in clean linen. Character more important than rank, indeed! What your sister needs is someone to teach her that her ways will not be tolerated in civilized society."

She fixed a freezing look on her son-in-law, but for once he did not quail before it. Instead he exclaimed, "You've got something there. Rosa does need a strong hand. And I've thought of the very man who can get her to cut line. I'll write to Julian."

The ladies stared, and Lady Orme demanded, "The Earl of Hawkley? What, pray, can *he* do?"

"Should think he can do anything. He's a devil of a fellow, Julian. A top sawyer, as I've said, and a bruising rider to hounds. Resourceful, too. Not the sort of fellow to cut his stick at anything."

Lady Orme was regarding her son-in-law with something bordering on respect. "But how can you be sure that the earl will help us?"

"Julian and I were at school together. What's more, he's a peer of the realm, now. He'll realize that if we all started consorting with shopkeepers and fur traders, we'd all be in the basket."

The viscount drew himself to his full five feet four inches. "Bound to see that he can't let the side down," he said earnestly. "And I'll tell you something else, Mama-in-law. If Hawkley can't handle Rosa and get her to see what's what, no one can."

Chapter Two

"Is nothing sacred these days?"

Julian Dane, fifth Earl of Hawkley, tossed the letter he had been reading onto his rosewood writing desk. The gilt-tooled leather surface of the desk was already buried in the letters, invitations, and bills that the earl's secretary, a spare man who appeared even smaller next to his lordship's six feet of brawn and muscle, had this morning been endeavoring to bring to his employer's attention.

"M'lud?" he inquired.

"Talking about my new neighbor, Beamler. The one who bought the Amber place."

"Oh, yes, m'lud. It was bought by a Mrs. Sample. A widow, I understand, and an American by birth."

An expression of the most profound distaste darkened the earl's countenance. "The sins of the fathers aren't just foisted on one's children, these days," he philosophized. "They affect the neighbors as well. To think that I used to ride to hounds with Amber and sat down to cards with the man. Then he gets himself knocked into the horse nails and sells his estate to a dashed American."

His secretary coughed diffidently behind his hand and pointed out that Mrs. Sample had apparently married an Englishman.

"A retired fur trader," scoffed the earl, "who turned merchant and speculator before cocking up his toes. Raff and chaff, Beamler, raff and chaff! I want nothing to do with the worthy Mrs. Sample."

He strode over to his study window, which looked down on a well-ordered garden. Beyond the garden lay meadows and trout brooks shimmering under fitful sunshine, and farther on there were farmlands and orchards that surrounded the village of Hawk-on-River.

The earl's ancestors had controlled this choice acreage for over two centuries. During that time there had been a blood feud or two, marriages that mingled Hawkley blood with the best houses in England, challenges, duels, and even a crime of passion that had resulted in the second Earl of Hawkley flying for his life to the Continent. But never before had the noble house been called upon to fraternize with Americans.

Hawkley continued gloomily, "Wish that Bevan and I hadn't gone to school together, but wishing won't mend fences."

"I'm not certain I follow, m'lud," Beamler said cautiously. "Does Your Lordship refer to the Viscount Craye?"

"The very one. Didn't travel in the same circles, but he makes it sound as if we were bosom bows." The earl nodded at the letter on his desk. "Craye's written me that his sister is visiting this Mrs. Sample. Asks me to keep an eye on Miss Rosamund St. Helm. A little too loud, that, Beamler!"

"Yes, m'lud. If I might make so bold as to ask, what will you do?"

Once more the earl surveyed his acreage. The skittish sun had burst out of the clouds, and after the recent March rains, the sight was irresistible.

"I'm going for a ride." Hawkley waved a nonchalant hand at the littered desk. "Take care of things here . . . That's a good fellow."

The secretary looked resigned. Though basically fair-minded and decent, his young employer seldom considered the convenience of his underlings. However, today he needed to bring a matter of some importance to the earl's attention.

"There is the matter of the tenant farmers, m'lud—" Beamler began.

But the earl was already striding out of the study and shouting for his horse to be saddled. He was going riding, and the world would have to cool its heels and wait on his pleasure. That was the way of the world, Beamler knew. The earl's late father—God rest him—had been cut of the same cloth.

Meanwhile Hawkley was calling for his valet. "My riding coat, Inchley, and my hat. Not that trumpery thing my sister sent me, either," he added sternly. "Maggie might think she knows London fashion, but I won't make a cake out of myself. I want my old one."

"Yes, my lord," murmured the valet. Hawkley glanced at the man and noted in passing that Inchley looked red-eyed and rather pasty in the face. But the announcement that Saladin was saddled and waiting at the door crowded out all other considerations.

A few moments later, Hawkley trotted his coal black stallion, which had been booted and spurred, past the gardens and made for the woods that formed the northern border of his estate. The March sun was bright, the air fresh and clean, and his spirits rose.

Hawkley Manor was not as princely an estate as some of his other properties, but the earl loved it the most. Perhaps this was because it carried happy memories of his late father and of his mother, now serenely ensconced in her own domain near Merton. Hawkley Manor also recalled happy childhood days with his younger sister, now married to his good friend, the Marquess of Hare.

And it was precisely because he loved this piece of ground, the earl thought, that he could not forgive Amber for selling his estate. It showed a profound lack of proper feeling for a man to gamble away his land, the symbol of his quality and worth. True, Amber had never been much more than a pigeon fancier, but even he should have realized that he had a responsibility to his ancestral name.

"And to his peers, dash it," Hawkley growled. "No man is an island, and all that rubbish. Now an American counter jumper's my next-door neighbor."

And as if that were not bad enough, here was Craye asking him to oversee his sister. Hawkley's heart sank. From memories of the viscount, he could almost picture his sister.

"Must be an antidote," he said, sighing, "tallow-faced, rabbit-toothed, and scared of her shadow. Never did care much for Bevan—stiff-rumped prig, come to that—but a fellow can't let the side down."

The enormity of this responsibility caused the earl to slow his horse. As he did so, he was aware of a sudden rustling in the underbrush nearby. When it came again, Hawkley drew rein and looked about him. He could see nothing, but when Saladin threw up his head and whickered, there was an answering whinny.

A trespasser? Hawkley's dark brows drew together as he

15

recalled that his estate had been plagued by a poacher for some time. The crafty villain had been making raids on pheasant and rabbit with impunity while his incompetent groundskeeper apparently stood by and twiddled his thumbs.

"Kittering's an idiot, but this time you'll have to deal with me, my buck." Grimly Hawkley dismounted and slipped softly through the underbrush toward a grove of spruce that grew nearby.

Now the rustling sounds were louder and there was an anguished, piercing yelp. At the sound, Hawkley's dark eyes hardened. He had the rascal now.

Just then a clear voice spoke. "Do not struggle so. I almost have you free."

The earl parted the evergreens and saw a fox swinging by its leg from a wire noose. A young woman in a fawn-colored riding habit was attempting to free the animal.

"I know that you're suffering," she was saying. "You haven't had water or food for some time, have you? I wish I could catch the brute who did this to you."

The fox saw Hawkley and gave a yowl of fear. Its rescuer turned, and the earl had an impression of coal black hair and amethyst eyes fringed with sooty lashes before she turned her back to him and got back to the business at hand.

"Have you got a knife with you?" she demanded over her shoulder.

Hawkley saw that the wire noose that had trapped the fox was attached by a rope to a tree. When he walked closer, he realized that the knots were too tight to be loosened and the rope too thick to break.

"I have a knife myself, but unfortunately I left it in the house," his companion explained. "I've tried sawing at the rope with this rock, but it's slow work and the fox is suffering."

"I think I can snap the rope." Hawkley grasped the ends

of the rope and tugged. The frayed hemp gave, and the fox fell to earth. As it lay dazed, the girl dropped to her knees and loosened the noose from about its leg.

The animal stared at her for a moment, then got up and limped away. She watched it disappear into the underbrush, then got to her feet to face Hawkley. "It doesn't appear to be lamed, thank heavens. Did you set this trap?"

"God, no." The earl looked with disfavor at the wire noose at his feet. "I don't allow these foul things on my land, either, but I've been plagued by a dashed poacher these last few months."

"The man deserves to be horsewhipped."

"I'd like to do the whipping," Hawkley agreed warmly. "A poacher's no better than a thief."

He could not decide whether her eyes were dark blue or amethyst as she regarded him soberly. "I meant that this type of trap is inhumane and causes terrible suffering to animals. I understand that people must trap animals for food, but there are ways and ways."

Hawkley could think of nothing else to say but, "So there are."

"Snarling Wolf hunted beaver with an ice pick lashed to a stick. His skill was pitted against the animal's instincts, you see, so that either of them could have won. Besides, Snarling Wolf respected his prey and gave it a clean death. Not like this."

She kicked at the wire noose and then looked up to smile. "Thank you for helping. It's a good thing you were strong enough to free Reynard."

With the sunlight dancing in them, her eyes were indeed amethyst, Hawkley decided. They looked at him directly, without any artifice, a fact that was not only surprising but also vastly refreshing, and her smile was like pure sunshine.

He liked the way she moved, too—with a crisp, quick step and an assurance that was still completely graceful. But all this talk about beaver and someone called Snarling Wolf could mean only one thing.

"I'm Rosamund St. Helm," she was saying.

Rosamund noted the astonishment in the tall gentleman's brown eyes as he took her outstretched hand. "Julian Dane, at your service. You are— Ah, you're *Bevan's* sister?"

"I am. And you must be his friend, the Earl of Hawkley."

Miss St. Helm's straight speech was unusual in a woman, but Hawkley thought that it added to her charm. Everything about her—from her well-fitting riding habit to the dashing plumes in her fashionable hat—was delightful. He looked her over with approval, then noted that her fine kid gloves had been lacerated by her morning's work.

"Are you sure you haven't been cut by that rock?" he asked worriedly.

"Quite sure. I've known how to deal with traps since I was a child."

"I forgot about that. No doubt you do."

Rosamund was warmed by the admiration in the tall earl's voice. She liked the way his brown eyes reflected his smile and the humor in his strong-boned face. The swift and efficient way he had dealt with the fox made a pleasant change from the mopes and fidgets of Bevan's friends.

Since Bevan had told her that he and Hawkley were old friends, she had been expecting the worst. Rosamund was truly relieved that Lucy Sample's nearest neighbor was not one of the stiff-necked aristocrats that England seemed to produce in large quantities.

"I will tell Mrs. Sample that I met you," she told him. "Perhaps you will come and take tea with us one day."

Dazzled by the brilliance of her smile, Hawkley forgot

what he thought of the American interloper and said heartily, "Capital. I look forward to seeing you again, Miss St. Helm."

They beamed at each other in perfect charity, and Rosamund felt an odd stir of reluctance as she said, "Now I must be on my way. Lucy and Anemone will be wondering what I am about, and Meadows will be as cross as crabs."

"Who is Meadows?"

"My groom. The old torment has been with the family since I was in leading strings, and he considers himself my social conscience. According to him, a lady does not ride alone." Rosamund looked rueful. "You can make book that he will rake me over the coals for stealing out without him this morning."

Hawkley briefly considered the various ladies of his acquaintance. None of them ever went riding without a groom in tow, and some would not even consider walking in her garden without an abigail in attendance. He wondered what his sister, the Marchioness of Hare, would think of a young woman who rescued wild creatures from a poacher's trap.

He glanced down at her as they began to walk through the clearing and noted that Miss St. Helm was tall for a woman. Most females of his acquaintance barely topped his shoulder, but this lady was only three or four inches shorter than he. The top of her glossy black head was on a par with his ear, and the earl speculated that if she raised her face, he could easily touch her lips with his.

So intent was he on watching Rosamund that Hawkley almost tripped over a root that snaked across their path. The astonishing girl beside him reached out a hand to steady him as if this were the most natural thing in the world.

"Be careful," she warned. "There are a great number of roots in these woods." She looked around her, adding wistfully, "The trees around York Factory were much taller, of course, but this reminds me of home."

The earl gave himself a mental shake and wondered what she was talking about. "York Factory is in . . . er . . . Canada?" he guessed.

"Yes. It's called a factory because the factor, the Hudson Bay Company's regional man in charge, lives there," Rosamund explained. "All the furs and trade goods passing to and from the company's holdings pass through York Factory."

Hawkley listened carefully to Miss St. Helm's descriptions of her Canadian home, which had apparently consisted of several buildings laid out in an H shape. York Factory seemed to have been an uncouth place with few comforts and no social amenities. And even though Lady Mary had started a small library, not many of the people could read.

How could Lord Jeremy have been so caper-witted as to allow his wife and child to live in such a place for *two days*, let alone *nine years*? "Wasn't it lonely there?" Hawkley wondered aloud.

"Never. There was Snarling Wolf and Tall Reed and Little Marten—" Rosamund broke off to explain, "Tall Reed is a Mohawk medicine man, and Snarling Wolf is a Chippewa hunter. He's my friend Little Marten's father."

"I meant to ask if there weren't any *English* people at York Factory." Hawkley was beginning to understand why Craye might have a problem.

"Some of the traders were English," Rosamund said. "There was Joe Cormack, and One-ear Sanderson, and— Oh, so many others. How could I possibly be lonely? And besides, there was the wilderness itself."

She fell silent remembering the forests and the sparkling lakes and the great expanse of Hudson Bay. She recalled the shy deer that lived in woods where the trees were as tall and as grand as church spires. She thought of the winter storms that buried the world in snowdrifts taller than a man. Beside such memories, the English woods seemed wholly insipid.

But she must not keep going on about Canada and her youth. It was not her custom to do so. Remembering brought little except homesickness, and besides, Cassandra and Lady Orme were indifferent to such reminiscences, while Bevan had made it plain that he did not enjoy such tales. Yet here she had been babbling about York Factory to the Earl of Hawkley, whom she had met for the first time not ten minutes ago.

"I am a sad rattle," Rosamund said, apologizing. "My sister-in-law tells me that I prose on too long and she is right. I'm afraid I've bored you, sir."

Whatever she might be, Miss St. Helm was no bore. "Certainly not," Hawkley said heartily. "I can understand why England seems tame. How long have you been back?"

"Four years, six months, and three days."

Hawkley grinned. "Doesn't sound as if you like it here."

"It is different in England," Rosamund admitted. "The people are different, too . . ."

Rosamund caught herself. She realized she had been on the point of telling the earl how stuffy she found the English upper class. But then, the Earl of Hawkley did not act like any aristocrat she had met. He was pleasant and a good listener. He seemed miles removed from people like the Duchess of Broon and Lady Orme.

"Hard for you to adjust, but you'll grow to like it here," Hawkley said, reassuring her. "Sussex, now, is a capital place."

From the way he looked about him, Rosamund could see that the earl loved his home as much as she had loved York

21

Factory. Turnabout was fair play, so Rosamund asked, "Did you grow up in Sussex?"

He nodded. "My father taught me to ride, hunt, shoot, *and* drive at Hawkley Manor. Don't live here all the year, of course. I maintain a residence in London. Now *that's* a splendid city, don't you think?"

To her, London had seemed overcrowded and full of noisome odors, but as she judged from the earl's expression, his impressions of the city were very different. "I am not used to city life," Rosamund said, temporizing.

There was a cough behind them, and a tentative voice ventured, "M'lord?"

A stocky, stubble-jowled individual was standing some distance away. He had whipped off his cap and was regarding the earl nervously. "I need a word with you, m'lord," he mumbled.

Hawkley's dark brows drew together in a frown as he recognized his groundskeeper. "What is it, Kittering?" he demanded.

The man approached somewhat gingerly. "Sorry I am to disturb you, m'lord. I dunno exactly how to say this, m'lord."

"Just say what's on your mind and be done with it."

Impatience rode the young earl's voice, and Rosamund's delicate brows rose slightly. That voice and that intonation were only too familiar.

The earl was using the selfsame tone in which Lady Orme reproved her underlings. It was the voice with which the Duchess of Broon had berated the gatekeeper's little girl. Once more, Rosamund realized, she was watching a member of the Quality bully an inferior.

The hapless Kittering was stammering that the poacher had managed to escape again. "He's that clever, m'lord.

22

He's got around my men. And what's worse, he's set traps right here in the north woods, right under our very noses."

Hawkley looked even more impatient. "I know what the man's done, Kittering. Just find the dashed blackguard and stop him from pillaging my woods."

"We're trying. But—"

"You're supposed to see that I'm not plagued by poachers. What else do I pay you for? Not to come whining to me." The earl's voice hardened as he added, "If you can't do your duty, I'll find someone who can."

"Yes, m'lord." Kittering was almost in tears. "I'm that sorry, m'lord. But the poacher's that clever, see, and—"

"Oh, get out of my sight!"

The discomfited groundskeeper fairly turned tail and ran. Hawkley glared after him for several minutes before turning back to Rosamund. "I'm sorry about that," he exclaimed. "Fellow's insufferable."

"It was insufferable, indeed," she agreed.

"Kittering's been trying to run that poacher to earth for months. If it weren't for the fact that he was my father's groundskeeper, I'd get rid of him."

"Do you mean that you talked to him in *that* way even though he's an old servant? One who has been in the family for years?"

The new note in her voice made the earl look at her. "Beg your pardon?" he asked.

"You need not beg *my* pardon," Rosamund retorted warmly. "Mr. Kittering is the one you mistreated."

"'Mistreated'!" repeated the earl in astonishment. "Dash it, the man's plainly inept—"

"So would you be if people were always shouting you down. Instead of berating the man, have you considered listening to him?"

25

"I *was* listening to him!" the earl protested, adding wrathfully, "Precious little he had to say, too. Fobbing me off with all those excuses—"

"I meant," Rosamund interrupted, "that you should listen to his ideas. And to the other servants' ideas, for that matter."

"Listen to *servants*?"

Hawkley was almost speechless. Rosamund said crisply, "Servants have ideas on occasion. And feelings, too. You humiliated Mr. Kittering in front of a stranger. If someone from your set had talked to you in that way, you would have sent him your cartel or knocked him down. But because Mr. Kittering is in your service, he's supposed to have no feelings."

The earl grew aware of the fact that his mouth was hanging open. He closed it with a snap. "Kittering," he said slowly and carefully, as though explaining matters to someone hard-of-hearing, "is my groundskeeper. He takes care of my grounds and my game. It's his duty. He's got a responsibility to deal with poachers, and he hasn't fulfilled that responsibility. I was bringing it to his attention."

"You were humiliating him." Rosamund looked down her small, straight nose at the earl. She had to tip her head backward and stare up at him in order to achieve this feat, but the effect was one of withering contempt nonetheless.

"Servants are human beings," she informed him. "They deserve to be treated with some measure of respect."

Bereft of speech by this piece of lunacy, Hawkley could only make a strangled sound in his throat.

Rosamund recognized that noise as one often produced by her brother. It meant that the earl was in a stamping temper. And as she looked up into the earl's now hard brown eyes, she realized that even though he had helped her with the trapped fox, Hawkley was a product of England. He was as much controlled by its pretensions as was Bevan.

In short, he was only another spoiled and effete aristocrat.

"I suppose," she said accusingly, "that you hunt foxes, too."

"Of course I hunt foxes. One thing has nothing to do with the other," Hawkley growled. "We're talking about Kittering's incompetence."

"Indeed?" Her soft lips curled. "I thought we were discussing your rudeness."

They were almost nose-to-nose. Hawkley realized that with her head tilted up as it was, Miss St. Helm's lips were indeed very close to his. But all thought of kissing her had vanished.

Instead, he glared down into her implacable amethyst eyes. She was unreasonable and insulting and completely in the wrong. No wonder Craye had despaired of such a termagant. For a moment Hawkley considered giving Miss St. Helm the setdown she richly deserved. Then, he remembered Craye's request—and his own manners.

With a stupendous effort, he pulled himself together, stepped backward, locked his hands behind his back, and said in a deadly-calm voice, "If you consider my behavior discourteous, I am sorry, madam."

Spoiled, effete, *and* sarcastic to boot. Rosamund bowed coldly and walked to her horse. Hawkley did not follow her or offer to hold her reins, but she did not need his help. Mounting with ease and grace, she cantered off without a backward glance.

"Dash and blast!" swore the earl.

For a moment he glowered at the rapidly disappearing horse and rider; then his sense of humor began to reassert itself.

So this was Rosamund St. Helm, the lady he was supposed

to bring up to the mark. "Suppose I'm lucky she didn't draw my claret," the earl said ruefully.

The task of reclaiming such a creature and rendering her socially acceptable would be a Herculean challenge. It might not even be possible. Hawkley winced as he recalled her frank speech, her admitted association with unsuitable persons, and her insane ideas about servants and underlings.

"The female's as mad as a March hare," Hawkley said musingly. "I should write to Craye and cry off. It's *his* sister. Let him deal with her."

Then he thought of the smile that had turned the blue of her eyes to the color of sun-washed violets. Perhaps, he thought, temporizing, it was not all the chit's fault.

Rosamund St. Helm had not only had the misfortune to have had a madman for a father, but she had also been brought up in an uncivilized land. How then was she expected to come up to the mark?

"Dash and blast that sapskull for saddling me with his problems!" The earl sighed. "Must keep an eye on his sister, though, I suppose. Can't let the side down."

He paused, hesitated, then made the supreme sacrifice. "I'll do it even if it means I have to fraternize with dashed Americans."

Chapter Three

When Rosamund returned to Amber House, the first thing she saw was her groom's scowling countenance. Meadows had positioned himself outside the main gate so that his mistress could not slip by him, and he was in such a state of agitation that the scant hairs on his head were standing almost upright.

He began to complain as soon as she came within earshot. "And ter think," he scolded, "that it was me what taught tha how t' ride, Miss Rosa. Nay, from what I see has come of it all, my sweet lady and my lord will be turning in their graves."

Knowing from experience that nothing would stop Meadows once he began his plaint, Rosamund waited in resigned patience.

"Haven't I taught tha that an English leddy cannot ride out by hersen? Nay, Miss Rosa," said Meadows, gaining momentum as he went along, "I was wi' thee in Canada, where tha lived for years wi' Mohocks and fur traders and such like riffraff, but tha'rt in England now. There's many here as will turn up their noses at a leddy that doesna follow the rules." He paused to add lugubriously, "Happen I'm too old. Happen tha needs a new and younger groom."

"Sneck up, do," Rosamund said, sighing. "You know very well that you are worth twenty ordinary grooms and that no one could possibly take better care of Isolde—or of me—and that we would be lost without you." She smiled at the old man, who sniffed loudly and attempted not to look pleased. "Stop raking me over the coals or I won't tell you about the fox I saved from the trap."

The telling took some time, and it was not till Rosamund had reached the stables that the old groom said musingly, "And so tha met the earl hisself, Miss Rosa. I ha' heard of His Lordship."

In the act of dismounting, Rosamund paused. "Have you indeed?"

"A sportsman, they say, who can take on Gentleman Jim hisself wi' the cuffs, but who has the lightest hands on the reins. He has a matched pair o' grays that His Highness, the Prince Regent hisself, would envy. Aye," Meadows went on, warming to the gossip, "it's said he's the spitting image of the old earl, God rest him, who died while still in his prime. I hear as the present earl's a pleasant gentleman and a good master as long as every man does his duty t' him."

Rosamund recalled the unpleasant scene she had just witnessed and wondered what his lordship, the earl, would say if he knew he was the subject of so much servants' chatter. "What about Hawkley's responsibilities to his servants?" she mused aloud.

Looking scandalized, Meadows told his mistress that such

thinking would not do in England. "There's them that's born t' be lords and leddies, and them that's born t' serve 'em," he lectured. "Nay, that's *my* job, sithee," he added as Rosamund attempted to lead her horse into the stables. "Th'art a leddy, think on. Go and tend to thy embroidery or read thy book and leave Isolde t' me."

Leaving Meadows in possession of the field, Rosamund retreated to Amber House. Here on the first-floor landing she surprised one of the underfootmen attempting to slide an arm around her redheaded abigail's waist.

"And himself thinking he's God's gift to females entirely." The girl giggled as the discomfitted footman hastily took himself off. "But what can ye expect from a bunch of hirelings? It's not much I'm thinking of them that is belowstairs, Miss Rosa."

In the few days she had been at Amber House, Rosamund had come to much the same conclusion. Apart from her own personal maid and Anemone's abigail, Lucy Sample had hired her staff from an employment agency, and they were hardly an inspiring lot.

"Are any of them mistreating you, Nancy?" she asked.

The girl gave a toss of her head. "I'd like to see anyone try."

She continued to gossip as she followed her mistress upstairs and helped her change out of her riding clothes. "That Mr. Bleak, the butler, is the worst of the lot, ma'am. Himself used to work for Lady Pomeran until she married last year. He gives himself airs and turns his nose up at Mrs. Sample because she was in trade and American-born." Nancy crinkled her own pert nose. "The footmen follow his lead."

Rosamund was thoughtful as she proceeded to the morning room, where the Samples, accompanied by a small, thin lady of indeterminate years, were sitting down to a late breakfast.

"There you are, dearie," called Mrs. Sample as Rosamund came into the room. "We would've waited on you, but Bleak said you'd already breakfasted."

Rosamund glanced at the butler who stood supervising the breakfast proceedings. He was a well-fleshed individual with an impressive carriage and a square, beefy face that conveyed such profound disdain that Rosamund itched to give him a lesson in courtesy. Instead she kissed her hostess's plump cheek and bade her good morning.

"*Is* it a good morning?" Anemone murmured, whereat the small, thin lady beside her halted in the act of conveying a piece of toast to her lips.

"Come, Miss Anemone, we must strive to be a ray of sunshine," she said reprovingly in a high, breathy voice. "Megrims in the young are not attractive."

"Hear that?" Mrs. Sample held out her fine china cup for more coffee, which was poured by a footman who equaled Bleak in arrogance. "Mrs. Devinter knows what's what, my girl, so you'd better listen to her."

The thin lady looked gratified and took more buttered toast. "I trust you had a pleasant ride, dear Miss St. Helm," she twittered. "Few things are comparable to the sight of dew sparkling on green meadows. In my youth, I, too— But those days are gone forever."

"I know what you mean," said Mrs. Sample sympathetically. "Old age brings aches and pains. Look at me. I used to get up at four of the morning and walk three miles to haul water for the cooking—with my musket tucked under my arm for fear I'd meet one of them bears. I was a slim bit of a gal, then, not like now."

A chuckle caused her ample frame to quiver in its morning

gown of deep blue muslin trimmed with lambsdown. The butler's countenance seemed also to quiver with distaste, and he looked down his nose.

Once again Rosamund held her tongue. This was Lucy's household, and if she was ever going to have any respect, Lucy herself would have to do something about her staff.

"One thing I'll never miss is getting up early," Mrs. Sample went on. "When Sample made his money I swore never to turn hand nor foot till ten o'clock—just like a highborn lady. Now ain't that something—me one of the swells?"

She beamed around the table, and Rosamund looked back affectionately at her hostess. Lucy had never been a pretty woman, with her blunt features and nondescript sandy hair, but she had good blue eyes, a ready laugh, and the strong physique suited to wilderness living. Since leaving York Factory she had put on weight and her broad American accent had softened somewhat, but she was essentially unchanged.

Mrs. Devinter was protesting. "No, no, Mrs. Sample. *Swells* is not the sort of word that a lady uses." She saw that the footman was about to remove the plate of toast and hastily snatched up the last piece as she added, "The word you are looking for is *quality*."

Lucy tried the word out on her tongue. "I'll try to remember," she said humbly. "It's ever so good of you, Mrs. Devinter, to 've answered my advertisement and come to teach me what's what. Without you the sw—the *quality* folks'd laugh their britches off at me."

Mrs. Devinter winced. Bleak looked disgusted. The attending footman screwed up his face into an expression of such contempt that Rosamund wanted to box his ears.

"Did you enjoy your morning ride, Rosa?" Lucy was continuing blithely. "When I was your age, I used to ride astraddle." Then, seeing the expression on Mrs. Devinter's

31

face, she added hastily, "Now, Rosa, don't you look the picture of health. You should ride out more often, Mona. Pale cheeks may be the fashion, but they give me the willies."

A sigh was Anemone's only answer, and Rosamund looked at her in some surprise. She had remembered Anemone as a sunny-tempered, vivacious child. Since her arrival at Amber House, however, Mona had done little save look morose.

The girl's blue eyes were lusterless, her pretty mouth seemed to have developed a droop, and she seemed totally without energy. Rosamund recalled that Anemone had recently returned from a year at a school where young women went to learn manners and deportment. Perhaps the Seminary for Gentlewomen had taken the joie de vivre out of her.

"I do not feel like riding," she was murmuring. "It is so exhausting."

"Seems to me you'd have more bounce if you did something other'n sit around and moan," Lucy pointed out. "No, no more coffee, Bleak. My innards'll swim if I drink any more."

With frigid bows, the butler and his underling took themselves off, and Mrs. Devinter hastily swallowed her mouthful of kidneys and eggs to explain that a lady never referred to such disgusting things as the inner workings of her body.

Lucy looked crestfallen. "I'll never get the hang of it," she said, sighing. "I try and try, but all I do is sound like a country cousin. You know, Rosa," she continued earnestly, "I thought it'd be easy to run Amber House—haven't I always run Sample's speculations and his business and that?—but them servants have me buffaloed. That Bleak, for instance. Always looking down his nose as if I was some kind of bug."

"Mama always said that a servant owes his employer respect and good service. Perhaps you need to take yours in hand," Rosamund said. Lucy looked dubious. "Don't you remember how you dealt with One-ear Sanderson at York Factory? He had an arrogant tongue till you took your broom to him."

Lucy's eyes kindled. "I'd forgotten about that! Well, now . . . if Bleak thinks he can give himself airs just because I'm not Lady Somethingorother, he's going to be sorry."

"Bravo!" Rosamund exclaimed. She glanced at Anemone to see if she would also offer encouragement and caught her sighing so deeply that the cherries embroidered on her white muslin morning dress seemed to quiver with woe. "Are you feeling unwell?" Rosamund asked in some concern.

"No—no, I am quite well, thank you," Anemone said. She pushed away her breakfast plate, which, Rosamund noted, had not been touched at all. "If I may be excused?"

"But you ain't hardly ate," her mother exclaimed. "Good gracious, girl. You didn't touch them nice scones Cook sent up."

Anemone gave her plate a look of loathing, got to her feet, and walked out of the room. Mrs. Devinter also rose to her feet. "I, too, must ask to be excused from this hospitable board," she twittered. "We must prepare the lesson for the day, must we not? Today we will review the etiquette used by a lady when she is introduced to a peer of the realm."

She started to leave the table, then turned to snatch up Anemone's uneaten muffins. "For the birds," she added brightly. "We must not forget the lesson taught us by our feathered friends. 'Birds in their little nests agree,' as Watts said."

She smiled, dropped the muffins into the capacious pocket of her black bombazine dress, and departed. Lucy watched her go with a wistful expression.

"Wonder as I'm ever going to have the chance," she murmured. "To meet the Quality, I mean. Oh, Rosa, it's bothering me something awful that I can't do anything about Mona's troubles."

"Do you mean that she's ill?" Rosamund asked, now thoroughly alarmed.

"I'll be straight with you, dearie. It's me that's the root of Mona's troubles. I ain't a lady, that's plain, and that rascally butler ain't the only one that thumbs his nose at me. For myself I care nothing, nor did Sample. We did honest work and earned honest brass. We was honest folk."

"Indeed you are," Rosamund agreed. She recalled her set-to with the Earl of Hawkley as she continued warmly, "I consider you far more respectable than some want-wits who have nothing but a title to their credit."

Lucy's smile was but a brief flicker. "You're sweet to say so, dearie, but that ain't the way of the world. Swe—I mean, the Quality look down at me. And though I took care for her to learn how to talk and act proper, they look down at my Mona, too."

"Does their good opinion matter so much?" Rosamund wondered aloud.

"Rosa, in England you're nobody unless you're Quality." Lucy gave a sigh that was almost as lugubrious as her daughter's. "That's why I put out an advertisement for a genteel lady to come and teach me how to talk and act, see? But for all Mrs. Devinter's cousin to the Honorable Maria Devinter, whose pa was a lord down in Shropshire, she ain't got dash like you do. I'm hoping that you can introduce Anemone to the right sort."

Rosamund's lips twitched into a wry smile. "My sister-in-law and her mother don't think I have 'dash.' They'll tell you that my behavior is improper, that I am a shocking ingrate who'll never succeed on the marriage mart. And since

I am on my way to being an ape leader, I don't see what I could possibly to do help Mona."

"Snakes, Rosa, you're no old maid," the outraged Mrs. Sample exclaimed. "Why, you're prettier than a picture. But that ain't here nor there. What I want is for you to give Mona your countenance. When the local gentry knows that Miss St. Helm as is related to the Viscount Craye is visiting me, maybe even that fancy earl what lives nearby may come to call."

Rosamund's eyes narrowed fractionally. "I seriously doubt it."

"Now that's what I mean, see?" Lucy went on dismally. "The Earl of Hawkley lives a stone's throw from us but to him we don't exist. He ain't even showed his face. Probably he's some dried-out stuffed shirt who talks through his nose."

"I would not waste time worrying about the earl," Rosamund said firmly.

"But I *have* to worry about the likes of him if I want Anemone to marry well."

How Hawkley would laugh at poor Lucy's ambitions—and he was not the only one who would. Rosamund could hear Lady Orme's shocked exclamations, Cassandra's protests, Bevan's outrage. "What sort of husband had you in mind?" she probed.

Lucy's eyes glistened. "A titled one'd be just dandy. Imagine my Mona being Lady Somethingorother! But," she went on handsomely, "as long as the man is a gentleman, I don't care if he ain't a duke or an earl. Could even be a younger son, see? He don't have to be rich 'cause I have a lot of brass myself."

She could well imagine the effect of this frank speech on someone like Hawkley. "But," Rosamund objected, "you were born an American, Lucy. You used to think that as long as a man is kind and decent, birth didn't matter. *I* believe that still.''

An unexpectedly shrewd look settled over Lucy's plump features. ''I can close my eyes and hear your father—God rest his soul—speaking. But then he was a lord, and you're a lady, so you can afford to talk about equality and suchlike. In England, there's them that is on the top of the heap and them that is stuck on the bottom. And I want my daughter to be on top.''

She paused and asked almost humbly, ''Will you help me, Rosa, for Mona's sake?''

Rosamund thought of her brother's household, of her sister-in-law's die-away disapproval, and of Lady Orme's constant carping. In Amber House it was different. Here no one frowned at her, or told her what to say, or found fault with her actions.

Here she could draw breath without feeling stifled; here she was free. It was ironic, Rosamund thought, that Lucy was pining for entry into the very system that she herself was trying to escape.

''I don't know what I can do,'' she said honestly, ''but if I can help, I will. Right now I'm going to see if I can coax Mona into going for a walk.''

Dropping a kiss on the top of Lucy's cap, Rosamund went in search of Anemone. Being told that the young lady was in the conservatory, she walked down the carved staircase and the ground-floor hall.

The hall was a gloomy place—hardly enlivened by the fact that the walls were covered with portraits of the former owner's ancestors. Apparently Lord Amber had not considered his forebears important enough to take with him when he exited the portals of Amber House. Rosamund wondered why Lucy did not banish the entire Friday-faced lot—but then surmised that she might consider that the berobed nobles gave the house an aristocratic atmosphere.

The conservatory was at the end of the hall. It was a much more cheerful place, bright with potted plants and flowers and even boasting a small fountain near which Anemone was sitting. She looked very pretty and pensive as she dabbled her fingers in the water, but as Rosamund approached she saw another enormous sigh shake her from head to foot.

"Good heavens," Rosamund exclaimed. "What is the matter with you?"

Anemone raised blue eyes that were so woebegone, Rosamund became truly worried. Sitting down beside the younger girl, she took her cold hands.

"Did something dreadful happen?" she asked. "Is it something you can't tell your mother?"

Another sigh gusted through Anemone, and she put a small hand to her heart. "Oh, Rosa, I am undone."

Rosamund did not have any desire to laugh at such dramatics. Anemone was not acting; she really was in great distress. "Can you confide in me?" she asked gently.

Anemone looked ready to sigh again but instead burst out, "Have you ever loved anyone?"

Rosamund thought of her parents and of Bevan, who, even though he was a sapskull at times, was still her brother. She thought of Little Marten and Tall Reed and the countless friends she had left behind at York Factory. But this was obviously not the sort of affection to which Anemone alluded.

"If you mean to ask if I have ever been in love," she replied, "the answer is no."

Anemone gave another of her sighs. "Then you cannot understand how I suffer. What I feel for Wilfred—I mean, Mr. Dilber—is too profound for mere words."

Enlightenment came. "Does Lucy know about this gentleman?" Rosamund inquired.

"That is the problem—he is not a 'gentleman.' " Anemone's lips quivered as she explained, "He was not born with a title or with a great deal of money. When I met him, Mr. Dilber was underclerk to Mr. Stooking, a grain merchant. Now he has risen to chief clerk and has a very good future . . . For all that Mama will not acknowledge that he exists."

Remembering Lucy's ambitions for her daughter, Rosamund silently agreed that Anemone was probably right. Lucy would never consider a mere clerk in a merchant's shop a suitable candidate for her daughter's hand.

Anemone continued, "Back when we didn't have a lot of money, Ma used to say that we were as good as anybody. Doesn't that mean that Mr. Dilber is as good as any gentleman? She—she forgets that *we* were in trade, too, and refers to Mr. Dilber as—as a jumped-up little turnip."

This time Anemone's sigh set her golden curls trembling. Rosamund remained tactfully silent. Though she had never been in love, she noted the courting rituals of her set. She had observed how lords and ladies married for wealth or convenience and then more or less discreetly pursued other inclinations from the shelter of matrimony.

"I will never forget Wilfred," Anemone was saying mournfully. "It is useless even to try. He is all that is kind and good. And—and he has such lovely blue eyes."

Rosamund said sensibly, "It won't help matters if you become pale and weak from lack of food and exercise. If you looked more the thing, Lucy might relent and listen to your side of the story." She smiled down at Anemone, adding, "It's a beautiful day. Why don't we walk in the garden, Mona, and you can tell me all about your Mr. Dilber."

Anemone brightened instantly. She threw her arms around Rosamund and hugged her tightly as she exclaimed, "Oh, Rosa, you do understand. I am so glad that you have come." Then she added darkly, "But Ma will never listen to me. She thinks that by dragging me away from Wilfred, I will forget him. She does not know I have sworn an oath to be true to him."

She gestured dramatically. "Let her parade all the lords in England before me. My heart is given to another."

In the days that followed, Lucy remained hopeful that the Quality would beat a path to Amber House. She insisted that her daughter always be dressed in the kick of fashion and that she do nothing more strenuous than work on her embroidery all afternoon.

"You've got to look like a gentleman's daughter," she lectured. "Mrs. Devinter says that young ladies embroider in the afternoons, so that's what you'll do."

Unfortunately the only person who came to visit Amber House was the local curate, an elderly gentleman who hoped that Mrs. Sample could see her way to contribute to the parish fund for orphans and widows.

"This won't never do," Mrs. Sample exclaimed. "We didn't buy this here property so that we could be snubbed."

Anemone's cheeks flushed a fiery red. "People snub us because we've gotten above ourselves, Ma," she protested. "I've told you and told you that I don't *want* to fit into polite society. All I want is—"

"You're too young to know what you want," Lucy interrupted. "What kind of thinking is that? I remember back in Canada when your pa lay in wait for a beaver for days before he bagged him. We just need another strategy, is all." She then added, "And call me Mama, not Ma. Mrs. Devinter says it's more genteellike."

She organized a shopping trip into town with Rosamund conspicuously driving a most genteel new phaeton. Once in town, Lucy told everyone she met that Miss St. Helm was being so kind as to take time out from her busy schedule to come and spend a few days with old friends.

"You know that her brother's a viscount," Lucy bragged loudly to all and sundry. "We was close friends in Canada, and Miss St. Helm ain't one to forget just because her blood's as blue as a robin's egg."

"Oh, *Ma*," Anemone said, groaning. She looked ready to die of mortification, and Mrs. Devinter appeared shocked, but Rosamund was amused. She had seen titled ladies who were even more direct when they wanted to marry off their daughters.

Whether or not Lucy's plan worked no one knew for certain, but a few days later Bleak entered to announce in patronizing tones that a gentleman had come to call.

Lucy took the card from the silver tray, looked at it, and gave a triumphant whoop. "There," she exclaimed, "didn't I tell you? Here's a real live lord come to see us. Lord Curtis Braden, the card says. Maybe you know him, Rosa?"

Rosamund shook her head. "But then there are many people I have not met," she pointed out.

"Well, never mind. He's one o' the right sort, anyhow," Lucy said stoutly. "Go on, Bleak . . . Show him up and get some refreshments ready for His Lordship."

She got to her feet and began to plump the cushions around the room. "Mona, you start embroidering . . . and mind you smile and look pleasant. Snakes, Rosa. I'm as nervous as a flea on a scratching dog. Mrs. Devinter, sit close by me, don't let me open my big mouth and make a bad impression."

Accordingly, when Lord Curtis Braden was admitted to the morning room, he was greeted by a tableau of Miss Sample sitting bolt upright on a settee embroidering determinedly while Mrs. Sample reclined upon a brocaded chair and attempted to appear unconcerned and sophisticated. At her side stood the vigilant Mrs. Devinter.

Standing back apace near the window, Rosamund took Lord Curtis Braden's measure. He was a good-looking man in his early thirties, tall and fashionably slender but with broad shoulders and a fine head of fair hair arranged à la Brutus. Further, he was nattily attired in a canary yellow waistcoat embroidered with flowers, a fawn-colored coat with a nipped-in waist, buff breaches, and well-fitting boots with tassels.

He bent over Lucy's hand and professed himself her most obedient servant. "Forgive this intrusion, ma'am," he said in a mellow tenor voice, "but I've newly come to Sussex and wished to make myself known to my neighbors."

"That's just dandy—I mean, right fine." Lucy's ample form struggled with the effort of rising to the occasion. "How do you do, Lord Braden. Glad to have you call, I'm sure."

She cast a hopeful look at Mrs. Devinter, received a nod of approval, and continued more confidently, "This is my daughter, sir. Anemone, dearie, meet Lord Braden."

She beamed as Lord Braden kissed Anemone's little hand as though she were a duchess. "Miss Sample," he announced, "Sussex is enriched by your presence."

"This is Mrs. Devinter—she's cousin to Honorable Maria Devinter from Shropshire. And *this* is Miss St. Helm." As Rosamund stepped forward to shake hands, Lucy added triumphantly, "She's the Viscount Craye's sister, y' know. An old family friend."

Lord Braden greeted Rosamund with a smile that was friendly without being presumptuous. He bowed over her hand and said that he had had the pleasure of meeting her brother and Viscountess Craye at Lady Hildermere's ball some Seasons past. "But I did not have the pleasure of seeing you before," he added. "I would have remembered if I had."

"I didn't often go to London for the Season," Rosamund explained.

"Rosa was brought up in Ontario," Mrs. Sample explained. "She don't like cities."

"It is London's loss," Lord Braden declared. "I hope, Mrs. Sample, that you and Miss Sample are not of Miss St. Helm's opinion. It wouldn't do to deprive the city of *three* shining stars."

It was nonsense, but charming nonsense delivered with just the right touches of admiration and humor. Mrs. Devinter twittered approval. Lucy beamed and said, "Well, my Mona's going to London this year for the Season. Sort of her day-boo, as you might say. No need to hide one's light under a bushel, I allus say. A pretty girl has to get noticed so that she can—"

She stopped short as Mrs. Devinter began to cough violently. Anemone looked mutinous and began to stab her needle into her embroidery. To ease the awkward pause that followed, Rosamund made polite conversation. "You live in Sussex, Lord Braden?"

"I am merely visiting, ma'am. I've recently returned from the Continent and couldn't resist enjoying spring in the country. Thoughts of an English spring have sustained me for many long months."

"You need more'n memories to sustain you. You need

something solid to put in your innar—stomach," Lucy exclaimed kindly.

As if on cue, Bleak and two underlings appeared bearing trays of potations and small cakes.

"Here's ratafia, but I daresay you prefer claret," Lucy said to Lord Braden. "Sample never could abide ratafia, said it gave him gas." Here she caught Mrs. Devinter's eye and added rather hastily, "So you was traveling, my lord? Where did you go?"

"Oh, Paris . . . Italy . . . Spain." Lord Braden sipped his claret. "But you are greater travelers, ma'am. You have come from the New World."

Just then the door opened once again and a footman entered with yet another card on the silver tray. Mrs. Sample picked up the card, turned almost magenta with excitement, and exclaimed, "Well, if that don't beat all! The Earl of Hawkley's come to see us."

Mrs. Devinter stopped short in the act of devouring her fourth cake. Rosamund exclaimed, "*What* did you say?"

"Here's his card, plain as day." Lucy turned to Lord Braden, adding happily, "He's a neighbor of ours."

"I am acquainted with the earl."

Even in her astonishment that the earl had actually come to call, Rosamund noted the odd note in Lord Braden's tone. She glanced at him and noted that though his lordship was still smiling, there was a set look in his handsome blue eyes.

She had no time to refine on this, for the earl was already striding through the door. He had probably been riding or driving, for he was dressed for the outdoors in a well-fitting gray riding jacket and buckskin breeches that smoothly delineated his huntsman's thighs and disappeared into the tops of riding boots. He bowed slightly to Rosamund before turning to Lucy and proclaiming himself her most obedient servant.

It was plain that Lucy was in heaven. Her broad face was wreathed in smiles and she could hardly sit still. She opened her mouth to respond, caught a warning stare from Mrs. Devinter, and almost choked.

"My lord earl," she managed to say, "it's good of you to call. We was—were wondering when we would have the pleasure of meeting you."

The earl bowed. Noting the supercilious expression in his eyes, Rosamund stepped forward to stand at Lucy's side. "No doubt," she said coolly, "pressing matters on your estate have kept you occupied."

Hawkley, who had been just about to utter that shopworn excuse, felt as though the wind had been taken out of his sails. He bowed once again and remained silent.

Lucy took all this at face value. "I suppose it ain't a joke being an earl and that," she said commiseratingly. "It's good to have you here, anyway, sir. I'd have come over myself but thought that might be too forward. Back home, you're so glad to have a neighbor, you'd ride miles to see him, but the English have a lot of funny rules."

Mrs. Devinter cleared her throat violently. "But let me introduce you to the other company," Lucy went on hurriedly. "You've met Miss St. Helm, haven't you? And this here lady is Mrs. Devinter, who's been teaching me how to behave. She's connected to the Shropshire Devinters . . . You might've heard about them."

Hawkley's bow to Mrs. Devinter was perfunctory. Without much interest, he professed himself Anemone's servant. Finally he turned to Lord Braden. For a moment he stared as though in amazement, and then his eyes hardened.

"This is Lord Braden," Lucy was proclaiming. "Lord Braden, this here is the Earl of Hawkley."

"The earl and I have met," Lord Braden said. "How do you do, Hawkley?"

The earl did not bow. He did not seem to see the hand that Lord Braden extended in his direction. In a voice that was as cold as the north wind, he said, "I hadn't thought to see you back in England."

Lord Braden smiled his charming smile. "I enjoy doing the unexpected," he confessed. "It keeps me from being bored."

"How long do you expect to remain in Sussex?"

"For some time." As though he had not noted the cutting edge in Hawkley's tone, Lord Braden added, "Miss St. Helm understands that I have long been deprived of an English spring."

Pointedly the earl turned his back on Lord Braden. Rosamund felt a prickle of indignation. Hawkley's high-handed manner recalled his rudeness to his groundskeeper. She had no idea why the earl had come to call, but if he was going to be odious, she wished that he had stayed away.

"Of course I understand," she said to Lord Braden. "Pray tell us about your travels abroad."

His lordship seemed pleased to talk about his adventures. He was witty and droll and had a storyteller's ability to fascinate his listeners. Or almost all his listeners. As Lord Braden regaled the ladies about an experience with bandits in Greece who had held him for ransom, Hawkley strolled away to examine a large cloisonné vase near the door.

To compensate for Hawkley's lack of manners, Rosamund smiled even more encouragingly at Lord Braden and said, "Your accounts are fascinating, my lord. I have never been to Europe."

"Nor I to the New World," Lord Braden answered back at once. "Could I beg the favor of hearing about some of *your* adventures, ma'am? The New World must be such a fearsome place—full of savages and wild animals."

"The tribes of the Six Nations—we call them the Iroquois—are often more civilized than we are," Rosamund replied equably. "The Mohawk Indians who lived near us were good neighbors. As for the bears, Lucy can tell you more about them than I can. She shot one just outside her home."

As Lucy gleefully plunged into the tale, Rosamund noted that the earl was staring hard at Lord Braden. Seemingly unaware of this concentrated gaze, that gentleman complimented Lucy on her narrow escape from the bear. "Canada must be indeed a wild place," he exclaimed. "You must be grateful you escaped to England, Miss St. Helm."

"Canada was home to me for many years," she replied quietly.

"I understand. No matter where or how humble, home is home."

The look Lord Braden gave her was sympathetic, and Rosamund felt a rush of warmth toward him. "That is what I think, also. There are so many rules and regulations in England."

She had spoken without thinking, and Mrs. Devinter looked up from a plate heaped with confections to protest, "But there must be *rules* or civilization would cease to exist. Do not tell me that there are no regulations in Canada, Miss St. Helm."

"Many! But they are rules that one needs in order to survive." Rosamund paused to add thoughtfully, "My sister-in-law once recited to me all the different edicts that had to do with a lady's dress. In York Factory, it was very simple—dress warmly in winter or freeze."

"And what did 'dressing warmly' entail?"

"First a mooseskin outer garment, then flannel-lined breeches—"

Rosamund broke off as Mrs. Devinter put a hand to her heart. "My *dear* Miss St. Helm," she protested, "that *word*!"

"I beg your pardon. I meant, *unmentionables* made of deerskin. I should add that these garments were all worn *indoors* to prevent one from freezing."

"And you miss such a place?" Mrs. Devinter sounded incredulous.

No one, with the exception of Lucy and Anemone, understood what she was talking about. To everyone else Canada was simply a wildland full of privation and misery. When the conversation returned to Lord Braden's travels, Rosamund quietly got up and crossed the room toward the windows.

From this vantage point she could see the gardens. Lady Amber had been a gardener of some repute, and already her daffodil beds were thick with budding flowers. Rosamund felt a tug of longing, but not for the showy English spring. The brief spring that came to York Factory had been a miracle, a wonder that mere words could not explain or describe.

"Miss St. Helm." Hawkley had come to stand beside her. "I'd like a word, ma'am."

His words were formal, his tone ominous. "What is it?" Rosamund asked warily.

"Must tell you something." Hawkley hesitated, searching for adequate words. "Put simply, it's about Lord Braden. I regret to say that he isn't the sort of man you ought to receive."

"Why is that?"

Hawkley had forgotten how direct Miss St. Helm could be. "He—well, dash it—" The earl broke off and tried again. "Can't go into details, but the thing is that Braden isn't the sort of man who should be received by respectable ladies."

Was he intimating that as an American, Lucy was not respectable? "I assure you," Rosamund said coldly, "that I have every confidence in Mrs. Sample's judgment."

About to point out that her confidence was obviously misplaced, Hawkley stopped himself. He had come to mend bridges with the St. Helm chit, not wrangle with her.

"Mrs. Sample may be an estimable woman," he said carefully, "but she wasn't born in England and isn't familiar with . . . ah . . . certain customs and codes of behavior."

Rosamund leaned her back against the French windows and regarded the earl attentively. "Has Lord Braden committed some crime or broken the law?"

"There are laws and laws."

Hawkley stopped short. He could not believe how stuffy he sounded, even to his own ears. But, he temporized, he could hardly tell the girl the more lurid details of Lord Braden's past.

Rosamund watched the earl's strong features harden with distaste. No doubt, she thought, Lord Braden had broken one of the innumerable codes of conduct with which the aristocracy tormented themselves.

"Unless you can tell me what Lord Braden has done to deserve condemnation," she pointed out, "I see no reason to shun him. It wouldn't be fair. If I heard gossip about you, for instance, I wouldn't believe it without proof."

"Gossip about me! Entirely different matter, that. There's nothing to gossip about," Hawkley exclaimed. He was torn between the understandable desire to shake some sense into

Miss St. Helm and a grudging admiration. She was being true to her code, even though that code was more suited to the wilds of Canada than to a civilized country. For a moment he was almost tempted to tell her the blunt truth.

Then he reminded himself that quite aside from the fact that he was no gabster, he had given his word not to reveal that truth. He glowered at Lord Braden, who was making Mrs. Devinter laugh with his imitation of a Venetian gondolier.

Rosamund followed the direction of his gaze and misread the earl's scowl. "Do you have something against Mrs. Devinter, also?" she asked.

"What? Why should I, when I don't know the woman?" Hawkley demanded in astonishment.

"Then why are you looking at her in such a disapproving manner? Mrs. Devinter is a gentlewoman in reduced circumstances who is trying to support herself. I think it's admirable—even if you don't."

"Never said I didn't think it admirable, dash it." Hawkley's voice climbed a notch as he added, "I was talking about Braden. The man isn't fit to be associated with."

Rosamund's eyes had developed a dangerous sparkle. "It seems that very few people seem important enough to associate with you, my lord. Perhaps you should go and live on a deserted island."

Hawkley tried in vain to think of some suitable retort. Rosamund had no such difficulty.

"Because of your rank and station," she went on, "you seem to feel that you have the right to blacken people's reputations. Perhaps Lord Braden is what you say and perhaps not. Either way I prefer to make up my own mind."

Hawkley was speechless. Never, *never* had a female spoken to him in such round terms.

Rosamund St. Helm was impossible, of course, but at the same time what a right one she would be if she weren't so damnably headstrong. Once more Hawkley felt respect competing with his sense of outrage.

"You must do as you like," he said stiffly. "Well, I've warned you. Can't do any more than that."

Rosamund was suddenly assailed by strong twinges of guilt. Certainly the man was overbearing, but she herself had been outspoken—perhaps even rude. And there was never an excuse for rudeness.

"I'm sorry," she said penitently. "I have been tongue-valiant, and for that I beg your pardon. I know that you meant your advice kindly. It's only that I need to make up my own mind."

Impulsively she held out a hand. For a moment Hawkley looked at that slender, capable little hand. Then he took it, and a smile gentled his face and warmed his eyes to a softer shade of brown.

"So you must," he agreed. "Rather tongue-valiant myself, come to that. I expressed myself badly. I need to beg *your* pardon, too, after all that dagger drawing. Shall we call a truce?"

It was not his fault, Rosamund reminded herself. The earl really could not help being the way he was. He had been cosseted from the moment he made his entrance into the world. As the heir to an earldom, he had been petted and bowed down to. He had no doubt been riding his pony in the Park—with servants in attendance—while she and her father were tramping the wilderness.

She smiled at him to show that she understood and said, "By all means, let there be a truce."

No woman who smiled like that should be consigned to

the devil, Hawkley thought. And with that thought came inspiration.

The realization of what he must do was simple and illuminating and made perfect sense. Rosamund St. Helm was no ordinary woman, and no ordinary tactics would convince her of the error of her ways. To affect change, he must wean her away from her fond memories of her life in Canada.

It was a challenge, Hawkley knew, but he knew he was equal to the task. For only when she realized that England had much more to offer than Ontario would this wild rose abandon her hurly-burly ways and begin to act as an English gentlewoman should.

Chapter Four

Wearing a determined expression, Hawkley strode down the stairs. "Not now, Beamler," he exclaimed firmly as he met his secretary on the second-floor landing. "I'm in a hurry."

The secretary looked troubled. "If I might make so bold, m'lud, there are matters that will not wait. The tenant farmers—"

"If there's a problem, talk to Wagonner." It was on the tip of Beamler's tongue to say that the earl's land agent *was* the problem, when Hawkley asked, "Is there a church at Hawk-on-River?"

"A *church*, m'lud?"

"A Norman church. That dashed Devinter woman mentioned that there was one in the neighborhood, and Miss St. Helm said she'd like to have a look at it." Hawkley grinned at the incredulous look on his secretary's face. "Dashed flat idea, come to that, but I promised Craye I'd keep an eye on his sister. Duty calls."

Duty, Beamler noted silently, had not called for some time. A full week had lapsed since his employer had paid his first visit to Amber House. Since then the earl had gone shooting with his brother-in-law, the Marquess of Hare, who with his wife had stopped at Hawkley Manor en route to their London establishment. The earl had also ridden to hounds twice, attended a turtle supper with several bon vivants, and won a wager with the Viscount Lake that his matched grays could best Lake's newly acquired bays in a curricle race from Cuckfield to Tunbridge Wells.

Apparently his old schoolfriend's request had not lain too heavily on the earl's conscience, Beamler thought. Aloud he said, "The church you speak of stands in Eisford, m'lud. But if you could allow me one moment, sir . . . The matter of the tenant farmers is most important. I should say, it is urgent."

Hawkley leaned back against the stair rail and surveyed his secretary thoughtfully. "You don't look the thing, Beamler," he remarked. "Dipping too deep last night?"

"You are pleased to joke, m'lud. I was up late last night, however. Our youngest had a fever."

Hawkley recalled vaguely that his secretary was married and had four or five children. "Called the sawbones, did you?" he wondered aloud idly.

"I beg you will not concern yourself, m'lud. It's the tenant farmers that require your attention. Eldridge was here yesterday."

Hawkley recalled that Eldridge was a middle-aged tenant farmer. "Why was he here?" he asked. "Wagonner's the one he ought to apply to."

"Apparently there is a . . . ah . . . problem of . . . ah

. . . communication. Eldridge said that he has applied to Mr. Wagonner for repairs to his roof, but that nothing was done."

Seeing that he had at last captured the earl's attention, Beamler added, "Eldridge is not the only tenant farmer to complain, m'lud. Many say that they have talked to Mr. Wagonner about their problems without result."

While his secretary spoke, the earl felt a twinge of conscience. He recalled that Beamler had been harping on some problem with the tenant farmers all week. He had never expected to inherit the earldom so soon—his father had been in the pink of health when he died—and he was constantly finding out that to be at the apex of a large estate was a complicated business.

"I'll get to the bottom of this," he promised. "Have Wagonner here at five o'clock. I'll deal with him."

When he spoke in those tones and frowned in that uncompromising way, the young earl looked and sounded exactly like his late father. A just master the late earl had been, but a hard one, Beamler recalled.

"Very good, m'lud." He hesitated for a moment and then ventured to add, "Mrs. Wagonner has been very ill of late. Perhaps that is why Mr. Wagonner has not been up to the mark of late."

"Personal matters don't mix with duty, Beamler. I need a land agent I can depend on. If Wagonner doesn't come up to snuff, I'll find a man who will."

Hawkley was still frowning as he went outside, but the sight of his gleaming curricle and his incomparable matched grays lightened his mood considerably. It had rained last night, but this morning only a few clouds hid the March sun, and there was hardly any wind to speak of. It was a perfect day to put in motion his plan to introduce Rosamund to the beauties of the English countryside. And today, Hawkley vowed to himself, Craye's sister was *not* going to cause him to fly into the boughs. No matter what outrageous thing she said, he was not going to draw daggers with her.

Rosamund St. Helm was like no female he had encountered before, which was undoubtedly why he had been thinking of her so much these past days. Recollections of her steady gaze and forthright tongue had pursued Hawkley as he went shooting with his friends, and a memory of how she had helped the trapped fox had actually cast a pall over his last two hunts. Miss St. Helm was opinionated, stubborn, *wrong* about so many things—and especially about Braden, who had surfaced in Sussex.

"Can't let the side down," he reminded himself. "Craye wouldn't like it above half if he knew what Braden was. I've got to see the game through."

But when the earl arrived at Amber House, the servant who answered the earl's knock at the door announced that no one was at home. Madam and the young ladies had repaired to a rented town house on Broad Street in London. With them had gone Mrs. Devinter and Mr. Bleak, and sufficient servants to see to their needs for the season.

This was an unexpected reprieve. "Even Craye can't want me to pursue his sister to London," the earl mused as he returned to his curricle. "Don't have time for it in any case, especially now when I've got to deal with Wagonner. Let someone else watch over Miss St. Helm and welcome. I wash my hands."

"Snakes, girls! Have you ever seen anything so elegant?"

Lucy Sample surveyed with satisfaction the parlor on the first floor of her rented London town house. Here in the Gold Room a Spanish chandelier presided over fine furnishings, artistic watercolors, ornate mirrors of gilt-framed pier glass, and silk French hangings. The satin curtains that framed the tall windows were a rich gold and the Persian carpet on the floor glowed like a jewel.

"I got it furnished. The place came lock, stock, and barrel from the Honorable Mr. and Mrs. Standhall," Lucy continued in tones of highest satisfaction. "Between you and me, dearie, the Standhalls may be high in the instep, but they're feeling the pinch. They didn't *want* to let the place to me, but they needed the brass."

She plumped down on a brocaded chair and ran a complacent hand over a French antique console that stood beside her. "This place *smells* of quality, don't it? It cost me a pretty penny, but you've got to pay to get value." She paused to add, "Now we're all ready to entertain."

"But, Ma, who are we going to entertain?" Anemone protested. "We've been here for ten days, and no one's come to call."

Mrs. Devinter clucked her tongue. "Miss Anemone, we must not be down-pin, must we?" she asked in a somewhat nasal tone. "And we must remember to say Mama instead of Ma. We cannot be accused of sounding common."

"That's the point," Anemone argued. "We *are* common. That's why nobody's come to see us."

Even more unbending than they had been in the country, the London Quality were completely ignoring the Samples. Mrs. Devinter, who was nursing an incipient cold in the head, looked somewhat dashed, but Lucy only smiled.

"I warn't born yesterday, and I know what's what. I've got plenty of brass, you've got good looks, and Rosa has blue blood. I'm mighty glad that you decided to come along with us, Rosa," she added earnestly. "You're a true friend."

Rosamund had not lightly made the decision to come to London. From her brief acquaintance with that city, she knew that she would detest an entire season there. But the thought of returning to Kent was an even worse prospect.

Besides, she could not leave the Samples when they needed her. "Don't you know some swe—lady or lord in London?" Lucy was saying hopefully. "Someone you could introduce Mona to, maybe?"

Since coming to the city, Rosamund had been daily racking her brains but without much result. "Bevan and Cassandra have many friends," she said. "I had hoped to ask for their help when they came to town, but Bevan writes that they are staying in Kent for some more weeks. I'm sorry, Lucy, truly I am."

Lucy looked disappointed for a moment, then brightened up. "Never mind, honey. We've still got Tim."

The one slim hope that the Samples had of enticing the Quality lay in the fact that Lucy had managed a minor miracle. She had hired a noted cook. Mr. Timothy Cressade was part French, part Irish, and had a temperament that trembled between exultation and despair. He was most sought after but was at the moment between employers, having recently told the Duke of March that he could no longer countenance His Grace's household. Besides, Lucy knew him.

"Sample and me knew Timmy when he was a slip of a lad and living near us in Norfolk," she had explained. "He was as thin as a toothpick, and his pa would go on the toodle and beat him regular. Many's the time he slept on a cot in the storeroom, poor little feller, and many's the time he ate at our table. Later, when he wanted to go into service to learn cooking, I gave him some brass to get started. Tim don't forget what little we done for him."

Mr. Cressade cooked divine meals, but so far he had cooked solely for his employer's household. "But one day they'll all come and eat Tim's vittles," Lucy said hopefully,

"It's still early in the Season. That nice Lord Braden said he was going to call, for instance."

"We must have patience," twittered Mrs. Devinter. "It is a virtue, is it not? Ah," she added brightly as an ormolu clock on the mantel chimed, "it is time for our morning chocolate."

Bleak, looking more disdainful than ever, entered the Gold Room with the chocolate and a plate of small cakes. Mrs. Devinter eagerly fell to, but Lucy waved the tray away. "Not for me. I'm fat enough already—and all this sitting and waiting isn't helping."

She paused as a new thought came to her. "Sitting and waiting never does any good, that's for sure. Look out the window, Rosa, and see if it's a nice enough day for a drive in the Park."

Obediently Rosamund walked over to the window. It was closed, of course, for even here on fashionable Broad Street an open window was an invitation to fog, smoke, and even more unspeakable smells. Rosamund felt a wave of claustrophobia as she looked down onto the street and watched the tops of landaus, hansoms, and sedan chairs rattling by. There was also an urchin who earned his living by sweeping the muck away from the streets so that people could cross without getting their shoes soiled.

But as she followed the sweeper-boy's movements, she noted that there was a tree growing close to the curb, a tree that had sent out green leaves. Spring had come even to London.

"It seems a fine day," she reported. "Would you like to go for a drive, Lucy?"

"Not me, dearie, but Mona needs to be shown off, so maybe you could drive her?" When Rosamund agreed, Lucy urged, "Now you go put on your walking-out dress with the puffed sleeves and that bonnet with the chip straw and them cornflowers, Mona. What about you, Mrs. Devinter? Will you chaperon the girls?''

Mrs. Devinter declined, saying that she still suffered from her cold and that it was in any case time for Mrs. Sample's lessons in elocution. "It will be perfectly respectable for the young ladies to ride out together, attended, of course, by a groom," she declared.

Accordingly, a half hour later Rosamund guided her hostess's phaeton and two cream-colored horses through the gates of Hyde Park. The warmth had brought out many Appropriate Personages who were driving, strolling, or even cantering down the stretch of tan by the carriage road.

Rosamund's spirits rose. The trees made a brave show with their new green leaves, some songbirds were chirruping in the branches, and even the attendant Meadows was seen to smile. Only Anemone remained gloomy in spite of her stylish walking-out dress and bonnet with cornflowers.

"Come," Rosamund said bracingly, "isn't this much better than being cooped up inside the town house?"

"Nothing can be better without Wilfred," Anemone replied. "I miss him *so* much, Rosa."

Rosamund glanced at her companion and was troubled to see tears welling in Anemone's eyes. "I can't believe that Lucy would do anything that makes you so unhappy," she said. "Perhaps if you talked to her—"

"I have talked to her. She only says that I am too young to know my mind." Anemone removed a scrap of lace from her reticule and dabbed at her eyes. "Rosa, can't *you* speak to Ma? I know that she will listen to anything you say because you're of the Quality."

Before Rosamund could react to this, a pleasant male voice

exclaimed, "Miss St. Helm, Miss Sample, your most obedient! What a pleasure to see you again."

Lord Braden was standing some distance ahead of them. He was carrying an elegant gold-tipped cane and was attired in a pale gray coat and matching breeches. His glossy boots were definitely a creation of the incomparable Hobbes, and the curly beaver he held in his nattily gloved hand could only have come from one of London's finest hatmakers.

Pleasantly surprised, Rosamund halted the horses and asked, "When did you reach London, Lord Braden?"

"I left Sussex at once when I heard that you had come to London. How could I not? The country was empty and bleak without your presence. You ladies took spring away with you and brought it to the city."

Lord Braden spoke this nonsense in that charming, humorous way that was all his own, his smile so genuine that Rosamund felt it easy to smile back, and even Anemone shed her tragic air. "I have been admiring you as you completed your first circuit around the Park," his lordship continued. "You are a most accomplished whip, Miss St. Helm."

"Rosa's the best driver there was," Anemone said proudly. "She even drove a team of dogs in Canada."

"Incredible! Miss St. Helm, I bow to your accomplishments."

While watching Lord Braden's graceful bow, Rosamund wondered what the Earl of Hawkley would have said under the same circumstances. No doubt he would have made some derogatory comment about the impropriety of a lady driving dogs.

Aloud she replied, "It was no accomplishment. Dog sleds were quite common during the winter around York Factory."

Anemone shuddered. "It was a wild place," she said. "Rosa misses Canada, but I—I like England better."

"I'm grateful for that . . . since it will keep you in this country," Lord Braden said courteously.

Just then a drum of hoofbeats announced a gentleman astride a handsome, coal black stallion. Obviously an excellent horseman, he was cantering down the stretch of tan with an assurance of manner that was almost arrogance.

"The Earl of Hawkley," Anemone exclaimed, surprised. "I thought he was still in Sussex."

Rosamund had thought so, too, but here was his lordship, as large as life. He drew rein when he saw them and doffed his glossy beaver to Rosamund and Anemone while announcing himself at their service. Lord Braden he completely ignored.

"Glad to have found you, ladies," Hawkley said. "Called in at Broad Street and was told that you had driven out toward the Park."

"So you came posthaste to save the fair ladies from the dangers of London," Lord Braden said jocosely.

The earl favored Lord Braden with a long, cool, silent stare that was as insulting as a slap in the face. Lord Braden's eyes narrowed, but he said nothing, and Rosamund felt her spine stiffen. Hawkley's arrogance had not abated one iota since their last meeting.

Disregarding Lord Braden, the earl went on, "The horses might catch cold if they stand idle. Drive on, ma'am, and I'll ride beside you."

The implication was clear: Lord Braden, on foot, could not keep up with them.

"Perhaps *you* should ride on, Hawkley," his lordship suggested.

"And perhaps you should go about your business," the earl retorted.

The two men looked daggers at each other. Afraid that at

any moment one might challenge the other to a duel, Rosamund said resolutely, "We have not concluded our conversation, Lord Braden. We will proceed—at a slow pace."

Lord Braden shot the earl a look of triumph. "You needn't fear for the ladies, Hawkley. Ride on if that's your pleasure."

"It's my *pleasure* to stay where I am."

Once more, the gentlemen glared at each other, and Rosamund devoutly wished that they would both take themselves off. Hawkley's arrival had charged the till now pleasant day with tension.

She was about to inform them that she and Anemone were going home when she suddenly became aware that she could not go anywhere. The carriages, barouches, landaus, and traps that had been proceeding sedately along the carriage row had all come to a halt. Pedestrians had also stopped walking and were craning their necks to see farther down the road.

"What is happening, Rosa?" Anemone asked, with curiosity.

There was a stir ahead of them and three men came walking down the road. Though their somber-hued coats and pantaloons were unexceptionable, they wore bright felt hats adorned with jaunty feathers. Their black hair hung over their shoulders and shaded hard, swarthy faces.

"What a villainous-looking trio," Lord Braden exclaimed. "Thieving gypsies, I have no doubt."

As if they had heard his lordship, one of the three men looked up and stared intently at Rosamund. He wore a dark red hat embellished with blue feathers and looked to be in his twenties. There was a blue tattoo on his chin, and his face was dark, proud, and hawk-nosed. His eyes were so dark that they seemed carved out of obsidian.

Lord Braden frowned. "Look how insolently the fellow stares at us. He should be taught a lesson in behavior."

Hawkley had been thinking the same thing, but his dislike of Lord Braden made him snap, "In England a cat may look at a king." He turned to Rosamund, who was staring at the savage trio in fascination, and added, "Shall we move on?"

"Yes," Anemone said, "let's!" She caught at Rosa's arm with nervous fingers as she added, "Oh, Rosa, I'm frightened. Let's go home."

"Jackanapes!" Lord Braden snapped. Then he added, "Good Lord, he's coming this way. Don't fear, ladies. I will protect you."

Hawkley frowned, but before he could say anything, Rosamund exclaimed, "There is something definitely familiar about those three men. Mona, am I wrong? Can it be that they are *Mohawks*?"

"From Canada, you mean?" Anemone peered doubtfully, but it had become hard to see through the crush of carriages and the growing crowd of pedestrians that had gathered around the dark strangers. Gentlemen and ladies stared, pointed, and whispered among themselves. Children pulled faces or made rude noises. Babies burst into tears.

Nor was the rapidly growing crowd composed merely of curiosity seekers. Rosamund's quick eye noted that a well-dressed young man was pretending to examine the swarthy strangers through his quizzing glass while at the same time dipping his hand into the pocket of a portly gentleman in a frock coat.

"Look there—a thief!" she exclaimed.

"Where?" Hawkley rapped out.

But before Rosamund could point him out, the pickpocket managed to jostle the man with the red hat against the portly gentleman he had just robbed.

"Hey! Look where you're goin', my good man," the stout man snapped.

Suddenly he clapped his hand to his pocket and began to shout that he had been robbed. "The demmed gypsies did it!" he bellowed. "Stop them! Don't let them escape!"

Several passersby seized hold of the three strangers, but with a savage cry, the man with the red hat broke loose. With movements that were both swift and savage, he knocked one man down and kicked a second aside.

Hawkley pushed himself and his stallion between Rosamund's phaeton and the man in the red hat, who threatened, "Go back, or I hurt you some more!"

"Leave them alone; those men are not thieves! You have let the real pickpocket get away."

Rosamund's voice did not carry above the noise the crowd was making, and Lord Braden cried, "The carriages have begun to move at last. Quickly, Miss St. Helm. Let us get away before violence commences."

He put a persuasive hand on Rosamund's arm, but she shook it off and instead tried to guide her horses closer to the fray. Behind her Meadows shouted a warning, and Anemone cowered into the cushions and began to cry.

"Stop this nonsense!" Hawkley shouted.

His voice had the impact of a thunderclap. The crowd actually stopped yelling and turned to stare at the earl, who continued, "This lady saw what happened. Another fellow was the thief, not the one in the red hat." He paused to ask Rosamund over his shoulder, "Where's this pickpocket now?"

Rosamund looked about the crowd. "I can't see him. He has escaped."

"Hang the dark-skinned devils," a gentleman in scarlet

regimentals suggested. Voices concurred, while others blamed the social evils of England on all foreigners.

"Silence!" commanded the earl.

Once again his voice cut the noise, and once more its authority held. "These men are innocent," continued the earl in ringing tones. "Let them go."

"That's what *you* say," shouted the stout man in the frock coat. "They didn't steal your purse, hey?"

Rosamund cupped her hands around her mouth and shouted, "The real pickpocket is a tall man in a green coat. I saw him put his hand in your pocket and then jostle you so that you fell against that man in the red hat. You're accusing him wrongly just because he is a stranger."

Red Hat showed his teeth in a grin. "That right," he exclaimed appreciatively. "Woman see better than rest of you squabs."

Just then several constables came elbowing into the crowd. They began to make for the three strangers, and their leader pointed at Red Hat with his truncheon. "You, there . . . Come with us quietly," he ordered, "or it'll be the wuss for you."

The big man crouched down in a defiant posture. "You try and take me," he snarled.

"What shall we do?" Rosamund asked Lord Braden, as the constables hesitated.

"Nothing," that gentleman said firmly. "The law will take care of matters, ma'am. Leave it to them and come away. They'll have a fair trial—"

"Fair? There is nothing fair about this situation." Rosamund let go of the reins and stood up in the phaeton, raised her fingers to her lips, and let out a piercing whistle. Then, as the crowd fell momentarily silent, she called out a few strange-sounding words.

65

The constables goggled. "Eh, what's that, now? It wasn't English," their leader exclaimed suspiciously. "What's that you're saying, miss?"

"Be quiet," Hawkley ordered.

The big man in the red hat broke into a smile. He drew himself up, raised one hand, and with unself-conscious dignity began to speak.

"He says that he is of the Iroquois Nation, a Mohawk Indian from Canada," Rosamund translated. "His name is Chief Storm Cloud. He is the leader of a delegation that has come to England on the invitation of His Majesty's government."

"What's 'at?" demanded the constable, while the stout personage in the frock coat was heard to wonder what the world was coming to.

"I don't believe that story for a moment," he shouted. "He's makin' it up. Hey? He picked my pocket. I *demand* justice!"

"Tha old mawworm—doesta dare question Miss St. Helm's word?" Meadows tumbled off his horse and creaked forward to stand beside the phaeton. "Sneck up, or happen I may draw my hand across tha face!"

While Hawkley stared at the ferocious old fellow in astonishment, Red Hat spoke again. Rosamund translated, "Chief Storm Cloud's companions are called Silver Beaver and Flying Crow. They are in London on official business and have papers to prove who they are."

"Let them produce the papers," Hawkley suggested. The constables looked doubtfully at each other. "I'm the Earl of Hawkley," he continued, "and I take full responsibility."

Then he stopped short, astounded at his own foolhardiness. He had never intended to involve himself in this idiotic business, much less stand guarantor for scruffy-looking savages. Trust Rosamund St. Helm, Hawkley thought grimly, to complicate something so mundane as a ride in the Park.

Meanwhile Storm Cloud and his retainers had produced impressive-looking documents and handed them to the chief constable, who took them, squinted doubtfully at them, and then announced to all that he was jiggered and had never seen the like in all his puff.

"Well?" Hawkley demanded impatiently. "Are they here on official business or aren't they?"

The chief constable scratched his head. "Yes, sorr. It appears so. But I dunno . . . All this about picking this gentleman's pocket, now . . ."

Storm Cloud bared his teeth contemptuously. "Squab, you pay attention," he told the head constable. "Woman with blue eyes tell truth. Not waste time. Go find real thief and take his scalp."

This suggestion caused the crowd to disperse rapidly. The carriages trundled forward, the pedestrian traffic recommenced to flow, and the constables beat a hasty retreat together with the frock-coated gentleman, who was demanding to know who would return his money to him. Storm Cloud watched this exodus with a grim smile.

"Good," he announced, "squabs all run away."

He gestured to his followers and walked forward until he stood directly in front of Hawkley's black stallion. The earl found himself looking down into the proud, dark young face. For a moment their eyes held, and then Storm Cloud nodded. "You are a chief, too," he said approvingly. "I like you."

From the expression in Hawkley's eyes, Rosamund felt sure that the earl was about to deliver a snub. Instead, his lordship's lips twitched. "Thank you," he replied. "What business brings you to England, Chief?"

"Come to learn about law of land . . ." The young Mohawk gave up the struggle and lapsed back into his own language.

"What are they saying?" Lord Braden asked. He was regarding the Mohawks with cold suspicion. "Really, Miss St. Helm, is it wise to stand here in the street and speak to such a— It isn't safe, ma'am. I beg you will come away."

Rosamund ignored him. "They are here to study real estate law," she translated. "Apparently Chief Storm Cloud and the other braves are a delegation sent by Chief Joseph Brandt. Since they have no idea of how to survey land, or write deeds, or collect rents, they've come to learn about our English land laws."

Remembering his own problems with tenant farmers, Hawkley felt a twinge of fellow feeling for Storm Cloud. Apparently Mohawks had troublesome tenants, too.

Rosamund was saying, "The Iroquois Nation, to which these braves belong, has a tract of land along the Grand River. It is too great an area for the women to farm, so they are thinking of acquiring white tenant farmers—"

"Just a minute," Hawkley interrupted, scandalized. "Do you mean to say that white settlers are going to be tenant farmers for these . . . er . . . Mohawks?"

A pucker had developed between Rosamund's brows. "Yes, of course. Why not? White settlers can farm, Mohawk warriors do not. It is not part of their tradition."

Storm Cloud and his two companions nodded. "Farming is for women, keep them in place," Storm Cloud added.

Hawkley could not help grinning at the look on Rosamund's face. She said something that made the Mohawk's eyes widen. Storm Cloud burst into laughter.

"You have spirit," he said approvingly. "Storm Cloud like you. We will be friends."

Rosamund felt a sudden sympathy for the three men. To a

Mohawk, London must be large and terribly bewildering. Remembering how she had felt when she first came to England, she asked Storm Cloud a question in his native tongue. "I asked him where they were staying," she then explained. "Apparently rooms have been provided for them while they study, but they are lonely."

Storm Cloud gestured to the west and then to the east and then put his hand on his heart. The gesture needed no translation.

If she allowed the young braves to go off on their own, they would almost certainly get into trouble again, and this time the consequences might be severe. "Do you think Lucy would enjoy visitors from home?" Rosamund asked Anemone.

"Great heavens, ma'am! Do you mean that you would invite *these* people to your home?" Lord Braden demanded in horrified accents.

"Why not? I'm persuaded that Lucy would enjoy hearing about Canada," Rosamund said.

"But, Miss St. Helm— These men are nothing more than savages," protested his lordship. "They are wild Indians."

Before Rosamund could frame an answer, Hawkley spoke. "They're strangers in a strange land, aren't they?"

Rosamund was not fooled. From the way in which the earl eyed Lord Braden as he spoke, she knew exactly why the earl had taken up her defense. But she also remembered how he had ridden forward to set himself between her and possible danger and how he had helped her free the Mohawks from the law.

"After all," Hawkley was saying piously, "we must be kind to strangers. Law of hospitality, and all of that."

The earl was most definitely a starch-shirted, high-in-the-instep member of the upper crust. Even so, Rosamund had to admit that he was someone who could be relied upon in times of trouble.

Chapter Five

As he was finishing his morning's toilette, Hawkley became aware that his valet was not himself. When the man had committed the extraordinary blunder of dropping his employer's gold cuff links, the earl turned to survey Inchley and found him exceedingly pale—except for two spots of red that burned in his cheeks.

"What's the matter with you?" the earl asked.

His valet looked frightened. "Nothing, my—my lord," he stammered. "I am exceedingly sorry, sir."

As the valet bent to retrieve the cuff links, Hawkley caught a strong whiff of spirits.

"Dash it, you've been drinking," he said accusingly. "No," he added sternly as the man began to stammer out a denial. "No use trying to gammon me. I know brandy when I smell it. Anything to say for yourself before I dismiss you from my service?"

Looking ready to burst into tears, the wretched valet mumbled something that sounded like "toothache."

Hawkley looked keenly at his man and decided that he was not lying. His hard face softened as he said, "Teeth can be the very devil. Remember a time once when I had the toothache and my old nurse packed me up with camphor and opium—nearly died of the stuff." He contemplated that memory for a moment, then added, "Lie down for an hour or two, why don't you?"

Surprised by the sympathy in the earl's tone, Inchley murmured his thanks. "I will be all right, my lord, as soon as the tooth is pulled. I am sorry to have disturbed Your Lordship with such a trifle."

"Oh, that's all right," Hawkley said good-humoredly, and added as an afterthought, "But don't nip too much brandy, especially in the morning. Won't do if you go on the toodle."

He took the gloves the valet handed him and walked out the door, whistling softly. Outside his Mount Street town house, his groom awaited with the earl's curricle.

"Where to this morning, m'lord?" asked the tiger, adding with the familiarity born of long association, "it's a fine morning wherever you've a mind to drive."

Hawkley looked about him. Mount Street, which had been so drab a few weeks ago, was now full of bustle. The sky was blue and the March sun almost made up for the smoke and dirt that rose from the city.

Perhaps because of the weather, the earl felt quite cheerful, even though he was on his way to call in at Mrs. Sample's. In fact, when he remembered that two days ago Chief Storm Cloud had defied the London constabulary with Rosamund St. Helm's assistance, Hawkley could not help grinning.

On the street corner a flower seller was selling spring

flowers. The earl threw down a coin and bought a cluster of violets. "Time she appreciated the offerings of an English spring," he said aloud.

He was still in good form when he arrived at Broad Street, where Bleak answered his knock with such a long face that Hawkley was astonished. The earl silently vowed that if any of *his* staff looked like this Friday-faced scrub, he would send him packing.

"Miss St. Helm in?" he demanded.

Bleak, who prided himself on recognizing True Quality when he saw it, became instantly obsequious and explained that the lady was most certainly at home and accepting callers. "If my lord would but wait a moment—"

A wild whoop reverberated through the house. "Dash and blast it!" Hawkley exclaimed. "What in hell's going on?"

Bleak's disgusted expression returned. "The . . . er . . . Mohawk gentlemen have come to call," he explained.

"No, have they?" Another whoop echoed through the stairwell. "Don't bother announcing me," the earl then said. "I'll see myself up."

Following the sounds, he proceeded up the stairs to a room on the first-floor landing, pushed open the door, and saw an extraordinary sight. The three Mohawk braves were shuffling about a hassock in the center of the room. Lucy Sample, her daughter, and Rosamund were watching their antics in fascination. Mrs. Devinter, sitting bolt upright in a wing-backed chair by the door, looked about ready to collapse.

"Well, I'm dashed," Hawkley exclaimed.

No one paid the least attention to him. The Mohawks went on shuffling and the ladies continued to watch. Suddenly Storm Cloud gave a loud whoop and leapt into the air.

"The dance," he announced, "is over."

He folded his arms across the chest of his blue coat and

stepped back. As he did so, Rosamund looked up and saw the earl standing in the doorway.

"Oh," she exclaimed, "we did not hear you come in. Chief Storm Cloud and his braves were giving us a demonstration of an Iroquois hunting dance."

"A dance?"

Hawkley looked so bewildered that Rosamund explained, "It is a ritual of the hunt. The animals have to be assured that their meat will be appreciated, their hair and hide and bones used to help the tribe. The hunters also praise the animals' bravery and thank them for the gift of themselves."

"You not hunt, Chief Hawkley?" Storm Cloud wanted to know.

Rosamund saw various expressions chase one another across the earl's face. "In England," she explained, "gentleman don't dance before they hunt."

"Huh," Storm Cloud grunted. He added dismissively, "Bet they not catch anything."

Mrs. Devinter had had time to recover. "But, *dear* Mrs. Sample," she twittered, "we have not yet greeted the earl. What can we be thinking of?"

"I don't know, I'm sure." Lucy bounced up from her chair and advanced contritely, her hand outstretched. "Sometimes I've got less manners than a goat."

"Mrs. *Sample*," interrupted Mrs. Devinter. "I beg that we watch our language. *What* will His Lordship think of us?"

Lucy bit her lip. "I done it again, didn't I?" She sighed. "I'll never learn to talk proper, that's a fact."

Rosamund was pleasantly surprised when Hawkley shook Lucy's hand, saying heartily, "Not a bit of it, ma'am. Hope you're enjoying London."

Lucy relaxed. "Not as much as we could be, thankee,"

she said frankly. "London'd be a right pretty place if it didn't stink so much of—"

"Mrs. *Sample*," moaned Mrs. Devinter. Lucy looked dashed but recovered quickly as the earl's smile became a grin.

"Those flowers are mighty pretty," she said approvingly.

Hawkley realized that he was still holding the violets. He presented them to his hostess, who said, "They put me in mind of the posies in the woods around York Factory. What do you say, girls?"

Anemone had lost interest and was gazing soulfully out of the window. She made no reply, but Rosamund took the violets eagerly. "How fragrant they are," she exclaimed.

Hawkley blinked. He had forgotten how extraordinarily beautiful Rosamund St. Helm could be when she smiled.

And her pleasure in the flowers was unfeigned. The earl had at one time or another presented nosegays to a veritable army of females, but he had never been faced by such genuine appreciation before. He found himself wishing that he had bought an armful of flowers for her pleasure.

Storm Cloud interrupted the earl's thoughts. "Back home, brave not bring flowers," he announced. "Kill deer, take to woman's wigwam. Can't eat flowers."

Bleak came in with the tea at this moment. Hawkley watched in astonishment as Storm Cloud called out an order to his retinue. Then he and his braves parted their coattails and sat down gingerly on chairs surrounding the tea table.

"The chief and his braves have asked us to help them practice," Rosamund explained. "Chief Storm Cloud is anxious to master the social art of drinking tea. No, Silver Beaver," she exclaimed as that brave seized hold of a cake and began to shove it into his mouth. "That will never do. Look at the earl—see how *he* does it."

Hawkley found that everyone was looking at him. Picking up a cake, he began to eat it deliberately.

The Mohawks all emulated the earl. Mrs. Devinter looked on mournfully as the cakes on the plate disappeared as if by magic.

"Gentlemen," she snapped, "do not *gulp* down their refreshments."

"These not refreshments. These are tea," Storm Cloud pointed out. "Watch now how we drink English tea."

Hawkley struggled to keep a straight face as the stern-faced braves lifted their teacups to their lips, elaborately crooking their little fingers.

"More difficult than hunting bear," Storm Cloud said, sighing. "Tea tastes like muddy water, too. What you think, Chief Hawkley?"

"I have to agree with you there, Chief Storm Cloud. Tea can be paltry stuff."

Hawkley's eyes danced with humor, and again Rosamund was agreeably surprised. When the earl had walked into the room, she had been afraid that he would look down his nose at the Mohawks. Instead, he was apparently going out of his way to be pleasant and helpful. He was even showing Silver Beaver how to dispose of his spoon so that it did not drop when he lifted up his teacup.

"How are the lessons on land management going?" Hawkley asked when this operation had been successfully completed.

Storm Cloud lapsed into his own language and Rosamund translated. "He says that they are trying to understand the English way of thinking. It's not easy, since Mohawks believe that land cannot be parceled and divided but belongs to everyone."

"They believe *what*?"

Rosamund was not surprised at the astonishment in the earl's voice. No landed aristocrat could appreciate the concept of land shared by all. She said, "My father, though he inherited a title after my uncle died, shared the Mohawk belief in many ways. He would have liked to make his new estate into common land, but that was not possible."

More than ever convinced that Jeremy St. Helm had been as queer as Dick's hatband, Hawkley protested, "But I thought that Storm Cloud was leasing *his* land to white settlers. That doesn't sound as if he believes in sharing land."

"Leasing land is a new idea put forward by Joseph Brandt, the leader of the six Nations Reserve. Chief Brandt feels that his nation must change with the times. Parcels of land have been sold to friendly settlers, but the property deeds were so badly drawn up that there has been trouble with the settlers and with squatters. Chief Brandt feels that acres of the land will be lost unless the Mohawks learn proper land management."

Flying Crow had commenced to slurp his tea and Mrs. Devinter was unsuccessfully attempting to correct him. She called upon the earl for assistance, and, leaving them at it, Rosamund got up and walked to the window.

As usual, talk about Canada had brought back a feeling of homesickness. Rosamund drew a deep breath of the violets that she was still holding and remembered cool woods where she had walked in the spring.

"How I wish I were home," she murmured.

Her need was so intense, the wish so fervent, that when she looked out of the window, Rosamund half expected to see York Factory. Instead, her gaze fell on a hansom rattling past.

"I can guess what you're thinking, but you haven't given England a chance," Hawkley said. He had left the tea drinkers and had come to stand beside her. "There's nothing as beautiful as an English garden in the spring."

"There are gardens at Craye," she reminded him.

"You haven't seen my mother's roses at Fairhaven Manor. I'd like to show them to you someday."

This last was so unexpected that Rosamund looked up at him in time to see the speculative look in his eyes. That look activated a suspicion that had been forming in her mind ever since the earl had sought her out that day in the Park.

"Did Bevan write to you and ask you to look after me?" she asked him.

The much too frank question caught the earl in an unguarded moment. "Yes, he did," he admitted. Then, hastily backtracking, he demanded, "Why shouldn't he write to me? Dash it, we're old schoolfriends and all of that. Naturally, he'd write to me."

Rosamund's eyes were sparkling ominously. "I can imagine what Bevan said in his letter."

Turning away from the earl, she stared blindly out of the window. She had suspected all along that Hawkley was not seeking her out because he wanted her company. Had Bevan asked the earl to bring her up to snuff? Had he begged Hawkley to make sure that his impossible sister did not make any social gaffes? The possibilities were endless—and shameful.

"It was kind of you, my lord," she told him, "but I free you from any onerous responsibilities. You can tell Bevan I said so."

Hawkley heard the brittle note in Rosamund's voice. He knew that her pride had been hurt, and he damned himself for being clumsy. "Not onerous," he assured her. "Pleasure, believe me. Really meant it about my mother's gardens." When she did not respond to this, he added, "There's

London to see as well. Lots of things are happening here in the spring. . . ."

Hawkley broke off as several tempting spring pastimes slid into his mind. But curricle racing and shooting and hunting were hardly suitable diversions for a lady.

"Like—like driving in the Park," he added rather desperately. "Did you drive out today?"

"No. Nancy had the headache, so I prepared a peppermint tisane for her." Seeing the earl's bewildered look, Rosamund explained, "Nancy is my personal maid."

"You mean that *you* nursed your *abigail*?"

"Yes, of course. What is so odd about that?"

Hawkley suddenly recalled his valet's pain-white face. The memory caused a pang of guilt that irritated him. He'd told the man to lie down, dash it all. He couldn't have been expected to hold Inchley's hand or put revolting compresses on his own valet's head.

"The thing just isn't done," he said aloud. "We don't take care of our servants; it's the other way around."

"But servants are people, too," Rosamund pointed out. "They work for us, but that doesn't mean that they are beneath us. There should be respect and caring on both sides."

Hawkley winced, but before he could pursue the subject, Bleak appeared at the door and haughtily offered the silver card tray to Lucy.

That fellow Braden again— But to Hawkley's relief, the names Lucy read out loud were unfamiliar. "Mrs. Chamondalay and her brother, Mr. Rupert Banks," she declared. "I don't know these people, but it's nice of them to call, whoever they are. Show 'em up, Bleak."

She beamed about the room, adding, "Feathers one day, chicken the next. We don't get one visitor for weeks, and now we have a whole bunch of swe—I mean, ladies and gentlemen, calling all at once."

But Mrs. Chamondalay and Mr. Rupert Banks were not what one would call gentlefolk. Rosamund instinctively knew this the instant they walked into the room. Though Mrs. Chamondalay's opulent form was resplendent in a lavender walking-out dress, bonnet of chip straw, and modish pelisse, there was something at once too obsequious and too bold in the way she presented herself.

"Dear Mrs. Sample," gushed Mrs. Chamondalay, "*so* good of you to receive us. *So* kind. May I present my brother, Mr. Rupert Banks?"

Mr. Rupert Banks was a fair-haired man with soulful dark eyes. His plum-colored coat, creamy white pantaloons, and waistcoat embroidered with gold flowers were all in the kick of fashion, and the bow with which he greeted the ladies caused Hawkley to eye him askance. Commoner, he thought. A bit of a leg, if I'm not mistaken.

Serenely unaware of his lordship's assessment, Lucy took at face value her visitor's assertion that she was related to Lady Forthingham and introduced the others. Mrs. Chamondalay gushed approval of the magnificently furnished drawing room, complimented dear Anemone's cerulean blue eyes, her delicate hands, and her lovely golden hair. Then she turned to Rosamund with protestations of esteem and assurances that she was acquainted with the dear Viscountess Craye.

"I had heard that you had come to London, Miss St. Helm," she said effervescently. "I have been impatient to make your acquaintance. I had heard that you were a beauty, ma'am, but I am persuaded that the reality far exceeds mere hearsay."

Vastly uncomfortable, Rosamund was grateful when Mrs.

Chamondalay turned her attention to the impassive Mohawks. "But what is this?" she exclaimed. "Are you having gypsies tell your fortunes, Mrs. Sample? I vow that is too enchanting."

As Lucy explained, Rosamund heard Storm Cloud mutter something under his breath. He and his braves stared pointedly at Mrs. Chamondalay, who declared that she was immensely diverted by the spectacle of such *savage* personages.

Then she added, "I collect that you are not familiar with London, Mrs. Sample. Have you yet enjoyed the pleasures of the city? No? In that case I beg that you will allow my brother and me to act as your guides."

Try as she might to be entirely open-minded and fair, Rosamund could not like Mrs. Chamondalay or her brother. Something about them reminded her of Robbie McKenzie, the fur trader that her father had distrusted back at York Factory.

"You must go to the opera and to Astley's Ampitheater," Mrs. Chamondalay said enthusiastically. "The opera is *so* divine. My brother and I will be delighted to escort you."

"Charmed," said Mr. Rupert Banks at once. "I will be enchanted to do so."

A leg—*and* a certain sharp, Hawkley decided. Ordinarily he would not have cared whether or not these commoners gulled Lucy Sample, but there was Rosamund to consider.

"The opera," Lucy was exclaiming. "I never saw an opera in my life. Have you, Rosa?"

Rosamund shook her head. "Papa never cared for such things."

"In that case, an experience awaits you, ma'am," Mr. Rupert Banks purred. "There is a performance of *Don Giovanni* tomorrow evening at the Opera House."

"Miss St. Helm has already consented to come to the

opera with me," Hawkley said abruptly. "Hope Mrs. Sample and Miss Sample will honor me by their company as well."

Rosamund stared at him. Lucy looked pleased and said, "Now, isn't that something, Mona? Us sitting in a real box. You do have a box, don't you, my lord?"

Assuring Lucy that he did indeed possess a box at the Opera House, Hawkley got to his feet. "Must take my leave," he announced. "Miss St. Helm, may I have a word?"

"Indeed you may," Rosamund exclaimed. As they walked out into the staircase hall outside the drawing room, she added, "I don't remember that we spoke of going to the opera, so I collect that your invitation was a ruse to protect me from Mrs. Chamondalay and Mr. Banks."

"Raff and chaff," the earl exclaimed. "If they aren't gazetted fortune hunters, I'm a rabbit sucker. Going anywhere with such scrubs doesn't bear thinking of."

Though she agreed with his assessment, his high-handed approach grated. "What makes you think that I *would* have gone anywhere with them?" Rosamund asked.

"Mrs. Sample was happy enough to accept their invitation. She's a wealthy woman, has an unmarried daughter. She ought to be more careful of whom she receives."

He shook his head so disapprovingly that Rosamund was aware of bristles forming under her skin.

"I realize you are trying to follow Bevan's instructions," she said coldly, "but pray remember that I'm no longer your responsibility. I'm perfectly capable of making up my own mind about people, sir."

First Braden and then the unspeakable duo in the other room—Rosamund St. Helm collected unsuitable *partis* the way a gambler attracted debts. She was impossible, stiff-necked, and as stubborn as a donkey. Hawkley longed to tell her that she was welcome to do as she pleased, for all he cared, but his promise to her brother held him back.

Suppressing a heartfelt desire to wring Craye's scrawny neck, Hawkley said, gritting his teeth, "If Mrs. Sample wants to go to the opera, *I* will accompany all of you."

Rosamund curled her lip. "How noble of you."

There was a crash from the room behind them, followed by a bloodcurdling whoop and the shuffling of feet. A second later, Mrs. Chamondalay came running out of the room. She was closely followed by a wide-eyed Mr. Rupert Banks. They skimmed past Rosamund and Hawkley and dashed down the stairs.

The racket in the drawing room ceased, and Storm Cloud appeared at the open door. "Squabs," he declared scornfully. "They didn't appreciate hunting dance."

He winked at Hawkley, then withdrew into the room. Rosamund tried to keep a straight face and failed. Her laughter pealed through the hall—and was so contagious that Hawkley could not help joining in her merriment.

"I'll take my leave of you, ma'am." He grinned. "Seems that I'm leaving you in good hands."

"It would appear that I have acquired another protector." Rosamund wiped her eyes and then added frankly, "I'm sorry if I was rude a moment ago, but you are somewhat to blame. You *can* be quite insufferable at times."

A few moments earlier, Hawkley might have taken offense at this candid assessment of his character. Now he merely nodded. "My sister Margaret tells me as much," he said. He followed this handsome admission by adding, "I meant it about escorting you to the opera. I warn you that it's paltry stuff, but Mrs. Sample seems to want to go."

On the point of declining the earl's offer, Rosamund hesitated. Lucy had truly seemed to want to attend the opera.

83

"If I do make one of your party we must understand each other," she told the earl. "You must promise me that you will disregard Bevan's letter. You need not feel responsible for me in any way."

She broke off, noting inconsequentially that though his lips had stopped smiling, Hawkley's eyes were still dancing infectiously. In fact, she was hard-pressed not to smile herself as she asked, "Are we agreed to that?"

"Agreed."

Lucy was in raptures over the earl's invitation. "This is *much* nicer than going to the opera with that Mr. Rupert Banks," she said. "After all, an earl's an earl. I can't say," she added judiciously, "that he seems much taken with Mona, but he's bound to know a lot of swells."

Even Anemone shed some of her tragic air at the prospect of going to the Opera House for the first time. She was more animated than usual, and her petite beauty caused several male heads to turn when she accompanied her mother and Rosamund on a whirlwind of shopping. But on the night of the opera Rosamund found her staring at the mirror with a woebegone expression in her blue eyes.

"I wish that Wilfred—Mr. Dilber, I mean—could see me now," she murmured.

Anemone's peach-colored tunic dress edged with gold was perfect for her delicate coloring, and a small cap of pearls and silk roses made her look both appealingly pretty and very sad.

Rosamund sat down beside her friend and slid an arm around her shoulders. "Hasn't Mr. Dilber written to you?" she asked gently.

"No." Like a child, Anemone wiped her eyes with the

back of her hand as she added, "Perhaps he has forgotten about me. I wish I could forget about him, too, but I can't."

Rosamund hugged the younger girl. She knew only too well how hard it was to forget. For a moment her thoughts were full of Canada and the freedom of the wilderness—and then she thought unaccountably of the way Hawkley's eyes danced when he smiled.

"Don't be so down-pin," she said briskly. "The opera is before us, and we mustn't keep the earl cooling his heels."

Hawkley was used to females who were fashionably late and so was pleasantly surprised to find the ladies already dressed and waiting for him when he came to escort them to the opera.

"Do you think we look all right?" Lucy asked anxiously as he greeted her. "I never been to an opera before and sat with all the swells."

She looked guiltily at Mrs. Devinter as she spoke, but that lady was engaged in arranging the folds of her own modest blue taffeta. Lucy had insisted that her mentor also attend the opera to make sure that she made no dreadful social gaffes.

"We must not forget our fan," Mrs. Devinter said, fairly chirruping. "No, dear Mrs. Sample, you must carry it *so*. Think of it as a rose that you waft back and forth through the air."

Gingerly Lucy took the large ivory fan. "Don't the girls look as pretty as a painted wagon?" she wondered aloud.

But even while Hawkley complimented Anemone's costume, he was admiring Rosamund. Her black hair was gathered in a heavy knot at the base of her slender white neck and ornamented with a spray of ivory roses, and her dress of dark blue figured lace over an ivory-colored satin dress brought out the color of her eyes.

"Magnificent," Hawkley said. He realized that he meant

what he said and that he was actually looking forward to an interminable evening at the Opera House. "Simply magnificent," he repeated happily.

Lucy was in heaven even before they had reached the Opera House. Once there, she wafted her fan back and forth while regarding her surroundings with wide eyes. "Have you *ever* seen so many folks?" she said, gasping.

There were, Rosamund had to agree, a great number of people. There was a large crowd in the pits where the common folk stood, chaffering one another and laughing, eating meat pies and spitting out orange seeds wherever they wished. Soaring above the common masses rose four tiers of boxes hung with crimson draperies and decorated in gold and white.

As Hawkley guided them to one of these boxes, Lucy fairly trembled with delight. She looked about her with such frank curiosity that several ladies and gentlemen turned to stare at her.

"Oh, Ma," Anemone pleaded, "everyone is looking at us."

"It's you they're looking at, Mona," Lucy retorted happily. "They can see that . . ."

Her voice trailed off as she came face-to-face with a heavily mustached, rail-thin gentleman in formal dress and an imposingly statuesque matron in maroon silk laced with pearls. Rosamund's heart sank as she recognized Their Graces of Broon.

The duke looked merely sleepy, but the duchess raised her lorgnette and studied the small party. Even as she bade Hawkley good evening, her haughty gaze swept past Mrs. Devinter, dismissed Anemone, and fastened on Lucy.

Centuries of noblesse oblige were in that frigid look. In one second, poor Lucy was being weighed, found lacking, and shunted aside. Rosamund felt the blood rush to her own cheeks as Hawkley returned the duchess's greeting and added, "Beg to present Miss St. Helm."

The duke, looking far afield, merely grunted. His duchess's eyes narrowed. *"Well,"* she exclaimed.

"I trust Your Grace is well," Rosamund replied calmly. She curtseyed, drawing Anemone down with her as she added, "May I present Miss Sample?"

The duchess said nothing, but red spots began to burn in her cheeks. The memory of what her darling child had suffered at the hands of the St. Helm chit was like vitriol. She started to sweep past without recognizing the brazen vixen but realized that by doing so she would insult Hawkley as well.

The Earl of Hawkley was popular with the fashionable set. Among his numerous friends he counted members of the royal house, to whom he was related on his mother's side. His title was even more time-honored than her own. Much as she would have liked to give Rosamund the cut direct, the duchess was not such a fool as to risk offending the earl.

"Miss St. Helm," she said, through her teeth. "I did not know that you were in London."

"She's with me, Your Grace," the irrepressible Lucy exclaimed. Then, as the duchess's lorgnette swung in her direction, she hastened to add, "I'm Lucy Sample, Your Grace. And this is Mrs. Devinter, who's related to the Honorable Maria Devinter of Shropshire . . ."

Her voice trailed off under the duchess's icy stare. "You keep interesting company these days, Hawkley," Her Grace of Broon then said. "My compliments to your mother."

"What did I do wrong?" Lucy wondered aloud as the duchess, followed by her lord, sailed past. She appealed to Mrs. Devinter. "What did I say?"

Mrs. Devinter rolled her eyes at the ceiling and intoned,

"We do *not* address a duchess in so familiar a way. We wait to be first presented. Oh, Mrs. Sample! How could you have forgotten that?"

Lucy blushed a fiery red, and Rosamund spoke quickly to spare her friend further embarrassment. "I think it is time to get to the box," she said. "The opera will soon begin."

Not to be sidetracked, Lucy craned her neck and looked after the departing duchess. "I made a mess of things again, didn't I?" she asked sadly. "I disgraced us all. Me and my big mouth."

Rosamund did not know what to say. She was grateful when Hawkley said cheerfully, "Not a bit of it, ma'am. The duchess was probably in a hurry to get to her own box, that's all."

He ushered them all into his box and then set about pointing out various peers. He was so amusing and attentive that even the discomfitted Mrs. Devinter was soon laughing at his sallies. When he looked and acted like that, Rosamund thought, Hawkley seemed like a different man entirely.

Soon afterward, the curtain rose and music began. Unlike most of the other patrons who kept on talking among themselves, Rosamund was lost in the beauty of the music. Though the story was somewhat racy and amusing, an undertone of tragedy captured her imagination and kept her breathless.

She was so immersed in the opera that she did not realize how keenly Hawkley was watching her. He could not take his eyes away from her face. He had, during the course of the years, occasionally escorted his mother to the opera. He had also attended the proceedings with his friends from time to time. But never before this had he seen anyone so lost in the music.

"Are you enjoying yourself?" he asked when the first curtain fell.

She wiped her eyes and drew a deep breath. "Is it necessary to ask? It is like—it is *almost* like watching a sunrise over the mountains in Canada."

Hawkley actually found himself wishing that he could have seen such a sunrise. "The sun rises in England, too," he said, temporizing.

"That music was too grand to be confined to a mere English sunrise." Rosamund smiled mistily as she added, "I have never enjoyed myself more. Thank you for bringing us."

Hawkley felt something tighten in his chest. In that second everyone else in the Opera House seemed to melt away so that he and Rosamund were completely alone.

"Thank you for letting me escort you here," he told her, adding softly, "If you hadn't, I'd never have known what a Canadian sunrise looked like."

His words and the tone in which they were uttered caught Rosamund unprepared. One moment she'd been thinking of the music she had just heard, and the next it was as if she had stepped out of the safety of the opera box into a country where there were no boundaries, no horizons, and no reality except the earl's intense gaze.

There was a footfall behind them, and an unfamiliar male voice. Turning with an effort, Rosamund saw three gentlemen in evening dress enter the box. The first two—a tall, robust-looking young man and a slender, languid-looking personage—were unknown to her. The third was Lord Braden.

Hawkley's initial smile of welcome disappeared as soon as Lord Braden stepped into his box. "What's that fellow doing here?" he asked, gritting his teeth.

The ardor in his eyes was replaced with displeasure, and his voice throbbed with irritation. His dark brows drew together as the robust young gentleman exclaimed, "So it *is* you, Julian. Maggie thought it was." He bowed with unfeigned curiosity toward the ladies, adding, "Going to present us?"

Without even glancing at Lord Braden, the earl performed the introductions. "My brother-in-law the Marquess Hare," he added, "and the Viscount Lake. What are you doing here, Nicholas? Thought you couldn't abide the opera."

"No more can I," replied the marquess frankly. "All Maggie's doing. We're to leave for the country tomorrow to see Mama-in-law, y'know—and what must she do but have a night on the town. 'Straordinary ideas, that woman gets. Dragged Lake along for moral support, and we met Braden outside. I say, Braden, I expect you already know Hawkley here—"

"I'd thought the opera was the last place you'd be, Lake," Hawkley interrupted. He turned his back on Lord Braden as he added, "Not at Boodles's or at Waite's tonight?"

The languid gentleman shook his head and drawled, "It's only because of my deep and abidin' friendship for Nicholas and his charmin' wife that I'm here." He smiled at Rosamund. "Do you find the opera somethin' of a bore, Miss St. Helm?"

Before Rosamund could reply, Lord Braden said, "For myself, I enjoy the performance. The music, the acting—it's an experience. Wouldn't you say so, Hawkley?"

Once more ignoring Lord Braden, the earl said, "It's Miss St. Helm's first opera."

"No, is it? 'Straordinary!" exclaimed the marquess. "Julian, Maggie's sent me to give you a message, but I forgot what it was. Come back to the box and talk to her yourself, there's a good fellow. Ladies will excuse you for a moment."

"That is not a problem," Lord Braden said suavely. "I will remain and entertain the fair."

"Yes, do," Lucy put in. Her awe of having so many titled gentlemen about her at one time was fading into a glow of deepest satisfaction. "Stay, Lord Braden, and explain what everybody was shouting about during the first act."

Inwardly Hawkley seethed. Though he would have dearly loved to throw Lord Braden out of his box, he could not very well cause a scene. Nor could he ask the man to leave without having to answer questions that were best left unasked.

"I'll see Maggie later," he said curtly.

The marquess shrugged and began to discuss a new horse that he was considering buying. Hawkley heard only one word in ten, for his attention was divided between Lake, who was drawling pleasant nonsense to Rosamund, and Lord Braden, who was explaining the opera to Lucy and Anemone. He gritted his teeth as Lord Braden stopped short in his explanations to observe, "Permit me to say that you look in high curl tonight, ladies. I couldn't keep my eyes off you during the entire first act—"

Hawkley could no longer contain himself. "You've got no business here in my box," he snarled.

The marquess stopped in midsentence and stared at his brother-in-law. Lake exclaimed, "Eh? What's the matter, Hawk?"

Mutely the earl eyed Lord Braden, who had gone white to the lips. His lordship's hands clenched into fists, and for a moment Hawkley was heartened. Perhaps the man would call him out? But it was a forlorn hope.

"I will take my leave," his lordship said.

"Nonsense, Lord Braden," Rosamund exclaimed. She could not credit Hawkley's rudeness. "As Lucy says, we need you to explain the first act."

Lord Braden smiled gently. "At another time, perhaps," he murmured. "I don't wish to linger where I am not wanted."

Rosamund looked from his lordship to the earl's hard countenance and got to her feet. "I feel the need for air," she announced. "Pray escort me, Lord Braden."

"No!" snapped Hawkley.

Rosamund turned and faced him. "You said something, my lord earl?"

The earl looked as if he was ready to explode. Lucy, not understanding what was going on but eager to cast oil on troubled waters, said heartily, "Sit down, Rosa, do. You, too, Lord Braden. You haven't explained why that lady was squawking on about her pa."

"Your wish is my command, ma'am."

Lord Braden smiled at the earl, who cast a smoldering glance at Rosamund before saying, "Come on then, Nicholas—Lake."

He then turned on his heel and stalked out of the box. Looking nonplussed, the marquess and viscount bowed to the ladies and also made their exit.

"Infamous!" Rosamund said breathlessly.

"It's my fault." A wry smile touched Lord Braden's mouth as he added, "I see that my presence continues to irk Hawkley."

"Why?" Lucy burst out. "What have you done to get the man's back up?"

"In Hawkley's eyes, I'm a commoner. You see, my mother was my father's second wife. She was a mere lady's companion and not gently born."

She should have guessed that it had something to do with class. Even so, Rosamund felt a sharp sense of disappointment. For a moment Hawkley had seemed so human, so genuinely decent and kind.

Lord Braden was going on. "There is more to my confession. When I was hardly more than a boy, I fell in love with the sister of one of the earl's friends. It was devotion of the most pure and respectful kind on my part, but the earl couldn't forgive the fact that I'd dared to raise my eyes to a peer's sister. He warned me away from the lady and assured me that if I ever came near her, he would horsewhip me."

"Well, I never!" Lucy exclaimed. "What did you do, Lord Braden?"

His lordship sighed. "I was very young and foolish. I challenged the earl to a duel. But the lady in question begged me not to meet Hawkley, and to save her from scandal I went abroad."

He broke off and smiled sadly. "We are all impetuous when we are young. I had hoped Hawkley would understand this, but he obviously hasn't forgotten or forgiven me for my 'social breach.'"

"I think that it is all very silly," Anemone broke in. Her cheeks were flushed, her small hands were curled into fists, and her eyes were bright. She went on breathlessly, "I don't think you did anything wrong, Lord Braden. People should be judged for who they are and not—not because of their birth. A *gentleman* in the grain business is every bit as good as a lord."

Somewhat hurriedly, Lucy got to her feet. "I'm stiff from sitting," she announced. "Maybe we could take a walk outside and loosen up our legs."

As Lord Braden rose to escort the ladies, he drew Rosamund aside. "Perhaps I shouldn't have spoken. I don't want to prejudice you against the earl, Miss St. Helm. He feels protective of you and wants you to associate only with the most correct people."

Lord Braden was being far more charitable than the earl, and Rosamund felt angry at herself for softening toward Hawkley. "What I do is none of his concern—" she was beginning, when Lucy stopped her.

"But we should *all* be rubbing elbows with the right people."

She paused and gave her fan a dramatic swish. "I can see it now—we've been going at things the wrong way. I'm going to have a party, and I'm going to invite all the swells. That way, Mona, you can make your proper day-boo into society like Mrs. Devinter says. I'll have a real party that'll make everybody sit up and take notice. Now, what do you think of *that*?"

Chapter Six

"I told you no one would come."

Anemone settled the flounces of her embroidered blue China crepe dress into one of the brocaded wing-backed chairs that had been set up in the drawing room. "You saw how the Duchess of Broon looked at us at the opera, Ma," she continued. "She thought that we were getting above ourselves, and so we are."

"Stuff and nonsense." Lucy's generous mouth folded into stubborn lines as she added, "I'm English now, but I was born an American. A lot of folks are smarter'n me and richer'n me, but I don't admit to anyone being better'n me. And don't you think otherwise, either, my girl."

She stopped, breathing hard, and glared at Anemone, who merely wondered aloud, "So where are all the guests?"

It was the night of Lucy's party, and so far none of the invited guests had arrived. This was a shame, for Lucy had thrown all her energies into planning what she hoped would be a most successful social event. She had prattled on about her plans to Hawkley on the way home from the opera and was not in the least daunted when his lordship spoke no word of encouragement—and indeed preserved an ominous silence. Lucy's spirits were not even dashed when Rosamund had been less than enthusiastic about the proposed assembly.

"We don't know anyone in London," Rosamund had pointed out. "Who would you invite?"

"There's them that has their names in the society papers for starters," replied the undaunted Lucy. "Hawkley pointed a lot of gentry out to me at the opera." She had paused to add, with unexpected shrewdness, "But I'm not inviting people like that Mrs. Chamondalay and her brother. They might think I was born yesterday, but they're 'squabs,' as Chief Storm Cloud would say. We're going to have nothing but swells at our party, starting with the earl and Lord Braden."

"It will be a waste of time to invite Hawkley," Rosamund had warned. Since the earl had stalked out of the opera box, they had exchanged a total of ten words, and he had not come anywhere near the Samples after that night.

Nonetheless, invitations had been sent out to unexceptionable ladies and gentlemen, and while the Sample household had been thrown into paroxysms of preparation, Lucy had set about the choosing of her daughter's attire.

"I don't see why you have to dress up as though you was thirty instead of twenty," she had protested when Rosamund refused to order a new dress for herself. "That ivory silk's dandy for every day, but this is an *occasion*. Snakes, dearie; you'll be fair put in the shade by all them ladies in their gems and jewels. And by the lords, too. Those fellers can knock out your eyes with the colors they wear."

Tonight everything shone or glittered. Tim Cressade, hovering between a nervous breakdown and inspiration, had produced wonders in his kitchen, and delicious smells filled the air. The servants had spent hours arranging potted plants and hothouse flowers and repositioning furniture, and the musicians that Lucy had hired for the evening had taken their places in a corner of the staircase hall. The footmen in their impeccable livery were waiting. Bleak, for once, did not have time to sneer.

"Well," Lucy said, "we're ready. The swe—I mean, the Quality are always late, that's all."

She twisted her hands in her new gloves and fiddled with the silk roses that the fluttering Mrs. Devinter had pinned in her hair. "I hope I look all right, Rosa. I hope I did right in not choosing that striped dress with the lace. I can't make any mistakes tonight, for Mona's sake."

Rosamund looked at Anemone, who had the faraway look of one lost in her own thoughts. She went over to Lucy, bent down, and took her hands in both hers. "Is all of this necessary?" she asked gently. "You know that Mona won't be happy with any of the lords or gentlemen that you choose for her."

Lucy's normally cheerful face took on a stubborn look. "I know what you're talking about," she replied, "but you needn't worry. Mona ain't talked about *him* for weeks. And tonight she's going to have her pick of lords." She added almost defiantly, "Mark my words, they'll come. They're late, that's all. They'll come."

"Truly, I almost wish we had gone to Mrs. Sample's."

The Marchioness of Hare tossed her chestnut locks, agreeably arranged in the Roman style, and paused to smile at the Viscount Lake, who had joined her and her marquess in a corner of the crowded drawing room. "I vow that I was tempted to accept the invite," she added. "Anything would have been preferable to dying of tedium."

She rolled her eyes at a far corner, where a Junoesque lady in a puce satin dress and bejeweled matching turban was holding court.

"*Anything* would have been more entertaining," the marchioness repeated, "but Hare would not let me accept Mrs. Sample's invite. He said that it wouldn't be the thing at all."

"What's not the thing, Maggie?" a deep male voice asked, and the marchioness turned to greet her brother with unfeigned delight.

"I didn't know you'd be here, Julian. I thought you had more sense than to come to one of Broon's assemblies. I vow that I am so bored, I have been regretting the fact that Nicholas made me throw Mrs. Sample's invitation into the fire."

Hawkley's dark brows rose, but before he could comment, his brother-in-law protested good-naturedly, "I didn't do no such thing. Just told you that it was 'straordinary to get an invitation to dine with a cit."

"A cit who's also an American," the viscount pointed out.

"Lord, Lake, don't breathe the word 'American' around Broon," the marquess warned hurriedly. "Man's as mad as a march hare on the subject. Hates the colonials. Things he'd like to do to them would curl your liver, Maggie. 'Straordinary, really."

"What is extraordinary," his lady said, sighing, "is that we all continue to come to Broon's assemblies. If the duchess were not so well connected, we would avoid her as we are avoiding the Samples." She paused. "But, Julian, why are *you* not at the Amer—that lady's soiree? You are so well acquainted with her charming houseguest, after all."

There was no mistaking the gleam in his sister's eye. In dampening tones, Hawkley reminded her that Miss St. Helm was merely the sister of a schoolfriend. "He asked me to look out for her from time to time," he added for good measure.

The marchioness looked even more interested. "I hoped you would introduce me to her at the opera, but you were odious enough to escape without doing so. I have heard that she rescued a pack of Mohawks in the Park, too. She must be an Original!"

The Viscount Lake changed the subject. "I did hear that the Sample woman had an excellent cook," he drawled. "He gave March the sack."

"Bamming us, ain't you? Cook giving a duke the heave-ho? 'Straordinary nonsense," marveled the marquess.

"My word on it, it's true. These cooks are wondrously independent. And as far as Miss St. Helm goes, she's a ravishin' brunet."

The marchioness turned on her brother in high excitement. "Julian, have you formed a *tendre* for Miss St. Helm?"

"Oh, dash it, no!" exclaimed the earl. "Good God, what an idea. Woman's impossible, Maggie—and so are you to believe such slum."

At this point several other personages joined their group. Under cover of the general talk, the marquess drew his brother-in-law aside. "Don't let Lake put the touch on you," he warned. "He's in dun territory again. Played all night last evening and lost every game. 'Straordinary how bad his luck is."

"Were you with him, Nicholas?" Hawkley knotted his brows in concern. "You should've tried to stop him. You know how he is once he starts."

"It's in the blood," replied the marquess sagely. "Lake's

father's a gamester, and his brother as well. Tried to talk sense to him, but he was in high croak, sure he was going to win. Now he wants to try some hell near Boar Square."

He paused for a moment, then cleared his throat to ask somewhat diffidently, "Meant to ask you, but haven't been able to get you alone. Thought Curtis Braden was a friend of yours. What was all that 'straordinary business at the opera t' other night?"

Hawkley's eyes were grim. "He's no friend of mine. Don't have anything to do with the fellow, Nicholas. He's a thoroughly bad hat."

"Well, I won't," replied the marquess equably. "Don't know the man, anyway. He came with us to your box that night because Lake's acquainted with him."

The earl did not reply. He was remembering the last time he had seen Lord Braden and how Rosamund St. Helm had ranged herself with the fellow against him. The memory still rankled. If Miss St. Helm preferred Braden's company over his, the earl thought wrathfully, the woman was beyond redemption.

He had deliberately stayed away from Broad Street all this time and busied himself with his many friends in London. Away from Miss St. Helm's insidious influence, he had enjoyed afternoons at Jackson's Saloon and at Manton's Shooting Gallery. And tonight, instead of attending Lucy's party, he had accepted an invitation to Broon's boring assembly.

Hawkley was considering how soon he could remove himself without being rude when he heard his hostess exclaim, "It is too shocking for words."

The duchess, surrounded by several of her guests, had drifted nearer. "I am shocked," she repeated. "I knew that the St. Helm gel was wild to a fault. How often has she been observed driving or riding in the city without so much as her groom in attendance? Wild, I say, and hot at hand. But she has outdone herself this time."

"What's Miss St. Helm done now?" Hawkley wondered aloud.

The duchess turned to see who had dared to interrupt her, and, seeing that it was Hawkley, deigned to explain. "All of London is talking about the incident involving her and some thieving savages," she said. "I hear she was nearly arrested in the Park."

Her long nose quivered, her small mouth screwed up to a malicious knot. The ladies and gentlemen around her nodded their heads and murmured horrified comment. Hawkley found himself protesting. "Your Grace is misinformed. I happened to be there when the incident took place, and I know for a fact that the Mohawks never stole anything. Good thing Miss St. Helm was there or an injustice would've been done."

Such was the duchess's indignation that the plumes on her turban bobbled. "I see that you continue to be in charity with the gel," she said icily. "I had not thought that you would be so easily taken in, Hawkley. And apart from her own actions, consider the person with whom Miss St. Helm is residing. One look at the Sample woman and her common manners were enough for me. I cannot credit it that even an American could be so vulgar."

Before Hawkley could frame a reply, the Duke of Broon, who had been standing nearby looking half-asleep, came to life with a jerk. "Quite right," he exclaimed. "Ha! War with the demmed Americans, is it? Shameful business. Let me tell you—"

At Hawkley's side, his brother-in-law groaned. "That's torn it. Man'll talk about nothing else all evening. Come away, Julian, and we'll—"

"Miss St. Helm," declared the duchess in a tone that cut across her lord's monologue, "has no idea of propriety. Imagine the sister of a viscount hobnobbing with half-naked savages. It is enough to make one cringe with disgust."

"Disgustin'," His Grace of Broon agreed promptly. "Everything about this war's an outrage. And the way our government pussyfoots around— I say, send in the demmed divisions. Man the demmed battleships. Wipe out the demmed rebels."

"But the Mohawks aren't savages," protested Hawkley. "They're guests of His Majesty's government."

"Damn the government!" shouted the duke. "Ha! Bunch of old women pussyfootin' around. Not one of 'em has any demmed guts. That business about that demmed ship, *Constitution*, attackin' the *Java* off the Brazilian coast— The Americans got the better of us only because our demmed navy's desperate for men. Only way they can get recruits is to kidnap 'em and impress 'em into service."

"Guests or not, they are savages. No doubt Miss St. Helm finds their manners refreshing," added the duchess nastily, "since *she* is also farouche. I truly pity Craye for having such a sister."

The spiteful words were uttered loudly and with conviction. Hawkley forgot that he had often expressed these same sentiments and exclaimed with some heat, "A touch too loud, that, ma'am. Miss St. Helm may have odd ideas, but dash it, she's a lady. As to Mrs. Sample, she's not an American any longer. She—"

"Demmed Americans are disguising frigates as line-of-battle ships. Gives them an unfair advantage," fumed the duke. "Demmed unsportin' of them. That's Americans for you. No sense of what's right and honorable. I tell you, we should wipe them all off the face of the earth."

The duchess raised her voice. "You may defend Rosamund St. Helm as you please, Hawkley, but she will never be given access to *my* company." She paused to add maliciously, "Do you know that they are calling her the 'Wild Rose' these days? It must be due to the common company she keeps. Birds of a feather, as they say."

"There's nothing common about Miss St. Helm," Hawkley snapped, and, hearing the note in his voice, the marquess plucked at his sleeve.

"Julian," he whispered. "I say, old fellow. Don't want to wrangle with our *hostess*. 'Straordinary bad ton."

Ignoring his brother-in-law, Hawkley said angrily, "You shouldn't listen to gossipmongers, ma'am. And Mrs. Sample's no colonial. Married an Englishman. Nothing common about her, either, come to that. She a kind woman, completely respectable."

"Respectable is as respectable does," the duchess fairly snarled. "Your dear mother would be grieved to hear you defend this—this hoyden, Hawkley."

"Nothing of the sort. She'd be the first to defend her." The earl added warmly, "Lady Constance is as loyal to her friends as Miss St. Helm is true to hers. And she hates backbiting."

The duchess was speechless. Her lord took advantage of her momentary silence to rumble, "Americans are crafty. They've got demmed spies everywhere, sent here to undermine the government. I tell you, I know what's goin' on."

Recovering herself, the duchess shot a final broadside across the duke's meandering. "I had not known that you were Miss St. Helm's champion, Hawkley. Since you are in such charity with her, I wonder why you did not accept the invitation to the Sample woman's soiree?"

"But I *am* going to Mrs. Sample's."

Hawkley stopped short as he realized what he had just said. He had not only accepted Lucy's invitation but had also championed Rosamund in front of dozens of witnesses. For a moment, he regretted what he could only consider a fit of insanity. Then, remembering what the duchess had said, he knew he would do it again if need be.

At his elbow the marquess was exclaiming, " 'Straordinary, Julian . . . Can't mean it." As his brother-in-law bowed to his hostess, turned on his heel, and began to stride through the room, he added plaintively, "You ain't really going to that American woman's? Ain't done, Julian. Not the thing at all."

Over his brother-in-law's shoulder, Hawkley caught a glimpse of the duchess's empurpled countenance. A fit of reckless madness seized him. "Why not?" he demanded in ringing tones. "As Lake says, Mrs. Sample's got a dashed fine cook."

On Broad Street, the minutes had long ago ticked into hours—and yet the ladies continued to wait. Nothing happened. No carriage rattled into the courtyard and no voices wafted up the stairs. Mrs. Devinter fell asleep in her chair and snored softly; Anemone's pretty dress became wrinkled; Bleak was heard to announce that he, for one, was not surprised that anyone who *was* anyone had given the Samples the cut direct.

At ten o'clock Lord Braden arrived. Rosamund went downstairs to greet him and shook his hand gratefully. "Thank you for coming," she said. "You are our only guest so far."

Lord Braden looked up at Lucy, who was waiting for him at the top of the stairs. She looked so forlorn that even the roses in her hair seemed to be drooping. "Then no one else has accepted Mrs. Sample's invitation? Not even Hawkley?"

Him least of all, Rosamund thought bitterly. Aloud she said, "Poor Lucy had her heart set on a grand party. I was afraid that something like this might happen."

Lord Braden shook his head sadly, then looked up again and saw that Anemone had joined her mother on the second-floor landing. "I will endeavor to cheer the ladies," he promised.

Before following his lordship up the stairs, Rosamund paused to look out of a many-paned window on the staircase landing. It was sleeting outside, and Broad Street had a dismal look. In that moment she truly hated the city and the peers who controlled it, the restrictions and rules that caused hurt to so many. Lucy was a finer woman than many a duchess or countess, but these ladies would never acknowledge her existence.

Suddenly Rosamund stared. A carriage had come rattling up to the door. Behind it came another carriage. And another.

"Lucy," she cried, "I believe that guests are arriving."

An enormous sigh shook Lucy. "It's kind of you to try and cheer me up, dearie," she said, "but it's all right. I can face the fact as I made a bad mistake."

"No, really, Lucy—they've come."

Rosamund's words were punctuated by a knocking on the door. She ran to the landing in time to see several gentlemen and ladies entering the vestibule.

The Marquess and Marchioness of Hare were announced first. Then came the Viscount Lake, Lord and Lady Pratt, and the Honorable Mr. Forthingay, who was the fourth son of the Duke of Chambers, escorting Miss Cordelia Temlar and her aunt, Lady Sutton. On and on they came, ladies and gentlemen from among the Top Ten Thousand, and behind all these glittering folks walked the Earl of Hawkley.

"I hope we're not too late, Mrs. Sample," he said.

"Well, I never," Lucy exclaimed in an awed tone. Then, beaming, she trotted down the steps to greet her company.

Rosamund stayed where she was. She knew that the gentry had not come in answer to Lucy's invitation and that somehow Hawkley had engineered this minor miracle. She did not know exactly why he had done it, but she was so grateful to him that she could have thrown her arms about him and kissed him.

But Rosamund soon realized that the evening was not an unqualified success. Though the guests were ushered into the gleaming drawing room and were plied by servants bearing salvers of potations and Tim Cressade's gourmet delights, there was an almost palpable constraint in the air. Lucy was so nervous that she could hardly speak, and Anemone looked bewildered and shy. The guests themselves exchanged speaking glances, and Lady Sutton was overheard whispering to her niece that they had but exchanged one boring social gathering for another with much less ton.

To make matters worse the musicians were playing slow, almost funereal airs. Rosamund had slipped out into the hall to ask them to strike up a more sprightly tune when she heard a step behind her. Turning, she saw that Hawkley had followed her out into the hallway.

Rosamund completely forgot how angry they had been with each other at the opera and went toward him with her hands outstretched. "Thank you a hundred times," she told him earnestly. "Thank you, for Lucy's sake. I know that no one would have come here tonight if it had not been for you."

Hawkley looked down at the lovely face that was raised to

his and felt an odd sensation of weightlessness. He forgot how often he had ground his teeth when he thought of the impossible Miss St. Helm.

"I didn't have anything to do with it," he managed to say. "My sister and my friends were desperate to escape Broon's boring assembly."

Rosamund shook her head. "You are telling whiskers. I think that Lady Margaret is charming, but I doubt if people would have come here if you hadn't intervened. I know that you did it for Bevan, but I am so grateful."

Looking down into eyes the color of sun-washed violets, Hawkley spoke the absolute truth. "Whatever little I did," he said, "I did for you."

Rosamund caught her breath. It was a mistake, for she had pulled into her lungs the distillation of Hawkley's clean scent. She realized how tall he was, how broad his shoulders were in his handsome black evening clothes, and how he was smiling in a way that made her feel suddenly giddy.

Their eyes locked and held. In that instant it felt as if the air about them seemed charged with static electricity. Rosamund felt as if she were being pulled forward by irresistible force. She felt weak in the knees and yet at the same time alive, so vibrant with energy.

She tried to rally. "Another whisker, sir. I know that my brother—"

"Oh, the devil fly off with your brother," Hawkley exclaimed.

There was more knocking at the door, followed by an outcry from the footmen. "My God," Hawkley ejaculated. "What's that?"

Up the stairs ran Storm Cloud, Silver Beaver, and Flying Crow. They were dressed in fringed deerskin jackets and breeches. Their faces were daubed with white and yellow paint, and feathered headdresses bobbled on their heads. Their chests were covered with beads.

"Hear there was potlatch, so we come to potlatch," declared Storm Cloud.

"What's a potlatch?" Hawkley whispered to Rosamund, whose reply was lost in the shriek of fright given off by the leader of the orchestra. He dived behind a potted plant while his comrades also scurried for cover.

"What's going on?" Lucy had come to the drawing room door. She stopped dead, staring at the Mohawks, who stalked past Lucy and entered the drawing room, which instantly exploded into curses, gasps, and squeals. Mrs. Devinter fainted dead away. The other ladies clung to their escorts, who hastily ranged themselves in defensive postures.

"Snakes alive! What's going on here?" Lucy gasped.

Rosamund could see the doubt and the beginning of hurt in Storm Cloud's eyes. The Mohawks had not been invited, but they had heard about the party and had assumed they would be welcome.

She could not allow their feelings to be hurt. Walking to the center of the room, Rosamund said formally, "Welcome, Chief Storm Cloud. Welcome, Silver Beaver and Flying Crow." She turned to the pop-eyed guests and explained, "This Mohawk chief and his companions have honored us by coming to our party. It is their first appearance in London society."

Everyone stared at Rosamund and then at the Mohawks. No one made a sound. In that awful stillness, Hawkley stepped forward and held out a hand. "Good to see you again, Chief Storm Cloud," he said heartily. "Let me introduce you to my sister, the Marchioness Hare."

The tension in Storm Cloud's fierce face relaxed. "Ah, Chief Hawkley. Your sister is here? Then I be introduced."

With great dignity he followed Hawkley toward the Marchioness and her astounded husband. But by now curiosity and interest had replaced the fright with which the newcomers had been greeted. One of the ladies let out a nervous giggle as she was introduced, but the Marchioness Hare's eyes were already bright with amusement and appreciation.

"Do you always dress like this, Chief?" she wondered aloud.

"These ceremonial clothes. Only for big potlatch or war," said Storm Cloud. With a princely air he allowed himself to be introduced in turn to the now fascinated nobility.

Rosamund blessed the Earl of Hawkley's presence of mind. She also blessed the Mohawks as the hitherto stilted party came alive. The gentlemen asked hundreds of questions about hunting and fishing in Canada. The ladies asked to feel the softness of the feathers, and vivacious Lady Pratt was delighted when Flying Crow took off his headdress and placed it on her head. Silver Beaver gave a rendition of a war whoop. Soon the guests were chattering with the Mohawks or about the Mohawks, and every constraint had fled to the winds.

Hawkley watched Rosamund mingling with the guests and saw that she was equally at ease with the Top Ten Thousand as she was with common folk. She had no hauteur, no airs or graces. In fact, she was charming.

"I'll take her to Fairhaven Manor," he decided aloud.

He smiled at the thought, but the smile died as he caught sight of Lord Braden. The man was talking and smiling with Anemone in a way that made Hawkley ache to draw his claret.

"You invite that man?" Storm Cloud had come to stand beside Hawkley and was following the direction of his gaze.

"No," Hawkley said shortly.

"That man is coward. He run and hide behind curtain

when we walk into room tonight. I see him!'' Storm Cloud paused, then added firmly, "In my country, we have way to deal with men like him."

"How?"

The Mohawk's grin showed all his teeth. "Take his scalp," he said.

Not for the first time, Hawkley appreciated what Rosamund had meant by freedom. With true regret, he shook his head. "Afraid it wouldn't do here in England, Chief."

But as he saw Braden using his charm on Anemone, he envied Storm Cloud. He knew that he, for one, would take a great deal of pleasure in scalping Lord Braden.

Chapter Seven

Rosamund was in her room putting on her bonnet when Lucy came trotting in.

"Rosa," she gasped, "you'll never guess what. We just got invited to the Countess of Standen's ball!"

She sank down onto the bed and regarded her companion with saucerlike eyes. "Imagine, Lucy Sample and her daughter being asked to go to a real ball," she said in an awed voice. Then she added, "You know who I should really thank, don't you?"

Of course she knew. What was more, Rosamund was about to discharge a part of her debt. Hawkley had asked her to drive out to take luncheon with his mother, Lady Constance, and she had accepted the invitation. Rosamund felt that she owed Hawkley that much for convincing his friends to come to Lucy's party.

"The Mohawks are the ones who should get the credit,"

Lucy was declaring. "They're the ones that the countess wants. And Lady Darcey, who invited us tomorrow night—she wouldn't even know we existed if it wasn't for Chief Storm Cloud."

There was much truth in this. In the days that followed Lucy's unorthodox but highly successful gathering, word about the Mohawks had buzzed around London. Chief Storm Cloud and his braves were the *on-dit* of every fashionable club and drawing room, and when no less a personage than the Duchess of Chelfordshire recalled that, in her grandmother's day, four American Indians had arrived in England and been lionized by society, the die was cast.

Here were these three highly entertaining Mohawks come once again to London! The gentlemen enviously recounted the braves' tales of hunting and fishing in an untamed land—while their ladies whispered behind their fans that Chief Storm Cloud was in every way so *savage* as to cause a delicious flutter in their breasts.

The Mohawks were being invited everywhere, with hostesses vying for their presence at their soirees, assemblies, balls, and routs. And because they refused to go anywhere without their friends, the Samples were being invited everywhere also.

"There's sure to be plenty of eligible lords and gentlemen at the countess's ball," Lucy was saying happily. "Mona'll make a hit, that's for sure."

Anemone was, at that moment, walking in the Park with Lord Braden—under the eye of Mrs. Devinter. "His lordship seems right taken with her," Lucy said complacently. "She looks more cheery, too. I told you Mona'd forget all about that grain clerk."

Rosamund paused in the act of picking up her pelisse. "Did you object so strongly to Mr. Dilber, Lucy?"

"He was a nobody," was the firm answer. "Mona's going to marry into the Quality." Then Lucy added, "Have a nice time with the dowager countess, dearie. It's a pretty day for a drive in the country."

Though tired to death of London, Rosamund had some reservations about meeting the earl's mother, and these doubts increased when she went downstairs and found Hawkley waiting for her in the ground-floor vestibule. He had his back to her, and there was something so rigid about his stance that Rosamund began to feel real misgivings. Supposing Lady Constance was cut out of the same cloth as the Duchess of Broon—

The thought made Rosamund stop short on the staircase, but it was too late for retreat. Hawkley turned and saw her, and the look that warmed his brown eyes caused Rosamund's heart, which had been slowly spiraling downward, to take wing.

As Lucy had said, it was a lovely day. Some distance from the city, they left the turnpike road behind them, and here in the countryside the air was full of spring, and the hawthorn hedges foamed with white. Further on, they passed meadows rich with wildflowers. Rosamund fairly leaned out of the curricle to admire the harebells, archangels, poppies, and daisies.

"How splendid it is," she exclaimed. "I can't believe that only a few hours ago we were in the city."

"Thought you'd appreciate an English spring."

Hawkley's tone bordered on smugness, and Rosamund checked her transports to amend, "The meadows in Canada were *incredibly* beautiful. There really is no comparison."

Even so, he was making inroads. With satisfaction, Hawkley noted the delight with which his companion greeted the changing scenery. "When you see my mother's gardens," he informed her, "you'll have to agree that they're beyond anything you've seen."

Soon the meadows gave way to a village of tidy stone cottages edged with flower gardens, a pleasant little church overgrown with climbing roses, and a pond where white swans glided.

Rosamund was charmed. "Has your mother always maintained a residence here?" she asked.

"Fairhaven Manor belonged to her family for generations. It was given to her great-great-grandfather—or was it great-great-great?—by one of the Tudor kings."

Rosamund felt a sudden check in her enthusiasm. With a lineage like that, the dowager countess must be truly formidable. She eyed the approaching manor house with some trepidation, but the manor, built of golden Cotswold stone, actually looked quite friendly.

Near the house stood an enormous cypress. "My mother told me that one of her ancestors brought a cypress cone home from the Holy Land and planted it here," Hawkley explained as they passed under the wide-spreading branches. "I'll wager you don't have anything like this in Canada."

As he spoke an old man in groom's livery tottered out to take the earl's reins. "Welcome, Master Julian," the gaffer said, wheezing. "Though I say it as shouldn't, you being the earl an' all now."

Hawkley grinned. "How are you, Gordons?"

"Still here, my lord." The old fellow sighed deeply as the earl dismounted. "I can remember when you and the late master—God rest his soul—came riding up this path together. Those were the days, Master Julian. Those were happy days."

He had heard this plaint many times before, so the earl only nodded. But as he went around the curricle to hand

Rosamund down, he chanced to glance at the old fellow's face. The tears he saw in Gordons's eyes touched something within Hawkley, and he, too, felt a sharp twist of regret for days that could not come again. He looked more attentively at the old groom and remembered Gordons as a smiling young man who had walked beside his first pony and comforted him after his first fall.

"D'you remember the time I came a cropper down by the fence?" Hawkley asked impulsively. "My father gave me a lecture on being a man and keeping my seat, but you dusted me off and let me cry on your shoulder." He paused. "Always wanted to thank you for understanding how I felt."

He put an arm around the bony old shoulders. "Glad you're keeping fit, Gordons. Wouldn't trust anyone else to lay a hand on these grays."

As the gratified old fellow led the horses away, Rosamund said softly, "That was a kind thing to do. Gordons loves you very much."

"Well, I care about the old fellow—"

Hawkley stopped short. He had always taken for granted that servants held their employers in high esteem, but the thought that he himself could care deeply for his retainers had never crossed his mind. He stared thoughtfully after Gordons, who had reached the stables and was joyfully ordering everyone about.

"After all," he amended, "Gordons was good to me when I was still a brat. Had my sister and me on horseback before we were out of leading strings."

He broke off as the manor door opened, then exclaimed, "Ah, there you are, Prescott. Mother expecting us?"

A butler, smiling and bowing with welcome, made haste to usher them into a room furnished in rose colors. Here a lady was reclining on a Chinese daybed with a fine Spanish shawl across her knees.

Constance, Dowager Countess of Hawkley, was a tall woman, with hair that had once been red-gold but that had now faded to a lovely peach color. Her eyes were as brown as her son's, and her long-lipped mouth was both strong and humorous. Though she was not at all beautiful, she exuded such warmth that all of Rosamund's reservations disappeared like morning mist.

Lady Constance apologized for not rising to meet them, explained that she was recovering from a trifling indisposition, then held Rosamund's hand for a long moment and looked into her eyes. "So you are Mary St. Helm's daughter," she said. "I have heard about you, my dear."

"Indeed, ma'am?"

The dowager countess laughed. "No need to look so worried. I never pay attention to London gossip. I meant that I was acquainted with your parents. Did you know that?"

"No, I didn't," Rosamund admitted. She added eagerly, "Please, tell me more, ma'am."

"Your mother and I came out in the same year, and though I did not know her very well, I liked her. Lady Mary Standell was lovely and kind—and she did not make judgments about people. Also, she had the most beautiful smile. Many gentlemen saw that smile and fell in love with her."

Hawkley, who had been strolling about the room, stopped short and looked thoughtfully at his mother.

"Did you also know my father?" Rosamund was asking.

"I met him only once or twice, but that was enough to persuade me that he was an Original." Lady Constance chuckled reminiscently. "Jeremy St. Helm was always doing or saying something that outraged the tonnish set. When he made known his intent to take his family away to Canada, people spoke of it for weeks. They were sure that Lady Mary would not go.''

"But she did go," Rosamund pointed out.

"It was hard for her. I met her just before she was to leave for the New World, and she confided in me that she was most sad to leave her son and England behind."

Rosamund was troubled. She had always assumed that her mother had loved Canada as much as she and her father had loved that country. "But Mother was happy in Canada," she said doubtfully.

"She was with her husband, whom she loved above all things. You have the look of her, Rosamund—I may call you that?—but there is more of a hint of your father in you also." Lady Constance smiled at Hawkley, adding, "You could not have brought me a more welcome guest, Julian."

Luncheon was a pleasant affair, with Rosamund and Lady Constance chatting like old friends. After the meal, the countess begged to excuse herself.

"My tiresome medical man insists that I rest for an hour after every meal," she explained. "Julian will take you through the garden, my dear, even though I am afraid that it is not at its best without the summer roses."

But no apologies were necessary. Rosamund found herself holding her breath as they strolled past beds of pinks and heather, azalea and lavender, violets and the white stars of marguerites. Willow trees trailed their long green branches into ponds that were edged with more flower beds. Among the many blossoms, Rosamund could see the buds of summer flowers awaiting their turn to bloom.

"Well, what do you think?" Hawkley queried.

Rosamund drew in a deep breath. "Do you need to ask?"

"Thought you'd like it." Hawkley looked about him as he spoke and saw a white rosebud that had come to bloom in a sheltered spot. He picked it and offered it to Rosamund. "The first rose of summer," he told her.

She took the flower as though it were some great treasure and smiled up at him in a way that took his breath away. No female, Hawkley thought disjointedly, should have a smile like that or possess so soft a mouth. There was no getting around the fact—lips like that invited kissing. The heady scent of flowers, the spring warmth . . . all rushed to his head so that his blood pounded in his ears.

The intense look in the earl's dark eyes confused Rosamund. One moment they had been talking about gardens, and now it was becoming increasingly hard to breathe. It was becoming impossible even to think. Rosamund attempted to pull herself together and marshal her thoughts, but the white rose in her hand trembled, and she could hear her heart pounding in her ears—

No, not her heartbeat—hoofbeats! And above the thudding of horses' hooves, they could now hear a man shouting.

"What in the devil is going on?" Hawkley exclaimed.

Just then, one of the housemaids came skimming down the lawn toward them. "Oh, my lord earl," she reported breathlessly, "my lady sent me out t' tell you that John Wilkes from t' village's come t' the house."

"What's the matter with John?"

"His son's took real bad." The housemaid dropped her voice to a scared whisper. "John think it's t' putrid throat."

Rosamund felt as though she had been struck a blow in the chest. It seemed as though the warm and lovely gardens had disappeared and that she was surrounded by winter desolation. Raging winds whipped through her memory and brought with them the smell of medicine and the sounds of pain.

Hawkley saw Rosamund go very pale and instinctively put

an arm around her waist to support her. "I'm going up to the house," he said quietly. "Will you wait here?"

She was still pale, but she shook her head. Then, stepping free of the protective circle of his arm, she squared her shoulders. "If it wouldn't be an intrusion, I'd like to come, too."

Together they walked back to the house and into the drawing room, where a stocky young man was sitting slumped over in a chair. The countess stood beside him, patting his shoulder.

"I heard there was trouble, Mother," Hawkley said.

Lady Constance tried to smile but could not quite manage it. "I'm afraid there has been some distressing news," she said.

The young man began to cry. Swiftly Hawkley walked across the room and gripped him by the shoulders. "What can I do, John?"

The man drew the back of his hand across his eyes and tried to pull himself together. "Master Julian," he muttered. "I mean, my lord earl—our Ned's in a bad way."

"John rode for Dr. Marland," explained the dowager countess, "but the doctor is attending a difficult birth in the next county. John then tried Dr. Gill, but he would not come."

"What do you mean, *wouldn't* come?" Hawkley demanded wrathfully. "Man's a dashed doctor, isn't he?"

"Dr. Gill's doctor for t' Quality," John said, without rancor. "He's afraid of t' infection if it's t' putrid throat. He wunnot come for such as us."

A society doctor would be reluctant to run the risk of infecting both himself and his noble patients. Rosamund watched the dowager countess and her son exchange glances and asked, "Are you sure it's the putrid throat?"

John Wilkes shook his head. "I dunnot know, miss, but I

fear it. T' fever's high, and Ned can't breathe. T' wife and me are afeard.''

"We need a sawbones for a diagnosis." Hawkley strode toward the door. "Gill will come for *me*."

The countess nodded. "Go, dear. Meanwhile, I will go home with John and help to nurse Ned."

She was reaching for the bellpull, but Hawkley caught her hand and held it in both his. "You mustn't go, Mother," he protested. "You've been sick yourself and haven't got the strength for it."

"Someone must go," the countess pointed out firmly. "I cannot ask anyone else to run the risk of contagion."

"I will go." Both the earl and Lady Constance stared at Rosamund, who explained, "We were subjected to the putrid throat in Canada, and I'm familiar with the disease."

It was this illness that had taken her mother's life. Hawkley felt a rush of admiration for Rosamund's courage, but added, "I can't allow it. There's no need you should be put at risk for our people."

"But I have done my share of nursing. I know I could help."

"Out of the question," Hawkley snapped.

Rosamund felt a flash of annoyance that turned to understanding as she saw the look on the earl's face. Hawkley was not acting like the lord of the manor; he was truly worried.

"I am the logical person to nurse the boy," she began in a reasonable tone. "Consider the fact that—"

"I *said*, no."

As soon as the words were out of his mouth, Hawkley regretted them. He knew well the lift of Rosamund St. Helm's chin and recognized the determined light in her eyes.

"I don't want to break straws with you," she said firmly.

"I know how worried you are." She turned to the dowager countess once more. "Please allow me to help, ma'am. I know I can be of use here."

"Julian is right. The risk to you, my dear—"

"I contracted the putrid throat as a child. The doctors said that I would probably not get it again." She paused and added pointedly, "We are wasting time."

The countess nodded. "Rosamund is right. We *are* wasting valuable time. Rosamund, you and I will go to the village together."

Hawkley began to argue, but Rosamund forestalled him. "Every campaign needs a general directing operations, Lady Constance. Don't you agree that you are the only one who can coordinate our efforts from the manor house?"

She looked at the earl, who agreed immediately. "In case of an outbreak of the disease, you'll be needed here at the house, Mother."

Seeing that the dowager was wavering, Rosamund added, "With your permission, I'll write a note to Mrs. Sample and send it by my groom. If Lucy thinks that you have invited me to stay the night here at Fairhaven Manor, she will not worry when I don't return home."

The countess started to protest, then broke off to smile wanly. "I can't gainsay the two of you, especially since what you say makes sense. Write your letter, my dear, and John will drive you into the village. Julian, dear . . . Pray hasten for the doctor."

As they both left the room, Hawkley drew Rosamund aside. "I know that you're doing this to spare my mother, and I'm grateful, but I won't have you put in danger, Rosamund."

"Don't worry about me, Julian." They were both so tense that neither of them realized that they had addressed each other by their first names. "Besides, it's my own decision. I have no one to blame but myself."

Stubborn, obstinate—and pluck to the backbone. Hawkley was uncertain whether he wanted to shake Rosamund St. Helm or hold her close to him. "I'm responsible for your safety while you're under my mother's roof," he reminded her grimly.

About to form some retort, Rosamund realized that she was still holding the white rose Hawkley had given her. She thought of Lady Constance's readiness to expose herself to contagion in order to help her people and of the earl riding out to bring back a doctor for his tenant's child.

Their ways were not her ways, but both Hawkley and Lady Constance truly cared about their people. Rosamund's voice was softer as she resumed. "Let us hope it's not the putrid throat after all. The doctor will know—*if* he comes."

"He'll come even if I have to drag him," was the grim reply. "And mind you, be careful. Don't take any unnecessary risks."

Meadows said the same thing, but in far more agitated a manner, and it was some time before he was prevailed upon to take the letter to Lucy and say nothing about a possible outbreak of putrid throat. After her groom's departure, Rosamund left at once for the village and soon arrived at the Wilkeses' neatly thatched cottage. She was descending from Lady Constance's landau when a wild-eyed woman came to the cottage door.

"Is t' doctor with you, John?" she cried. When the situation was explained, she sagged against the doorframe and began to sob. "Oh, Lord. Our Ned'll pike away for sure now."

Rosamund went up to the woman and took her shaking

hands. "I'm Rosamund St. Helm, Mrs. Wilkes. I've come to help if I may. Will you take me to your son?"

Her voice was both compassionate and firm, and the mother reacted to the unconscious authority in it. "Come in, then . . . Come in, ma'am. Ned's in here."

There was only one large room inside the small but spotlessly clean cottage. Rosamund's quick eyes took in a few bits of furniture and water boiling in a kettle on the hearth. Blanket curtains had been suspended from the ceiling to set apart the sleeping areas.

Behind one of the curtains was a narrow bed on which lay a boy about six years old. Heavy breathing tormented his small frame, and a sense of pity and horror filled Rosamund as she realized that the child probably had the same disease that had killed her mother.

It took an effort of will for her to approach the bed and say cheerfully, "Hello, Ned. My name is Rosamund, and I've come to help you get better."

The child stared dully at the pretty lady who was smiling down at him, but he was too sick to respond. Rosamund rested her cool hand on his forehead and tried not to wince as she felt the fever almost singe her skin. She then ran both hands gently over his neck, her heart sinking further as she felt the distended lymph nodes.

"Is it t' putrid throat, ma'am?" the mother asked anxiously.

"I don't know," Rosamund replied. "I'm no doctor. But there is no foul odor and no nasal discharge, either, so that is a hopeful sign." She smiled down at the boy and said, "I want to look into your mouth, Ned. Will you let me do that?"

"Do as t' pretty lady says, Neddy," his mother pleaded. "Do it, lambie."

Ned's throat was both alarming and reassuring. There was

no viscous white membrane, but Ned's throat was alarmingly red. Once more Rosamund fought down her memories and her fear.

"We must bring the fever down," she declared. "I see that you have been sponging him down with cool water and vinegar, Mrs. Wilkes. Let me help you. Has he been drinking water?"

The child became delirious and thrashed about. In spite of the constant sponging, Rosamund could feel Ned's fever spiking upward. "It's not coming down," the mother whispered. "I dunnot know what else we can do, ma'am." Then she added sadly, "Ned's not the first one I've borne—and lost. I dunnot want to lose him, too."

"We aren't going to lose him." Rosamund sounded so fierce and determined that the mother was somewhat heartened. "You are worn out with nursing, Mrs. Wilkes," she continued in a gentler voice. "It won't do if you fall sick yourself. I am here now—rest for an hour or so. I promise to call you if there is any change."

Too worn out to argue, the woman obeyed. Wilkes stayed up with Rosamund for some time, but he, too, was desperately tired. When she told him that he needed his strength, he did not protest but stumbled to his bed on the other side of one of the curtains.

Left alone, Rosamund watched the day fade into the long English gloaming and continued to sponge Ned's hot little body. She sang to him, told him nonsense riddles, and despaired as his fever continued to rise. In the silent cottage she could hear nothing except the boy's ragged breathing and the sound of the wind outside. It reminded her of the bitter wind that had blown the night her mother died.

Suddenly she heard the clatter of horses' hooves. Leaving the sickbed, Rosamund hurried outside and almost fell into

Hawkley's arms. She looked out into the darkness, but there was no one in the earl's curricle.

"The doctor?" she questioned.

"Couldn't find Gill," was the grim response. "He'd left for London—probably as soon as he heard there could be putrid throat nearby."

He held her by the shoulders and looked down at her tired face. "Is it very bad?"

"Yes," she said frankly. "Yes, it is."

"There's another doctor in the next county who's willing to come, but he can't leave a surgery. My groom's stayed with him and will guide him here."

"I hope he will come soon. Ned is so small, and he isn't strong. Without a doctor's care I think he'll die."

There was a catch in her voice, and under his hands he could feel her tremble. Hawkley would never have believed that Rosamund St. Helm could be afraid, but there was fear in her eyes.

The fear was not for herself, Hawkley knew, and his voice was husky as he said, "I came back because I thought you might need help. We'll fight this thing together. Tell me what to do and I'll do it."

Behind her, Rosamund could hear Ned's coughing, and the sound seemed to paralyze her will. In a low voice she said, "I don't know if there's anything we *can* do. My—my mother had this terrible fever, too. The doctors and Tall Reed did everything they could, and dear Lucy nursed her so faithfully. But in the end Mama fell into a deep sleep and did not wake up."

There were tears in her eyes. Hawkley put his arms around her and held her to him. "Steady," he whispered. "I'm here, Rosamund."

Rosamund felt the comfort of that hard clasp and for a

moment rested her cheek against Hawkley's hard shoulder. His touch and the sound of his deep voice gave her strength and renewed her spirit so that she felt her weariness ebb away—and with it her sense of hopelessness.

Hawkley saw her renewed determination in the way she pushed away from him, in the way she lifted her chin and squared her shoulders. Rosamund St. Helm was ready to do battle—with death, if necessary.

"We're not going to lose the brat," he vowed.

Their eyes met—and in the earl's dark gaze Rosamund saw a determination that matched her own. Like comrades-in-arms facing the enemy, they marched into the cottage together; Hawkley resolutely removed his coat and rolled up his shirtsleeves. "What do you want me to do?"

In the hours that followed, while the exhausted Wilkeses continued to sleep, Rosamund blessed the earl's strength and endurance. Even when her own muscles cramped, Hawkley seemed tireless. He sponged the child, hauled cool water from the well outside, and held Ned in his arms while she made him drink.

"Ned must drink as much water as possible," Rosamund explained. "Tall Reed told me that if a feverish person does not drink, his body loses valuable fluids."

"Wish your friend Tall Reed were here right now— Damn that quack Gill," Hawkley growled. "John and his wife have buried three children already. Losing this one will kill them."

"You know a great deal about the family."

"John and I played together as boys." But, Hawkley recalled, such camaraderie had ended abruptly when he went away to school and became aware of the differences between a tenant farmer and the son of an earl. In fact he had hardly spoken to John Wilkes until his mother returned to live at Fairhaven Manor.

He did not know he had spoken this thought aloud until Rosamund asked, "When did your mother return to these parts?"

"Two years ago— That is, after my father died." He added thoughtfully, "He was killed in a hunting accident at Hawkley while I was in London. Driving my curricle—racing Lake, as a matter of fact—when it happened. I've often thought that if I'd been there with him, I could have done something to save his life."

Rosamund looked up at his altered tone and saw the shadowed look in the earl's eyes. Impulsively she reached out to take his hand in hers. "I understand," she said gently. "That's exactly the way I felt when Mama died. They sent me away because I was sick, also, and I thought—oh, for *years*—that if only I hadn't left her side, she might have lived."

He put his hand over hers, and they sat in silence for a long moment. "Every inch an earl was my father," Hawkley then said musingly. "A good man but a high stickler. Believed in the divine right of kings. Believed that that right extended to the peerage. He cared about his people in his own way, but he'd never have—"

Hawkley broke off, but Rosamund knew what Hawkley had meant to say. The late earl would never have dreamed of sitting by the sickbed of one of his tenants' brats. He would have taken care of his people—treated them justly and fairly— but there would not have been any personal touch.

She had not expected that Julian Dane would have done any of these things, either, but Rosamund noted how gentle his hands were as he sponged down the hot little body. "Not a bit of it," he said cheerfully, when she asked him if he was not fatigued. "Stayed awake all night playing cards plenty of times—*and* rode to hounds in the morning, too. Led the field, what's more. A man's got to have some dashed stamina. Well . . . time to bathe the poor brat again.''

Rosamund nodded wearily and bent over the sick child. Suddenly she bit her lower lip. ''What is it?'' Hawkley demanded.

Instead of answering, Rosamund felt Ned's forehead and his neck. ''Oh, dear God,'' she whispered.

Hawkley saw the tears well up in Rosamund's eyes and felt pain knife through him. Ned's tormented little body had gone quite still. It was over, and now it was up to him to break the news to John and his wife. If that blackguard Gill had come with him, it might not have come to this.

Then he saw how pale Rosamund looked, and his anger subsided. ''You did everything you could,'' he told her. ''More than everything. It's not your fault that the boy's dead.''

''Dead?'' Rosamund looked up in astonishment and then began to smile through her tears. ''But he's not going to die. The fever's broken, and he's sleeping soundly. Oh, Julian, Ned's going to get *well*!''

As she spoke, there were the sounds of carriage wheels and horses' hooves outside, and an irascible voice snapped, ''Easy with my bag, my good fellow— Easy, I say!''

''There's the sawbones!'' Hawkley strode out of the room, and Rosamund hastened to wake the Wilkeses and tell them that the miracle had occurred.

The doctor, a small, weary-looking individual in a rumpled frock coat, confirmed this miracle. ''This is not putrid throat but some childhood ailment. Sometimes young children have high fevers that ape the more virulent diseases.'' He smiled reassuringly at the parents and added that when the child awoke, he should be fed a broth made from chickens.

"I'll go strangle one of them hens right now," John Wilkes said, and his weeping wife thanked God, Miss St. Helm, and Master Julian in the same breath and swore that the moment her lamb awoke, the broth would be ready for him.

Watching the happy parents, Rosamund felt a lump rise in her throat. She knew that if she stayed here any longer, she would begin to weep herself, so she left the others listening to the doctor and slipped outside. Dawn was breaking, and the morning sun illuminated the little village. Dew glistened on the flowers by the cottage door and songbirds were chirping in the hedgerows.

She heard a step beside her and realized that Hawkley had joined her. "Isn't it a perfect morning?" she asked.

He agreed but added, "Mother won't have slept all night from worrying. We'd better get back to the manor house."

Their ride back to Fairhaven Manor was somewhat delayed at the onset, for the entire village turned out to ask for news of Ned Wilkes. "I never thought the sun could feel so wonderful," Rosamund said when they were at last clear and driving through the meadows.

Hawkley halted the horses and they looked over the dewy landscape. A meadowlark was fluttering in the almost translucent blue sky. A faint mist, like silver smoke, lay over the fields.

The earl drew a deep breath. "When I first saw Ned Wilkes, I didn't think there was a prayer that he'd get well."

"I didn't, either. I should have remembered that there is always hope," Rosamund said resolutely. "Once, Snarling Wolf was clawed by a bear. Everyone was sure that he would die, but my mother sat up with him, and Tall Reed came and gave him herbs and poultices and sang the old songs until he became well."

Listening to her, Hawkley realized once again how different Rosamund St. Helm's life had been. Tonight he had seen her steel and her tenderness, and he had at last understood. This woman was no hurly-burly female flying in the face of all that was correct. She was a magnificent creature!

No wonder her brother was frustrated. He was trying to mold Rosamund to fit one of the neat pigeonholes into which well-born Englishmen fit their women. Craye did not realize that this was like trying to make a mountain pretend to be an anthill.

"That dashed idiot," Hawkley said aloud.

She turned to look questioningly at him, and for the first time he saw the dark lines under her eyes. A surge of protectiveness filled him—together with a tenderness so great that it was almost painful.

He was looking at her in such a way . . . Rosamund's heart seemed to contract until all that was left was a throbbing core within her deepest self. She could not turn away from the bright light in Hawkley's eyes.

"We should be going back." She had meant to speak firmly, but her words came out in a quiver that ended abruptly as Hawkley gathered her into his arms.

His arms were strong—and well remembered. Rosamund felt as though this was where she had longed to be all her life. Here there was no sense of lack, or homesickness, or loneliness. Here was security and excitement and the joyous realization that she had come home.

And then he kissed her, and all these thoughts shivered away. Rosamund felt herself lifted out of time and place to a universe where no one existed but the two of them. Here the sun was golden and there was only the scent of hawthorn and the caress of the spring wind.

For a moment the magic held. Then one of the grays flung up its head and snorted, and like a thunderclap, reality returned. To his horror Hawkley realized that he was kissing Rosamund. He was kissing her in the open road as if she were some common serving wench.

And this was the woman he had promised to safeguard! The exhilaration of holding Rosamund in his arms faded before the enormity of his offense. Hawkley tried to think of some rational apology for his outrageous behavior, but his tongue would not move and his brains seemed to have taken French leave.

"Forgive me," he managed to say. "Don't know what— Beg that you'll forgive me, Miss St. Helm. It's been a—been a dashed trying night." Then he paused to add, "But that's no reason to act as I did."

Rosamund's heart, which had been singing with the larks, plunged like dead weight. Hawkley was apologizing as though this kiss had meant nothing more than some embarrassing social gaffe.

She had felt his kiss in her soul. But perhaps her emotion was only excess emotion generated by the camaraderie she and Hawkley had shared through the long night.

"Don't regard it," she said aloud. "Stress makes one act in peculiar ways. I'm told that fur traders who had many adventures in the wild become closer than brothers."

Not trusting himself to speak, Hawkley snapped the reins over his grays. As he drove, Rosamund closed her eyes to the breathtaking morning and wished with all her heart that she was safely back in Canada, where she belonged.

Lady Constance was so relieved and delighted by the good news that she vowed that she felt years younger. "And now you must lie down and rest," she told Rosamund. "Your groom has brought back word from Mrs. Sample that you are to enjoy yourself at Fairhaven, and I cannot send you home looking pale and wan.''

Rosamund could not in courtesy refuse the dowager's invitation. She washed and then lay down obediently in a comfortable guest room, but sleep would not come. And later, when they sat down at a late luncheon, she found that her appetite, too, had taken French leave.

Not so the earl. He was in high curl as he regaled his mother with stories of London, a curricle race he had won, and his sister's latest extravagances of dress. Nowhere could Rosamund see a hint that the earl was in any way disturbed.

Feeling uncharacteristically dispirited, she was grateful when Hawkley suggested that they return to London that afternoon. Lady Constance was genuinely regretful.

"You must come back and visit me," she told Rosamund. "This has not been a peaceful visit, and we must promise ourselves a long cose. Bring her back when the roses are blooming in May, Julian."

But of course, she would not return in May or any other time. In spite of the beautiful afternoon, Rosamund's spirits remained low, and they did not improve when they reached London. It had begun to turn dark, and the wind that blew across the city had a gritty feel to it. The clouds had rolled in as they drove, and now it was starting to drizzle. Rosamund pulled her pelisse around her and was grateful for the blanket that the earl had wrapped about her knees.

She was telling herself that she would feel better when they reached Broad Street when she became aware of a disturbance ahead. A woman, obviously drunk, was staggering along the middle of a nearby street. As Rosamund watched, a well-dressed man came up behind her and shoved her out of his way. The woman lost her footing and fell into a gutter.

"Oh, base!" Rosamund exclaimed.

Hawkley was intent on navigating the crowded street and did not reply, but Rosamund turned her head to see what had happened to the poor woman. She noted that the gentleman who had pushed her there did not even give his victim a passing look, but strolled nonchalantly into one of the many establishments that lined the street. As the man turned his head, Rosamund was astounded to see that it was Lord Braden.

It was only a fleeting glimpse. As she stared, his lordship—if it had truly been Lord Braden—disappeared into the building.

"What is this street?" she asked. "St. James Street . . . I have heard Bevan talk of it. Isn't that where the clubs and the gambling houses are?"

Hawkley nodded. "No place for a respectable female to be," he added as an afterthought.

She said nothing, and Hawkley felt a welling of protective feeling as he saw how tired she looked. He wanted to put an arm around her and draw her close to him, and the strong emotions that followed this thought confused him.

He was not—could not—have come to care about Rosamund St. Helm. It was not possible. Hawkley told himself that he was concerned about her only because Craye had asked him to watch over his sister—and knew that he lied.

"Oh, dash and blast it," Hawkley muttered under his breath.

Rosamund did not even hear. She was still wondering whether or not she had really seen Lord Braden push a woman into the ditch. Perhaps, Rosamund told herself, I was confused. Lord Braden, so sympathetic and kind, could never have acted in that reprehensible way.

She felt weary to tears and was grateful when they reached Lucy Sample's town house. She was even more grateful when Hawkley escorted her to the door and announced that since he had business in Sussex and must leave early in the morning, he would not come in to pay his respects to Lucy.

Handing her cloak to a footman, Rosamund went upstairs to the first-floor Gold Room, where Lucy was turning the pages of the *Mirror of Fashion*. When she saw Rosamund, she jumped up crying. "Now, dearie, here you are home again. Tell me everything. Did you have a good time with the earl's mother?"

"Lady Constance was charming," Rosamund murmured so listlessly that Lucy frowned.

"Snakes, dearie, you look beat." She hugged Rosamund, who had the almost uncontrollable urge to rest her head on Lucy's plump shoulder and burst into tears.

With an effort she stemmed the foolish tears, stepped back, and surveyed her friend. Lucy's ample form had been corseted into a striped taffeta evening dress trimmed with costly lace. Jewels glittered on her décolletage and there were several rings on her fingers.

"You look very fine," Rosamund exclaimed. "Are you going out?"

"Lady Darcey's crush," Lucy reminded her. She added smugly, "Chief Storm Cloud and the others are coming to fetch us in a little bit, so we'll make what Mrs. Devinter calls a 'grand entry.' Won't you come with us?"

Rosamund shook her head. "I'm a little tired," she said. "You and Mona—and the Mohawks, of course—must do the honors at Lady Darcey's. Where is Mona?"

Lucy's grin was full of satisfaction. "Changing her clothes. She's had company all afternoon, see. The Honorable Mr.

Paget and Lord Stanforth and Lord Braden all called on my baby."

"Lord Braden," Rosamund murmured.

"Sure. Anyone can see he's real taken with Mona." Lucy gave Rosamund a playful poke in the ribs. "I'd better go up and see what's keeping her, though. The Mohawks will be here any minute."

When Lucy had gone, Rosamund wondered what she ought to do. She was not sure that she had really seen Lord Braden on St. James Street, and to say anything to Lucy would be irresponsible.

It could not have been he, she told herself. How could it? Lord Braden would never act that way.

An insistent knocking on the door roused her from her thoughts, and a few moments later Bleak haughtily admitted Chief Storm Cloud. The young Mohawk was dressed in black evening clothes but sported a crimson waistcoat embroidered with roses. There were silver buckles on his shoes.

Rosamund complimented him on his attire and asked, "Where are Silver Beaver and Flying Crow?"

"They already gone to Lady Darcey," was the succinct reply. "Wanted to talk with you."

Rosamund was surprised. "Has anything happened, Chief?"

Abandoning the cumbersome English tongue, Storm Cloud lapsed into rapid Iroquois. "I grow tired of being stared at by fools on the streets," he said. "The English talk, talk, talk—about stupid things. The last time I was at one of these dinner parties, a man described what he called a hunt. Can you imagine that grown men and a pack of dogs run after a single fox—and often do not catch the fox?"

He shook his head at such idiocy, then resumed. "The air in London is bad. When the wind blows, it brings unclean smells. Also, the clothes that these English wear pinch at the wrong places."

"I understand," Rosamund said sympathetically.

"I don't want to go to Lady Darcey tonight, but my braves are looking forward to it. Silver Beaver has gotten a swelled head because the English squaws make a fuss over him. Flying Crow is young and stupid and likes to shock the English by giving war whoops and showing-off dances. He doesn't realize that we are mere curiosities to these people. Lately I have taken to walking about on the waterfront dreaming of home."

Rosamund nodded somberly, and the young Mohawk bent a speaking look on her. "You alone understand how I feel," he said.

Perhaps she had become more stuffy than she realized, Rosamund thought. It disconcerted her to have the young chief look at her so intently.

"In a few weeks I will be finished here and can go home," Storm Cloud said. "Don't you want to go home, too?"

Rosamund discovered that her mind had begun to wander and that she had been thinking not of Canada but of morning sun and an English meadow. The memories were fully as disconcerting as Storm Cloud's stare.

"Why dwell on something that can't be helped?" she said briskly. "I am here in England, and in England I will stay. I must make the best of it."

With some relief she saw that Lucy was coming down the stairs. "I am not going to Lady Darcey's tonight," she told the young Mohawk, "but I am glad you are here to accompany Lucy and Anemone."

Storm Cloud did not argue, but while the ladies were being helped into their wraps, he turned to Rosamund once again.

"You are too fine a woman to remain in this uncivilized

country," he said softly in his own tongue. "Remember that all things are possible."

And leaving Rosamund staring after him, he strode out of the room.

Chapter Eight

It was past three in the morning, but Rosamund lay wide awake in her bed. Lucy and Anemone had long since returned from their evening at Lady Darcey's, the house was shut and barred against thieves, and the servants had gone to bed.

Though she was usually a sound sleeper, Rosamund was kept awake by a tangle of disturbing images. There was the shock of seeing Lord Braden push that poor woman into the gutter. There was the look Chief Storm Cloud had given her when he talked about returning to Canada. And then, there was Hawkley.

Rosamund turned over on her pillow, but this did not keep her from recalling the taste and feel of the earl's lips. And she remembered how, after that passionate kiss that had left her universe reeling, he had simply excused his behavior as excess fatigue.

She did not understand the earl. He kept her off balance. He infuriated her. Yet he could also make her laugh, and he had nursed Ned Wilkes as gently and as compassionately as Tall Reed might have done. Sometimes he looked at her intently—not as Storm Cloud had done tonight but in a way that caused her knees to feel weak—but that was probably all for Bevan's sake. She could well imagine what her brother had said about her in his letter.

Rosamund sat bolt upright in bed, picked up her pillow, and hurled it across the room. It skittered against the window and landed with a *plop*, and she began to laugh. "What a fool I am," she said ruefully. "Now I'll have to get out of bed and fetch my pillow."

She padded across the cold floor and bent to retrieve her pillow. As she did so, she glanced idly out of the window and was startled to see a man standing by the steps of the house. She could not see his face because it was so dark and because he was well muffled into a hat and cloak, but she sensed that he was watching the house.

Here was a thief, or perhaps a glassman or snakesman employed by robbers to break into Lucy's house. Rosamund gave the bellpull a hard yank, and, pulling on her robe as she went, hastened to knock on Lucy's door.

Lucy received the news with the fortitude of a woman who had shot a maddened grizzly and had dealt summarily with drunk and disorderly fur traders, truculent Iroquois, and poisonous snakes. Nightcap aquiver, she jumped out of bed, shoved her feet into stout shoes, and demanded, "You've roused the servants, Rosa? Good! Let's go get that skunk."

Footsteps pounded on the stairs as the footmen, struggling to do up their shirt buttons as they came, rushed up the stairs. Bleak, his superior air for once dissipated by alarm, followed on their heels, and behind these stalwarts scurried the Sample ladies' abigails, Nancy, the housemaid, parlormaid, cook, housekeeper, and the little potboy, who was still in his nightshirt.

"Oh, what is happening?" Mrs. Devinter's door had popped open to disclose that lady swathed in a voluminous night robe and cap. "Dear Mrs. Sample, what is afoot?"

"Rosa has found a man outside watching the front side of the house," Lucy explained tersely. She added, "Go and get him, you lot. Don't make any noise or the skunk will get away."

Nancy scurried to Rosamund's side as if to defend her. The housemaid and chambermaid grasped each other's hands in terror. The parlormaid uttered a faint shriek. Mrs. Devinter clutched her heart and slid to the floor in a faint.

"Never mind her," Lucy ordered the pop-eyed footmen. "Get on with it. You, girls," she added to the maids, "take care of Mrs. Devinter."

Rosamund, closely trailed by the vigilant Nancy, followed the menservants down the stairs and up to the front door, where a pale-faced Bleak begged her to stand clear.

"This could be an Ugly Customer, ma'am," he warned.

But when the door was thrown open, no intruder lurked outside. "He must have heard us and taken to his heels. He can't have gone far," Rosamund said, urging them on.

Bleak held a lantern high while the footmen charged into the darkness. Watching them, Rosamund said, "He must have been a burglar. From the way he was watching the house, he was most certainly after something."

"Who was after what?"

Anemone, looking like a sleepy kitten in a white satin dressing gown trimmed with swansdown, had ventured out onto the staircase landing. She yawned prettily as she asked,

"What is all this noise, Ma? And what's the matter with Mrs. Devinter?"

That lady, who was sitting in a chair and being fanned by Lucy's maid, uttered a hollow moan and wailed, "Criminals are going to murder us in our beds."

"Rosa saw some polecat standing out in the street watching the house," Lucy explained. "He's gone now."

"He was watching *our* house?" squeaked Anemone.

Just then the footmen returned to report that there was no sign of the intruder. " 'E must 'ave legged it when 'e 'eard us coming," the senior footman said apologetically. "Shall us call the watch an' all, Mr. Bleak?"

The butler looked toward Lucy for clarification, but that lady shook her head. "This is London," she said practically. "If we was to worry about every varmint that's hanging about the city, we'd never get a wink of sleep. He's probably miles from here by now anyway."

Remembering the intent way in which the man had been watching the house, Rosamund was not so sure. "Perhaps the footmen should keep watch during the night," she suggested.

"Good idea. Lock up tight, Bleak, and let Edward and Benjamin each take a turn at watching the street." Lucy turned to her daughter. "Mona, you quit looking so scared and go to bed. You, too, Mrs. Devinter. We'll be all right with the footmen on guard."

Even so, Rosamund remained awake until dawn, when she dozed off only to be awakened by a pair of jarveys shouting underneath her window. With a heavy head she went down to breakfast and found Mrs. Devinter attacking a plate heaped with eggs and ham, chops and kidneys.

"I had always thought London to be a civilized place," she said, sighing. "My kinswoman, the Honorable Mrs. Maria Devinter of Shropshire, enjoyed coming here in past Seasons. But now I see that London has become a wicked place."

"No more wicked 'n most," Lucy said heartily. "Now you just put something in your innards and don't you worry none about that skunk from last night. Why, back at York Factory we had a lot more to deal with than a puny robber—"

She broke off in surprise as Anemone fairly bounced into the morning room. Her cheeks were pink, her eyes were bright, and she was humming. "Well!" Lucy exclaimed. "Somebody's looking spry today. I told you that you'd have a good time at Lady Darcey's party, dearie."

Eagerly she began to relate Anemone's triumphs. "There were so many swe—ladies and gentlemen there, Rosa! The Honorable Mr. Paget and young Lord Stanforth both kept asking Mona to dance. And then there was the Honorable Mr. Claude Somethingorother, whose father is a marquess, begging to have the honor of calling on us. Let me tell you, Mona's going to have her choice of lords."

She sank back in her chair and beamed at her daughter, who was piling her plate with buttered toast. "You should have come with us, Rosa," Anemone said, giggling. "You should have seen Silver Beaver dancing."

Rosamund could not get over the change in Anemone. It was as if the sun had suddenly shone through thick clouds. "Who did Silver Beaver dance with?" she asked curiously.

"No one. He danced the cotillion all by himself." Anemone giggled again. "I don't think Chief Storm Cloud liked it, because he just folded his arms and looked stern and *savage*. I am persuaded that he was missing you, Rosa. He told me that you were the only female in London worth killing a deer for."

Somehow this disclosure was not reassuring. "I am the

only one who can speak his language," Rosamund pointed out.

Lucy was still savoring Anemone's triumph. "Mona was the prettiest gal there, and everybody was taken with her."

Anemone made a little face. "Except for the Duchess of Broon."

"Oh, her." Lucy's brow furrowed as she went on. "I don't hold with talking bad about people behind their backs, but that duchess sets my hackles up. She looked right through me like I wasn't there! And her husband the duke muttered and fumed about the war with America. I'm English now, Rosa, but it made my skin crawl to hear the duke say he wanted to drown all the 'colonials.' "

She contemplated this unpleasant memory for a moment and then added more cheerfully, "Maybe Their Graces won't be at the Countess Standen's ball tomorrow night. Now, what will you girls do to keep busy? I'm going to lie down with a pineapple juice compress on my face—the *Mirror of Fashion* says that takes away wrinkles."

Rosamund suggested a drive in the Park. Mrs. Devinter pointed out that it would very likely rain but was overruled by Anemone, who exclaimed that it was an excellent idea.

"And it'll do you good, too, Mrs. Devinter," she added cheerfully. "You're looking down-pin this morning."

Half an hour later Rosamund was driving Lucy's phaeton around the Park. "Isn't it a beautiful day?" Anemone said enthusiastically.

In point of fact it was gloomy and none too warm for April. But as she trotted her horses around the Park Rosamund noted that several gentlemen and ladies, many of them unknown to her, bowed to them. Anemone explained, rather smugly, that she had met all these people at Lady Darcey's.

"So you have taken London by storm." Rosamund smiled. Anemone looked pleased.

"That's exactly what Lord Braden said to me." She dimpled.

Rosamund suddenly felt uneasy. "Was Lord Braden at Lady Darcey's last night?" she asked.

Anemone shook her head. "I don't think so, but then there were *so* many people. I'm persuaded that he'll come to call today, however. Ma likes him."

Rosamund felt even more uneasy. "What about you, Mona? Do you like him, too?"

Mrs. Devinter clicked her tongue primly and pointed out that young ladies did not discuss gentlemen in such a familiar way. "Well, I do like him. He makes me laugh and is sympathetic, too," Anemone countered. "Oh, Rosa, I'm glad we came to London. It is a *most* romantic city, don't you think?"

Before Rosamund could respond to this, she heard a peremptory voice call her name, and, looking up, saw an imposing barouche advancing toward them. It was driven by a man in livery and sported a ducal crest. "Her Grace of Broon," Mrs. Devinter exclaimed. "And that must be her dear little girl."

The duchess was resplendent in emerald armozeen frogged with gold. A bonnet with sweeping green feathers shaded her imperious visage. Beside her, looking deceptively demure, sat her daughter, Charlotte.

"What can she want with us?" Anemone wondered aloud. "At Lady Darcey's last night she completely ignored us."

Rosamund would have liked to ignore the duchess but knew that she could not in courtesy do so. Accordingly she slowed the horses and bowed slightly. "Your Grace."

The duchess noted the cool poise of Rosamund's bow and

she smiled sourly. "I have noted your progress in London society, Miss St. Helm," she said. "You are becoming an *on-dit* these days. I was remarking to Lady Darcey last night that it is entirely like you to set London by the ears."

"How entirely like Your Grace to be so perceptive."

Very few people dared to speak so crisply to the duchess or meet Her Grace's fulminating eye with such directness. Her Grace frowned. "Don't be pert, miss," she snapped. "I have your interests at heart when I say that you must remember how we are judged by the company we keep."

Anemone stirred uneasily. Rosamund's eyes had begun to sparkle dangerously, but she said nothing. Emboldened by this silence, the duchess continued, "To give you words with no bark on them, your brother would be horrified by what goes on at Broad Street."

The duchess had pitched her tones so that she could be heard by some half dozen interested passersby. Gentlemen stopped to look at Rosamund and Anemone through their quizzing glasses. Ladies, driving by on their perch phaetons and landaus, slowed their horses to wonder what was going on.

Rosamund's hand had tightened on her whip, but she only asked, "Is that all, Your Grace? The horses are getting tired of standing."

"Stay, Miss St. Helm. I have not finished. You force me to tell you something disagreeable." The duchess leaned forward to add with relish, "Your hostess, it seems, cannot regulate her household. That woman in your phaeton—the one who gives herself airs and social pretensions and puts about that she has noble connections—is an Impostor!"

There was a choking gasp from Mrs. Devinter. Glancing at her, Rosamund was horrified to see that she had turned the color of putty.

"She is *not* related to the Honorable Maria Devinter," announced the duchess triumphantly. "I inquired of a friend of mine who lives in Shropshire, and she has written to tell me that the Honorable Maria Devinter has no living relatives!" She regarded the trembling Mrs. Devinter with withering contempt. "No doubt this brazen liar felt that it would be easy to fool a mere American."

Charlotte suddenly leaned over the side of the ducal barouche and pulled a horrible face at Mrs. Devinter, who began to cry. Anemone, looking shocked and bewildered, attempted in vain to console her as the duchess swept on, "A fraud and an American—I am persuaded that the two are well matched. Even Hawkley will have to agree that for a sister of a peer to keep such company is indefensible."

"Mrs. Sample," Rosamund retorted, "is much more of a lady than you are."

The duchess opened her mouth, but no sound came out. Heedless of the ripples of horror that ran through the small audience that had gathered about them, Rosamund continued. "Lucy is a kind person, unlike Your Grace, who obviously takes pleasure in hurting people. I believe," she added heatedly, "that common decency and kindness are worth more than a trumpery title."

Without waiting to see the duchess's reaction to this statement, Rosamund turned the horses around and began to drive away, nearly upsetting a Bond Street tulip who was mincing across the Park. No one in the phaeton said a word until Mrs. Devinter whimpered, "Oh, what are you going to do?"

"Is what that horrible woman said true?" Rosamund demanded.

Mrs. Devinter nodded miserably. "My name is Dewinter, not Devinter. My parents were poor folk who died early. I— I was a governess for many years, but when my health gave out, I lost my position. I had few savings and was forced to go to the workhouse, where I nearly died of hunger."

So that was why the woman always stuffed herself with food. "How horrible," Anemone was exclaiming. "But why should you want to lie about your 'noble' relatives?"

Mrs. Dewinter dabbed at her eyes. "I was afraid that if I didn't lie, I would not get the position with Mrs. Sample." She added humbly, "It is dreadful to be hungry."

"You must tell Lucy everything." Rosamund was still so angry that she could hardly keep her voice steady. "Otherwise someone is sure to carry tales." Her voice softened as she added, "Please, don't cry, Mrs. Dev—Mrs. Dewinter. Lucy is not at all like that griffin. And—and we all have done things that we cannot be proud of."

It was a grimly silent group that returned to Broad Street, where Lucy was endeavoring to entertain callers in the drawing room. She welcomed Anemone's return with relief, exclaiming, "Those lords have come to see you, not me. Go in there and— What is it, Rosa? Why do you need to see me alone *now*?"

Reluctantly she followed Rosamund to an adjoining room, where an agitated Mrs. Dewinter was waiting to confess. "I lied because I knew you wanted someone genteel and well connected," she said, sniffling. "I know there is no excuse. I—I will pack my bags and leave at once."

She turned to leave the room, but Lucy, who had been looking by turns bewildered, concerned, and indignant, forestalled her. "You'll do no such thing! Leave me with the countess's ball coming up tomorrow and a roomful of swells waiting to spark Mona? Who's going to tell me what to say or do, I'd like to know!"

"But everyone will know the truth about me," Mrs. Dewinter wailed. "No one would want to associate with a liar, Mrs. Sample. I am of common stock."

"Well, so am I," declared Lucy. "You'll stay right here and bad cess to that duchess. But," she added, "you ought to have trusted me and told me the truth, Mrs. Dewinter. I'd have understood."

Mrs. Dewinter wept tears of relief and gratitude into her sopping handkerchief until Rosamund suggested diplomatically that she would go into the drawing room to be with Anemone. "That's right," Lucy exclaimed. She gave Mrs. Dewinter a bracing slap on the back, adding, "Now, you pull yourself together, that's a good soul, and let's go chaperon my girl. There's three young lords in the drawing room drinking sherry, and if we leave them at it any longer, they may get too drunk to see straight."

Leaving Lucy and Mrs. Dewinter to do the honors by Anemone, Rosamund started upstairs to change out of her driving costume. As she reached the second-floor landing, Lord Braden was announced.

He looked up at her, saying, "Miss St. Helm, my homage. I've been worried for you. I heard that you had a set-to with the duchess in the Park."

"Bad news has good legs," said Rosamund dryly. "I suppose that the Wild Rose's latest exploit is already on everyone's lips."

"No one who knows you will believe a word against you," Lord Braden vowed.

His lordship was genuinely concerned. His fine eyes expressed only kindness. Could this kind and sensitive gentleman have viciously pushed a woman out of his way?

It was not possible. She must have made a mistake, Rosamund thought. It was dark, after all, and she had seen the man for only a second. She must have seen someone who only *looked* like Lord Braden.

"I know you must have been in the right," he was saying, "but there are bound to be a few who'll deplore your conduct." He paused. "The Earl of Hawkley believes in noblesse oblige. It would be hard for him to understand why you acted as you did."

Rosamund recalled the duchess's cutting reference to Hawkley. "If you will excuse me," she said somewhat stiffly, "I must go and change."

Lord Braden's eyes conveyed perfect understanding. "I'm sorry I brought up disagreeable matters." He added delicately, "Miss Sample told me that you are all invited to the Countess Standen's ball tomorrow evening, but in light of this . . . ah . . . contretemps, you may not wish to subject yourself to stares and slurs. I would be delighted to escort you and the other ladies to the theater if this is your pleasure. *The Merchant of Venice* is playing, with the divine Mrs. Siddons as Portia."

But Rosamund knew that she could not run and hide, and Lucy was of the same opinion. "Once you get thrown from a horse, you've got to get up on right away or you'll be scared forever," she said. "I won't tell *you* to go, Mrs. Dewinter, but the rest of us have to make a push." Then she added hopefully, "Maybe that dratted woman won't be there."

But this seemed a forlorn hope. The countess's ball was one of the high points of the Season, and next evening when the Sample ladies' closed carriage arrived at her ladyship's fashionable residence, it was quickly surrounded by carriages, landaus, traps, phaetons, and curricles that were waiting to gain admittance through the gate.

Lucy eyed this massive portal askance. "Looks like we was going to church," she exclaimed. Then, as they finally gained admittance, she added, "Snakes, girls. How many footmen work for the countess, anyhow?"

More than twenty footmen, bewigged and liveried, stood on either side of a crimson carpet that led to the house. This dwelling had been built in the sham-Gothic style by one of London's famous architects and boasted an octagonal tower with several spires, turrets, and flying buttresses. Inside, the same mock-medieval mood prevailed. Torches flared in the great hall where the guests were assembled, and armorial bearings and the stuffed heads of various animals graced the rough stone walls.

Lucy looked around her with critical eyes. "It must be hard to heat this place in winter, but then I guess swells like the countess don't have to worry about things like that. Steady, girls. Here's that master of ceremonies announcing us."

Conscious of many watchful and speculative eyes, Rosamund followed her companions into the great hall, where they were received by their hostess. The countess was far too well bred to show any apprehension as she greeted her guests, but Rosamund saw her glance toward a corner of the crowded room. Her heart sank as she recognized the Duchess of Broon.

"Be careful," she whispered to Lucy. "That woman will do or say something spiteful if she gets the chance."

"Sticks and stones," Lucy said, but she looked nervous. "You said that Hawkley was in Sussex, and I don't see Lord Braden anyplace. Too bad. It'd be nice to see a friendly face."

Would Hawkley be friendly? But Rosamund had no chance to pursue this thought before there was a stir among the guests and the Mohawks entered the great hall. In spite of their very English evening clothes, they exuded a kind of pagan animal magnetism as they stalked over to greet the countess.

Once having bowed over his hostess's hand, Storm Cloud came directly up to Rosamund. "Did I do that well?" he asked in his own language.

"Very well, indeed, Chief. You are a true English gentleman."

Storm Cloud took Rosamund's hand and lifted it to his lips. "All thanks to you," he said. "Without your help, we would have been in prison for picking pockets."

"We should talk in English," Rosamund said. "It is not polite to talk a language that others cannot understand."

Storm Cloud grunted but obediently switched languages. "Here come Chief Hawkley," he announced.

Rosamund's heart beat sharply as she turned to see that the earl, together with his pretty sister and her marquess, had entered the great hall. When had Hawkley returned from Sussex? she wondered. And had he heard of the incident in the Park? She was heartened by the way the Marchioness of Hare smiled and bowed to her across the great hall, but she could not catch Hawkley's eye.

A group of the Mohawks' admirers surrounded them at this juncture, and as Rosamund stepped backward out of the crush, she heard Hawkley's voice at her elbow. "I need to speak with you," he said.

She knew him well enough to sense that he was disturbed. Deliberately Rosamund met his eyes as she whispered, "And I need to speak with you."

Hawkley was by now used to Rosamund's direct speech. He should have also been inured to the fact that her eyes were almost the color of violets, and that her mouth was like a rose petal. She looked lovely in her straight gown of palest blue lace over satin, so lovely indeed that he wanted nothing more than to catch her up in his arms and escape with her from this tedious ball.

Hawkley had gone to Sussex to give himself some needed distance from Rosamund. He had meant to stay at Hawkley Manor for several days. But today he had had a long and distressing interview with his land agent, during which Wagonner broke down and confessed that he had been using the earl's money to pay doctors and buy medicine for his sick wife.

"The doctor costs so much—and medicine is even more," Wagonner had said, sobbing. "I have been a criminal, but my poor Alice knows nothing. She's innocent of any wrongdoing."

A month ago, Hawkley might have called the police. He would certainly have dismissed Wagonner from his service. But this morning he had heard the despair in Wagonner's voice and had actually blamed himself for being so unapproachable that his people could not come to him for help.

So he had given Wagonner another chance and offered to help his sick wife. The man had sobbed like a child and fallen on his knees to kiss the earl's hand. If Hawkley had not prevented him, Wagonner would have kissed his feet.

Hawkley felt an odd tightening in his chest when he thought of that scene. He was both exhilarated and exhausted. After the emotional storm, he had called for his curricle and driven back to London, driven harder and faster than he had done in any race, because he had wanted to see Rosamund. All the reasons why he wanted to avoid her had disappeared, and all he could think of was that she was the one person who would understand how he felt and could advise him on sensible ways in which to help Wagonner.

Rosamund, watching the earl's face, thought she knew why so many emotions were shadowing his dark eyes. She decided to take the bull by the horns and said, "I suppose you have heard about my set-to with the Duchess of Broon."

Still lost in his thoughts, Hawkley did not reply at once, and, misreading his silence, Rosamund went on. "I know that Mrs. Dewinter lied to us, but she was forced to do so. And at any rate, it was none of the duchess's business, and the way in which she exposed Mrs. Dewinter was cruel. That's why I told her that I thought Lucy was more of a lady than she was."

Lingering memories of Wagonner's incredulous gratitude dimmed suddenly as Hawkley realized what Rosamund was saying. "What?" he demanded. "What's that?"

Rosamund's heart sank, but she kept her voice even. "The Duchess of Broon is a wretched human being."

Hawkley asked her to repeat her story. As she retold the incident in the Park, he began to grin. "So you put paid to that griffin?" he asked appreciatively. "Well done. The woman's a dashed gorgon."

The humor in his voice and the approval in his eyes reached Rosamund like the friendly touch of a hand. She was conscious of a lightness, as though some weight had been lifted from her heart.

"Then you don't disapprove of what I said? Lord Braden intimated that you wouldn't understand—"

She stopped at the altered expression in Hawkley's eyes. "Have you been listening to that fellow again?" he demanded in a completely different voice.

He was talking in that odious, toplofty way again. Unwilling to lose the rapport that had bound them a few moments earlier, Rosamund tried to explain. "He only meant that some members of your class are sure to disapprove."

"*Your* class, too," he reminded her. "Which is more than I can say for Braden."

Rosamund was troubled by the earl's hard tone. "You are

being unjust," she protested. "He can't help it if his mother was not nobly born."

"His mo— Is that what he told you?" Hawkley's brows drew together in a dark scowl. "Who's listening to gossip now?"

"I don't know what is gossip and what is not. I do wish you would answer my questions," Rosamund said, somewhat crossly. "Collect that I asked you about your reasons for disliking Lord Braden before this, and that you refused to answer me."

"The man's a dashed liar, and that's not the worst of it. He's a gamester and the worst sort of rake who would—"

Hawkley broke off abruptly. "Go on," Rosamund exclaimed.

"I've said too much already," Hawkley retorted. He was disgusted that Braden had once more disturbed the good feeling that he and Rosamund had been sharing—and even more appalled that he had come so close to breaking his word.

"But you have not said enough! If Lord Braden betrayed someone or hurt someone, please tell me."

Rosamund searched Hawkley's dark eyes, and, looking even more troubled than Rosamund, Hawkley shook his head. "I truly can't tell you any more. Sworn to secrecy by a friend. But, believe me, the man's a dashed bounder."

Rosamund felt a sinking of her heart that did not come simply from what the earl had said. It was a feeling—an instinct—that warned her that Hawkley was right.

"Demmed Americans! Sweep 'em all into the sea!"

The explosive voice belonged to the Duke of Broon, who was standing a few feet away. The crowd near him began to edge off, among them the languorous Viscount Lake, who exclaimed, "The seaside's very fine this time of year. Are you thinkin' of sailin', Your Grace?"

His valiant effort was in vain, for the duke was deaf to anything save his favorite topic. "Americans are all around us," he rumbled. "Curse 'em. Spies for the demmed colonials, every one of 'em."

Rosamund looked hastily about and saw that Lucy was standing in a corner distinct to the Marchioness of Hare and some other ladies. Anemone was surrounded by a group of admiring gentlemen. Hopefully the duke would run out of fire before either of them heard him.

But His Grace was just warming to his subject. "Demmed colonials need to be taught a lesson. Get 'em on the run! Send battalions to clean the demmed lot of 'em out. Sweep 'em into the sea."

His voice echoed around the great hall, and Rosamund saw Lucy turn around. Several other voices now joined that of His Grace's. Some of the speakers were bored young bucks who wanted to stoke up the verbal fireworks. Others were of the same opinion as the duke and advocated throwing any Americans who might be in England out of the country.

Rosamund was appalled. She started to go to Lucy, but His Grace's next words stopped her in her tracks.

"The *London Times* tells us to strike at the demmed Americans and chastise them. Down with the savages, I say."

"Americans are not savages."

Rosamund's protest shattered the silence that had followed the duke's last roar. "What's this?" boomed His Grace of Broon. "What's the girl sayin' about the demmed Americans, hey?"

"You are wrong in saying that all Americans are savages," Rosamund replied earnestly. "They are fighting for their homes and their country. You would fight for England, sir, wouldn't you?"

"Balderdash!" the duke shouted. "Colonials can't fight.

Cowards and knaves, the pack of 'em. Ha! We'll smash 'em down—"

"Collect," Rosamund interrupted, "that America beat England to its knees in 1776."

There was a deadly silence—broken by a hiss like that of an enraged goose. Turning her head, Rosamund found the Duchess of Broon smiling at her.

"Pray, Miss St. Helm," said the duchess in a poisonously sweet voice, "are you saying that His Majesty should bend his knee before America? Are you intimating that we should give the Americans carte blanche to take what is ours?"

To her distress, Rosamund realized that everyone was staring at her, and that Hawkley was watching her with an unreadable expression in his eyes. "I was merely pointing out—" she began.

"But of course," said the duchess in her venomously dulcet voice, "you would be disposed to champion the Americans. Mrs. Sample, with whom you reside, is an American."

"I'm not anymore . . . I married an Englishman." In her distress, poor Lucy's accent was more foreign than ever. "I'm a law-abiding woman who's loyal to the crown."

"And I suppose we must believe you?"

The duchess sneered as she spoke, and it was that sneer that tipped Rosamund over the edge. "You know nothing about it, Your Grace," she cried.

Her Grace of Broon looked down her aristocratic nose. "Pray explain yourself."

"It is you who should explain," Rosamund flung back. "You have made an accusation against my friend, Mrs. Sample, who is now a loyal Englishwoman. You have been discourteous to her. You may think, ma'am, that your birth and station permit you to be unkind whenever it pleases you—"

"This is England," snarled the duchess. "In England there is law and order."

"There is also a great deal of rudeness," Rosamund shot back. "You owe Mrs. Sample an apology, Your Grace. You owe *Americans* an apology."

"Come," exclaimed a shocked new voice—the Viscount Lake. "Doin' it too brown, there," he drawled. "At war with America, after all."

"Being at war does not mean that we can bully helpless people," Rosamund said, trying to explain. "Surely you agree that having a title is not a license to behave without conscience? We all have feelings and—and value. Indeed, we are created equal in spite of the accident of birth."

The assembled guests shook their heads. Men and women whose titles stretched back centuries drew together in mutual disapproval of such heresy. The Viscount Lake looked pained. The pretty Marchioness of Hare looked uncertainly at her husband, who exclaimed, " 'Straordinary idea, that!"

"If you persist in such ridiculous notions," the duchess said coldly, "you will find no friend in England, young woman. You are turning your back on your peers. You are a traitor to your class!"

Rosamund saw a score of disapproving faces swim out at her. Then she saw Hawkley, and the look on *his* face caught her like a blow. His eyes were the eyes of a hostile stranger. For a moment those stony eyes met hers—and then he turned his back on her and walked out of the grand hall.

You are turning your back on your peers. You are a traitor to your class. As she watched the pretty Marchioness of Hare also turn away from her, something tightened inside Rosamund's chest. Suddenly she felt cold and alone and far from home.

It took all her courage to walk over to Lucy and say quietly, "It's time to leave. Come, Mona. We will get our wraps."

"We go, too," Storm Cloud announced. He rolled an angry eye toward the duke. "I am tired of the company of squabs."

He nodded to his braves and they all followed Rosamund and the Samples out of the drawing room. As they went, Rosamund felt an ache in the region of her heart. It had nothing to do with the fact that she had probably slammed the door forever in the face of polite society. It had everything to do with the cold look that Hawkley had given her before he turned his back on her.

This time, she knew, Hawkley would not forgive her, and though Rosamund told herself that the earl's opinion of her should not have mattered a whit, she knew that it did matter.

Hawkley paced his room. He was frowning black thunder and felt worse. In fact, he had never been as badly shaken as he was now.

Tonight he had watched Rosamund pit herself against a spiteful woman whose influence in society was well known. She had the courage of her convictions, had more pluck than a dozen men, but she was wrong. Dead wrong.

She had flown in the face of all he had been taught, against all he held dear. The worst of it was that he had been tempted once more to come to her aid.

"Dash and blast," swore the Earl of Hawkley.

Rosamund St. Helm had turned his life upside down. She had broken down truths he had accepted since birth. She had changed the way he dealt with his underlings, had made him believe that he enjoyed the company of cits like Lucy Sample. And Rosamund had made him question his God-given birthright.

In short, the wretched woman had infected him with her madness. Because of her, he now actually worried about the feelings of his servants and underlings. Because of Rosamund, he had almost given credit to the lunatic idea that everyone was created equal.

"Of all the slum to have believed in." Hawkley groaned. "I must have been mad."

His instinct of self-preservation had asserted itself at long last. It was warning him to get away from Rosamund St. Helm while he still had any sense—or any friends—left. He had to distance himself from her before it was too late.

Hawkley started to shout for Beamler, then changed his mind and instead strode over to his desk. Then, too agitated to sit down, he tore a sheet of paper out of the pile, seized a pen, dipped it into ink, and began to write.

Chapter Nine

Rosamund looked out into the dreary morning. It had rained for the past three days, and the drains were overflowing. The malodorous streets were awash with dirt and muck, the buildings on Broad Street looked dingy, and the passing hansoms and sedan chairs had a dreary, downtrodden air.

"How I hate this city," Rosamund muttered.

She closed her eyes and tried to conjure up sustaining visions of Canada, but memories of the wilderness around York Factory seemed hazy and dim. More vivid was the recollection of a brilliant morning when meadowlarks sang and wildflowers were pearled with dew.

"Why, Rosa . . . You look down-pin this morning." Anemone had come into the morning room. "Do you have a headache?" she continued solicitously.

Anemone herself looked very well indeed. In spite of the miserable morning, she was rosy and smiling and all but skipped up to the window. "How green the trees are," she trilled. "London is so delightful in the spring. Don't you think so, Ma?"

Lucy, attended by Mrs. Dewinter, had followed Anemone into the morning room. In sharp contrast to her daughter, Lucy looked mired in gloom. She walked heavily to her chair by the breakfast table and plumped down into it.

Looking at her hostess's unhappy face, Rosamund was racked with guilt. She knew that she had ruined all of Lucy's hopes of a good marriage for Anemone.

Since the Countess Standen's ball, all calls, notes, and invitations had ceased. Save for Lord Braden, who continued to call, the Samples had been summarily ignored by the Quality. And even though Mrs. Dewinter blamed herself for her employer's social ruin, Rosamund knew better.

She went over to Lucy and knelt down by her chair. "I'm so sorry," she apologized. "It is my fault that we are in disgrace."

Lucy patted Rosamund's shoulder. "Don't you be thinking that. You was only standing up for me, dearie. It's not your fault that the Duke of Broon has a head like moldy cheese." Anemone giggled. "There's nothing funny about it, though," Lucy said reprovingly. "All this expense of coming to London and the effort to get us noted by the swells—wasted. To think that my daughter was nearly married to one of the gentry."

"Not one of them offered for me," Anemone pointed out.

"No, but they would have in time," Lucy retorted. She added in an aggrieved tone, "It makes me really mad to think of all them young bloods calling on us and guzzling good food without nary a one coming up to scratch. But the good book's right, I suppose. It says not to put your trust in swells."

161

"Princes," corrected Mrs. Dewinter automatically. " 'Put not your faith in princes.' "

Nor in earls. Rosamund tried hard not to think of the look that Hawkley had given her before he turned his back on her.

"I've made up my mind," Lucy went on, "that we should pack up and go back to Sussex."

"No!" Anemone cried so violently that the others stared at her. "I mean that we've paid the rent for this town house for the whole season, Ma. It'd be a waste of money if we left now."

Gloomily Lucy pointed out that while it went against the grain to lose brass, it was no use throwing good money after bad. "And that's what we're doing here," she concluded. "Snakes, that cook hisself is being paid more than an ordinary man'd see in his whole lifetime."

She was interrupted by a knock on the outer door, and some moments later, Bleak entered. Since the Samples' disgrace, Bleak had been more insufferable than ever, and there was barely concealed insolence in the voice in which he announced that Lord Braden had sent up a note.

"He probably ain't going to call here anymore," Lucy said gloomily. She handed the card to Rosamund. "You read it, Rosa. I don't have the stomach for it."

Rosamund opened Lord Braden's note. In a bold, distinctively ornate hand Lord Braden excused himself profusely for calling at this early hour but added that he could not bear to wait another moment. He therefore begged a private moment with Mrs. Sample to discuss a matter close to his heart.

Lucy's eyes grew as round as saucers. "Snakes!" she gasped. "Matter close to his heart . . . It can't mean what I think it means?"

"When a gentleman asks the parent of a young lady of marriageable age for a private interview," Mrs. Dewinter twittered, "it usually means that he is about to declare himself."

Lucy turned bright red and uttered a muffled shriek. "He's come to offer for you, Mona."

Anemone looked stunned. Mrs. Dewinter clasped her hands and raised her eyes to heaven. Beaming, Lucy bounced up from her chair. "Tell His Lordship as I'm coming, Bleak," she commanded the butler.

Pausing only to straighten her morning cap, Lucy exited. Anemone, who had gone very pale, whispered, "Rosa, he can't possibly have come for that. Ma has to be wrong. He wouldn't—I mean, he knows—"

Mrs. Dewinter burst into transports of delight. It was, she caroled, a heaven-sent opportunity. All was well that ended well. Dear Lord Braden was the finest, the kindest, the most noble of men— Did not Miss St. Helm agree?

Remembering what Hawkley had told her about Lord Braden on the night of that disastrous party, Rosamund said nothing. Anemone clutched her arm.

"If he offers for me, I'm in the soup, Rosa. I—"

She broke off as her mother reentered the morning room. Lucy was beaming from ear to ear, and every ounce of her ample form oozed triumph.

"Oh, my baby," she exclaimed. "I'm so happy, I could dance a jig. That dear man's asked if he can pay his addresses to you. It's a dream come true."

She rustled over to her daughter and clasped her to her ample bosom. "You're going to be Lady Braden. Go down to him now; he's waiting."

Lucy went as pale as ashes and then flushed a fiery red. "I can't," she whispered. "I—I need time to think."

"Think about what?" demanded Lucy. "Thinking has made a lot of girls turn into old maids. Females ain't made to think." She gave Anemone a little push. "Go on . . . *Now*, dearie."

Anemone wailed, "I'm going to be sick."

She ran out of the room and could be heard throwing up down the hall. Mrs. Dewinter scurried after her, and Rosamund also started to follow, but Lucy stopped her.

"No, I'll go. It's my fault. I broke things too sudden." She started to leave the morning room, then paused to ask, "Rosa, will you go tell Lord Braden that Mona ain't feeling herself? He's an understanding man. Ask him to come back later."

She then trotted off after Anemone, leaving Rosamund to go downstairs to Lord Braden, who was waiting in the first-floor parlor. She entered the Gold Room softly and found him standing by the unlit fireplace. His boot rested on the hob, his hands were clasped behind his back, and Rosamund noted that he was smiling complacently.

He looked up when she came into the room and at once came forward, his hand outstretched. "Miss St. Helm," he exclaimed. "Good morning, ma'am. Have you come to wish me happy?"

"Mona is not feeling well," she explained. "Her mother is with her now."

While he expressed concern and regret, Rosamund looked hard at Lord Braden. He met her eyes so frankly, he smiled so openly, and his handshake was firm. He was handsome, came from a good family, and he was accepted in society. Could Hawkley be mistaken? she wondered.

"I will call on Miss Sample another time," Lord Braden was saying. "I'm desolate that she isn't feeling well. Pray convey my deepest homage to her and my hopes that she will be well soon."

Rosamund said that she would do as he had asked and

watched from the window as Lord Braden walked out of the house and into the street. There, she saw him stop, look back over his shoulder, and smile that complacent smile again—the smile that was almost a smirk.

Rosamund waited until his lordship had hailed a passing hansom and driven away. Then she went upstairs to look in on Anemone, who was lying down while Mrs. Dewinter fussed about with pillows and burned feathers and Lucy positioned an ice pack on her head.

"You just lie there and be still," Lucy was saying contritely.

Anemone shifted the ice bag and looked appealingly at Rosamund. "Has he gone?"

Rosamund nodded. "But," Lucy said bracingly, "he'll be back. After all, I gave him permission to spark you."

Mrs. Dewinter winced at the word but said only that she would tell Anemone's abigail to bring up a peppermint tisane; then she left the room. Urging Anemone to rest, Lucy drew Rosamund out of the room also.

"She'll be fine," she said. "If a lord proposed to *me*, I'd be so nervous, I'd fall down flat in a faint."

"Are you so sure that it's only nerves?"

"What else could it be?" It was amazing how Lucy seemed to have recovered, Rosamund thought. Her eyes were snapping, her cheeks were round and rosy, and her whole body exuded confidence. "To have a lord offer for you—that's something out of a fairy tale."

"What if Mona doesn't want to marry Lord Braden?" Rosamund persisted.

Lucy's pleasure did not dim. "Oh, shoot. You're thinking of that Wilfred Dilber again, ain't you? Mona's gotten over *him* a long time ago."

Rosamund hesitated. She did not want to alarm Lucy with

hearsay, which was all Hawkley's assessment of Lord Braden might be. And she was not *sure* that she had seen his lordship push a woman into the gutter, either.

She was not certain about anything, and yet she could not let matters lie. Rosamund needed to find out the truth about Lord Braden once and for all, and there was only one person who could enlighten her.

She considered taking Lucy's phaeton or the closed carriage on this pressing errand, then decided against it. She did not want the servants to speculate or gossip. She needed to seek Hawkley out as swiftly and with as few people knowing about it as possible.

But she had reckoned without Meadows. When Rosamund, dressed and booted for riding, arrived at the stables sometime later, the old fellow bristled with outrage. "Th'art never going riding in the *rain*?" he demanded. "Hasta gone soft in the head, Miss Rosa?"

Meadows looked carefully at his mistress. She was wearing her deep purple habit and an expression that reminded him of the way Mr. Jeremy had looked when he announced that he was planning to leave England to go and live with savages.

In short, she was up to no good. "Why would I saddle Isolde?" Meadows lectured. "No leddy I knows'd go skittering around in such weather. It's raining pitchforks and shovels, sithee, and tha'll catch thy death. If tha *must* go, take t' phaeton, else t' carriage—"

He broke off sharply as Rosamund, without offering any argument, began to saddle her horse herself. "There is a good reason why I must ride out today," she told him, and the very quietness of her voice made the old groom narrow his eyes. Now, Meadows thought, Miss Rosa looked like her lady mother.

Sometimes he had been able to get around Mr. Jeremy, but Lady Mary was another matter. Her sainted ladyship had looked like gossamer and moonlight and had more steel in her than any ten men. Meadows remembered how Lady Mary had wept her eyes out for a month at the thought of leaving her son and England, but that once in Canada she had never shed another tear and never looked back.

Bristling and grumbling under his breath, he saddled Isolde. But when Rosamund said that she was going to ride alone and that he should stay home out of the wet, the old fellow let forth such a volley of objections, lamentations, and accusations that she agreed to let him accompany her.

Though the rain had gentled to a fine misting, few people were out on the streets. A dingy hansom passed them, and a sedan chair drawn along by soggy carriers. Disregarding Meadows's demands to know where they were going, Rosamund cantered grimly on.

She had written out the invitations to Lucy's party and thus knew Hawkley's address, but once on Mount Street she slowed her horse. "Going to turn back?" Meadows asked hopefully from behind her. "Tha'rt wetter than a fish, sithee."

Rosamund did not answer, for she was being seized by misgivings. She had not seen Hawkley since that night of the Countess Standen's ball. She was sure he would not want to see her, was not even sure whether he would talk to her, and the memory of how he had turned his back on her made her bite her lower lip. But, remembering Anemone's happiness, Rosamund gritted her teeth and trotted her horse down the street.

She had not gone too far before she saw a familiar curricle in front of the earl's fashionable London residence. Next moment the door of the house opened and Hawkley himself appeared on the top step. Rosamund spurred her horse forward, calling, "My lord earl!"

She was too far to see the expression on his face, but she could read the sudden tension in him. For a moment she was afraid that he might not even acknowledge her, but then he said something to his tiger and strode through the rain toward her.

Finally he stopped and looked her over in ominous silence. "Sir," Rosamund said, "I need to talk to you."

She looked a perfect wreck, Hawkley thought. Her handsome riding habit was wringing wet under her cloak. A water drop was suspended from the tip of her nose, and her black hair, which was escaping from under her bedraggled shako, had the dull sheen of wet silk.

And she looked cold. He had meant to greet her with freezing courtesy, but when he noted that her slender, gloved hands were trembling, he could not help but exclaim, "You'll catch your death in this dashed rain! What are you thinking of, riding in weather like this?"

Under his curt words there was concern, and Rosamund took heart. "I must ask you a question. It is of the utmost urgency, so I beg that you'll answer it truthfully."

Her eyes were like drowned violets, and under the sheen of rain her cheeks glistened like mother-of-pearl. Hawkley, who had never had any use for poetry, found himself recalling some obscure line that he had read back in his salad days—something about a lady's beauty eclipsing the moon.

Pushing aside such inappropriate thoughts, he charged, "I thought you cared about your animals. Your horse will catch cold even if you don't."

"That is unfair," Rosamund replied evenly. "I suspect that you have hunted in much worse weather and taken no thought to either the dogs or your horses—or to the fox, either.

My horse won't take any harm, I assure you. I'll rub him down myself."

Which was the kind of sheep-brained thing this outrageous female would do. "What's your question?" Hawkley rapped out.

His voice was so frigid that the raindrops caught in his thick brown hair seemed to freeze into bits of ice. Rosamund drew a deep breath and took the plunge. "You have more than once warned me against Lord Braden, but there is no proof that he has *done* anything. I know that you have made a promise not to reveal any particulars, but couldn't you give me some hint that will help me discover the truth for myself?" When he shook his head, she added, "You see, he has offered for Anemone. Lucy is delighted, but I have grave doubts . . ."

Her words trailed away, and Hawkley found himself caught between the devil and the sea. He thought of the vow of silence and the code by which he lived, and yet the thought of Braden marrying an innocent young girl was horrifying.

"Lord Braden has a past," he said at last. "He's a gamester who used up his inheritance and beggared his family. He also very nearly ruined a lady."

Rosamund's eyes narrowed. "Is there some proof I can take to Lucy?"

Hawkley shook his head. "No one knows except the principals and myself. I've given my word to say nothing, so there's nothing to be done. But I *can* say that if Miss Sample were my sister, I'd never allow Braden within a hundred yards of her."

"Lucy will not believe me without proof." Rosamund looked so unhappy that Hawkley felt a desire—insane under the circumstances—to put his arms around her and comfort her. For a moment the thought of holding her was almost irresistible—but then he reminded himself of what had happened at the Countess Standen's ball.

He clasped his hands behind his back and spoke stiffly. "I understand your concern for Miss Sample, but I'm honor bound not to say any more."

"But isn't there some way to—to convince the principals to break their silence?" Seeing that Hawkley was already shaking his head, Rosamund cried, "I don't know who the lady is, but I *do* know that if I were in her place, I would go to hell itself to help save another woman."

Her voice rang with such conviction and passion that Hawkley, who had been on the point of returning to his curricle, looked back at her sharply. Rosamund read condemnation in his steady, silent gaze and felt her heart sink.

He did not understand her. He would never understand how she felt. Talking further was worthless, so she turned Isolde's head and cantered away, feeling cold and bereft, as if she had lost her best friend. Absurd, really, since Hawkley had never been her friend.

Rosamund drew a deep breath and forced herself to return to the matter at hand. Though the earl had not answered her question, he had definitely helped to make up her mind. Somehow she must try and convince Lucy that Lord Braden was not a fit husband for Mona.

As Rosamund had feared, Lucy was not convinced. She shrugged aside what Hawkley had said and allowed that most men had "pasts."

"Sowing their wild oats," she said tolerantly. "I shouldn't be talking about such things to you, dearie, you being an unmarried young lady and all, but I already know that Lord Braden wasn't an angel in his youth. He told me this morning that he'd been a wild young buck. I guess he always felt he wasn't as good as the rest of the swells because his ma wasn't gently born."

"This has nothing to do with his birth, Lucy. Hawkley has said that Lord Braden very nearly ruined a lady."

"Did Hawkley give you any details?" Lucy demanded heatedly. "Well, I don't believe him. Earls tend to look down their noses at other people, and swells like Hawkley are more like to give a girl like my Mona a slip on the shoulder rather than to make her an honest offer."

She paused, breathing hard. "Lord Braden wants to marry Mona all right and proper. I won't cry down a man for the sins of his youth—nor for gambling a bit, either."

As far as Lucy was concerned, the matter was closed, but Rosamund could not accept this. She knew instinctively that Hawkley was no liar—and that unsavory skeletons were rattling about in Lord Braden's closet.

If there had been more time, she could have hired someone to watch his lordship and dog his footsteps, but there was no time. Lucy was already talking about an announcement in the *Gazette* and an early wedding. Anxious not to lose the only lord that she had netted for her daughter, she was pressing ahead at full speed.

No, there was no time. "So I will have to follow him myself," Rosamund said under her breath. "I'll start at St. James Street, where I saw him push that poor woman into the gutter. I think I know which gaming house he entered. If I can find out something about Lord Braden that I can take to Lucy, that should end his suit. But Hawkley told me that no lady would be seen on St. James Street, so I must go as a man."

In Canada Rosamund had occasionally slipped into buckskin breeches and jacket and accompanied her father into the wilderness. Lady Mary had protested vigorously, but Lord

Jeremy had had his way and had taught his daughter how to ape a man's long strides and how to meet danger head-on.

And she had need of this training—because stalking Lord Braden through London was potentially more dangerous than any expedition in the wilds. Not only were there criminals and press-gangs loose on the dark streets, but Lord Braden might also turn vicious if cornered.

"I will go armed," Rosamund decided.

On her twelfth birthday Snarling Bear had given her a bone-handled knife that could fit easily into the palm of her hand. It had proved useful in so many ways that she always traveled with it. Rosamund went to her box, found her knife, and withdrew it from its leather sheath; the play of light on the sharp blade made her feel more confident.

Now to find her costume, and for this she needed her abigail's help. But when Rosamund explained to Nancy what she planned, the abigail crossed herself several times while entreating the holy saints to bring sanity back to her mistress. "And anyway, ma'am," she added in horrified accents, "where am I to get a man's clothes, entirely?"

"The footmen are too tall, so you must filch some of Meadows's clothes," Rosamund instructed. "I'll call him to the house and ask him some questions, and in the meantime you must get his shirt and breeches. Make sure that they are old ones so that he won't notice the theft."

"Holy saints above, will you listen to yourself? You shouldn't know about breeches, never mind wearing them," Nancy cried, scandalized.

"If you can't help me, I'll steal the clothes myself," Rosamund said, with such determination that her abigail promised compliance.

Accordingly a furiously indignant Meadows was summoned to the house, where he answered questions about Isolde's welfare for ten minutes. At the end of that time, Nancy put her head around the drawing room door and nodded to signal that the deed had been done.

Dismissing her spluttering groom, Rosamund went upstairs and surveyed the garments that Nancy had purloined. They were a pair of ancient tweed breeches much too big around the waist, a shirt that would hang down to her knees, and a cap covered with grease and mud.

"You could never be a successful cutpurse, Nancy," Rosamund said, sighing. "These are dreadful rags."

"It's all I could get, ma'am," retorted her abigail. "Maybe now you'll forget the whole idea?"

Rosamund ignored this hopeful suggestion. "I will wait until everyone is asleep," she said. "I'll need a hackney, but I can't hail it too near the house."

She cut such a sorry figure in Meadows's castoffs that she had difficulty in getting a hackney to stop for her. Once that was accomplished, the man looked at her askance when she ordered him to ride to St. James Street.

Overcoming the jarvey's objections by offering him more money, Rosamund started on her quest. When they arrived at St. James Street, she had the hackney drive slowly up and down the road until she spotted the gaming house into which Lord Braden had gone.

"What is this place called?" she demanded.

"It's one of the gaming 'ells. A place where you oughtn't ter know abaht, young sir," reproved the jarvey. He was now convinced that his passenger was a sprig of the gentry out for an evening's sport. "They'll get their fambles on yer silver feeders before you can turn around twice. Best you stay out of it."

Rosamund took out a gold piece and held it tantalizingly under the jarvey's nose. "I can't go in dressed as I am, so you must do it. Find out if Lord Braden is there. You will be paid," she added as the man reached for the coin, "*after* you do your errand."

Muttering darkly against peevy rich coves that would slamguzzle an honest cabman, the jarvey went away and came back with the news that Lord Braden was indeed there. "The flash cove's gaming," he reported. Then, having bitten his gold coin and found it genuine, he added more cheerfully, "What next, young sir?"

"Now we wait. You will be well paid for your time," Rosamund went on, "so you needn't worry."

The wait was a long one, for Lord Braden seemed to be enjoying his evening of gambling. It was not till some hours had passed that the doors of the gaming house opened once more to disgorge his lordship.

He was dressed to the nines in a handsome cloak over evening clothes, but he looked pale and strained in the lamplight, and his mouth had a pinched look to it. "Been losing," the jarvey commented sagely. "They allus looks that way when they've given up a lot of their vowels."

Rosamund waited until Lord Braden had hailed a hackney and rattled off. Then she ordered, "Follow them."

They clattered down a street and then another. Finally Lord Braden stopped his conveyance in a run-down area of the town, where Rosamund's jarvey rebelled. "I don't twig what your lay is, young sir," he lectured, "but Boar Square ain't a place fit for honest folk. Either we leaves now or you'll pay me and get down."

Afraid that her quarry would get away, Rosamund did not stop to argue. She paid the driver and then hastened down a narrow alley after Lord Braden. Though intent on the man she was following, she could not help but note how her footfalls echoed in the quiet of the dark, malodorous place. There was menace in the silence, and Rosamund's resolve almost faltered. Then she thought of the pinched look she had seen around Lord Braden's mouth, and the idea that Anemone might be chained to the man for life kept her moving forward.

Shifting Snarling Bear's knife more securely into her palm, Rosamund followed the alley until it opened into a small square lit by a single streetlamp. By this imperfect light Rosamund saw Lord Braden walking toward one of the buildings that ringed the square. As he climbed the steps, a shadow appeared at the door, and a young voice quavered, "It's you, Papa!"

Papa?

Rosamund flattened herself against the wall as Lord Braden snarled in a voice she had never heard him use before, "Damn you, you little idiot! I told you never to call me that. Where's your mother?"

"Working late again at the milliner's," said the child at the door, sniffling. "A young leddy is 'aving 'er come-out and Mam and t' others 'ave been working all night for the 'ole week."

"I need to speak with her. I'll wait inside."

Rosamund watched the two go into the house. After a moment, she ran up the stairs and put her eye to the small window. Through the dirty pane she could see the insides of a small room. It looked very poor and cramped but was furnished with a pathetic semblance of good taste.

An armchair stood before a small stove in the center of the room, and here sat Lord Braden, at his ease, while a small boy knelt on the floor to pull off his lordship's boots. Now that she could see him, Rosamund could see that the child resembled Lord Braden.

"The villain," Rosamund said, seething. "That deceiving, conniving, disgusting beast!"

The sound of approaching footsteps sent her hurrying back down the stairs to hide in the shadows. Soon a woman trudged out of the alley and into the square. She paused wearily for a moment before she climbed the stairs leading to the same house Lord Braden had entered, and by the uncertain lamplight Rosamund saw that she was young and quite pretty but drooping with weariness. She was dressed plainly and carried a market basket over her arm.

When the woman had crept up the stairs, Rosamund once more hurried up to press her eye to the window. She nearly fell from her perch as she saw Lord Braden embracing the woman.

Now he was kissing her. Rosamund felt physically ill. It was not difficult to guess that this young woman was probably Lord Braden's mistress and was supporting him with her hard work.

"He's come to get money from her after losing at cards," Rosamund said, still seething.

No wonder Hawkley had warned her about this man! Boiling with anger, Rosamund hastened away from the disgusting sight she had witnessed. Lord Braden had a ladybird. Not a plump and spoiled barque of frailty in some neat little establishment but a woman who worked hard for her meager wages. And there was the little boy, too—the son who was not permitted to address him as father.

Was Mona to be leg-shackled to such a blackguard? "Never," Rosamund swore.

She was so angry that she did not feel the menace of the alley that led away from Boar Square. She was hardly even aware of her surroundings until she heard footsteps behind her. Heavy and purposeful, they stopped when she halted and advanced again when she began walking. Rosamund quickened her steps—and the footsteps also picked up speed.

Lord Braden had seen her and had come after her. Rosamund thought of his lordship's hard face and the voice he had used to the boy, and her heart gave a painful beat. Then she reminded herself of what she had learned in the Canadian wilderness.

"The best defense is an offense," she whispered.

A thick fog had drifted over the alley, making it doubly hard to see, and, after all, she was dressed in men's clothes. Instead of letting Lord Braden frighten her, she would intimidate him.

Resolutely she turned and faced the darkness. "Who's there?" she demanded in as gruff a voice as she could produce.

For answer, there was a snicker that turned her blood to ice.

"Now look 'ere! We've got a nice young cove ready for the plucking, Willy," a harsh, unfamiliar voice rasped. "You're going to like life in 'is Majesty's Navy, my lad."

And then, before she could cry out or run, they were upon her.

Chapter Ten

As one of the ruffians caught her around the neck, Rosamund reacted instinctively. In a maneuver that Snarling Bear had taught her, she kicked back at him, connecting with the knee. He yelled and loosened his hold on her; she spun loose, only to find her escape blocked by his confederate. As he lunged for her, she struck out with her knife.

There was a shout of pain, her attackers fell back, and Rosamund took to her heels. "Don't let 'un get away. After 'im, Willy," she could hear one of the villains shout. " 'E's hurt me leg, 'e 'as. I can't run."

She could run very well. Perhaps she could outrun him. Rosamund could hear the man called Willy puffing and swearing behind her and hoped he would curse even more so as to exhaust his wind. In spite of the fog she could see that she was approaching the entrance to the alley. If she could win through to the main street, a hansom driver might be passing even at this late hour.

Grimly Rosamund sprinted on. Suddenly something scurried out in front of her so that she stumbled over it and lost her footing. She was up again in a flash and running—but it was too late.

"I've got yer now," a harsh voice said, panting, and a hand clamped over her mouth. Her knife went flying as she tried to twist free of the arm around her waist, and her flesh crawled as she felt her attacker stiffen. "Gorblimey," he gasped, "you ain't no cove."

Up until now there had been no time to feel fear. Now, as he fumbled at her breasts, terror rushed through Rosamund and filled her mouth with bile. As her attacker started to drag her back into the depths of the alley, she clamped her teeth down on the palm of his hand.

He howled and released her mouth, and she let out a blood curdling war whoop that Snarling Bear had used. Surely someone would hear *that*—

The fearsome cry broke off, smothered by her attacker's hand. "I'll squeeze the puff out of you. Play your tricks on me, will yer?" the man called Willy snarled. "Yer'll be sorry when Maggot and me gets through wi' yer."

She kicked and fought, but he held her in such a way that her kicks and her elbows could find no purchase, and as he hauled her back toward his confederate, he described the things that he and Maggot would do to her.

"And when we gets through wi' that," Willy said, gloating, "we'll slit yer throat. That's what we do to morts as play their tricks on us."

He broke off as footsteps began to echo in the dark alley. Purposefully and quickly they approached them. "Maggot?'' Rosamund's captor called. "Clap your glims on wot we got 'ere—"

Then the words were strangled back into his throat as iron hands seized him and lifted him off his feet. In the next second, Willy was hurled against the alley wall. He sagged down against it, unconscious.

" 'Ere, Willy. What's the matter wit' yer?"

The second villain had no chance to scream as a fist caught him cleanly on his jaw. He said "Oof," and collapsed to the ground.

Rosamund had been on her hands and knees searching for her knife. As she finally found it, she heard Hawkley's tense voice demand, "Are you all right?"

Rosamund did not bother to ask why Hawkley was there. She was beyond questions. Nauseated and shaking in every limb, she sagged against the dank alley wall.

"I'll have the watch come around to collect these bastards," the earl was saying. "Probably a press-gang that kidnaps 'volunteers' to serve in the King's Navy. The navy must be in a bad way if it employs such thatchgallows to do its dirty work."

He picked up his curly beaver, which had fallen in the fray, and dusted it off. "Good thing I heard your battle cry," he went on. "I knew there was only one man in London who could have made such a noise. But what are you doing in this neighborhood, Chief? Dashed unsafe place to be."

He thought she was Storm Cloud! Rosamund was grateful. Even in her befuddled state of mind, she was blazingly aware that she didn't want to have the earl see her dressed in a groom's clothes.

She managed a grunt that she hoped was a fair imitation of the Mohawk's voice, and Hawkley went on, "Never come down this way myself. Lake—you remember my friend, don't you?—got a maggot in his brain that he wanted to try a gambling hell nearby and dragged several of us here with him, but one look at the place was enough for me." He paused to ask, "You seem played out, Chief. Are you hurt?"

Rosamund shook her head. If only he would go away—but then she thought of the two men who had attacked her. If Hawkley went away, she might be assaulted again.

She shivered violently, and the earl spoke in an altered voice. "You *are* hurt. Lean on me and we'll— What in hell is going on?"

Hawkley grasped Rosamund urgently by the shoulders and attempted to stare down into her face. It was too dark, but he knew her by the subtle perfume she wore, by the feel of her slender, warm body. "What in hell is going on?" he repeated.

Numb and unprotesting, Rosamund allowed herself to be dragged out of the alley and hustled under a streetlamp. Once again Hawkley stared down at her. *"You,"* he grated. Then he added urgently, "Are you hurt? Did those bastards hurt you?"

Naked fear was in his eyes, and Rosamund felt a bubble of happiness rise in her. She forgot her terrors of a moment ago. She forgot the feel of vile hands on her body. All she knew was that Hawkley cared—truly cared—for her safety. She tried to tell him that she was unhurt, but her numb throat would not form the words.

She shook her head instead and a few curls, freed from Meadows's grimy cap, drifted across her cheeks. She looked so beautiful in those incongruous clothes, Hawkley thought hazily. She could have been badly hurt—would have been, if he had not left Lake and the others gaming and decided to walk until he found a hansom. The thought of what those two villains would have done to Rosamund terrified him past bearing, and without thought he reached out and gathered her into his arms.

Their kiss was primal, as wild and as elemental as storm and sea and wind. Rosamund felt herself being whirled into a vortex of sensations and emotions over which she had no control. Nor did she want to control them. All she wanted to do was to be held and to hold, kiss and be kissed.

Her lips were as sweet as honey, as intoxicating as brandy. Hawkley felt his body and spirit merge into a rapturous response to the beautiful girl in his arms. "Rose," he whispered against her lips. "My beautiful Wild Rose—"

There was a rasping cough in the near distance. Hawkley ignored it. It came again. " 'Ere, then, sorr," exclaimed a scandalized-sounding voice. " 'Ere, now."

Reluctantly Hawkley and Rosamund broke apart and blinked into the beefy face of a constable. Behind the constable were two underlings, both of whom were avidly gawking.

"What's going on 'ere?" demanded the chief constable. "Some reported that there was a 'orrible screaming going on, but I didn't expect to find nofink like this."

Rosamund was too numb to realize that she could be recognized and compromised in her scandalous costume, but Hawkley was not. He also grasped another and more immediate problem. The constable was regarding him with horror and disgust because he thought that Rosamund was a man!

Pushing her behind him, he faced the law. "It's about time you came," he snapped. "My . . . er . . . younger brother here was attacked by brigands in that alley and fainted dead away. Thought he'd cocked up his toes. I was endeavoring to bring him around when you came."

From the look on the constable's face, the man didn't believe a word he'd said. "Is *that* so?" he said, sneering.

"Go and look in the alley if you doubt me." Hawkley's voice was laced with sarcasm, made imperious with centuries of noblesse oblige. "Hurry up, man. You can't be so incompetent that you want those villains to escape."

Obviously seething, the constable jerked his head at his underlings, who cautiously entered the alley. He and Hawkley then eyed each other with mutual suspicion until the minions of the law emerged from the alley.

"Well?" barked the chief constable.

"There's two coves in there, sorr. Big, ugly barstids," reported one of his underlings. "One of 'em's been cut up, and they'st both 'olding their 'eads and moaning."

"Let 'em finish moaning in the roundhouse," the chief constable decreed. He tugged at his mustache and looked doubtfully at Hawkley and at Rosamund, who was partially visible behind the earl. "The thing is, I dunno what to do with these 'ere two."

Rosamund opened her mouth to explain but closed it as Hawkley kicked her sharply in the ankle. "I'm sure that there are many things you don't know," he drawled. "However, even you should realize where your duty lies. Now, go and do it while I take my brother home."

He held the chief constable's eyes with his own until the man looked away. Mumbling something about decadence and damnable catamites under his breath, the man gestured to his followers. "Let's go, then, lads."

Then he paused. "I'll need you and *your brother* to come around to the roundhouse to make a report . . . *sir*," he said sarcastically.

"Not possible. Brother's ill. So would you be if you had to breathe the air in this place. I'll come to the roundhouse myself in the morning." When the policeman hesitated, Hawkley snarled, "Be off with you and stop annoying your betters."

Stunned as Rosamund was, she could still feel the lash of the earl's voice. As the still doubtful but temporarily cowed constables left the scene, she managed to ask, "Why did you have to treat him that way?"

"Because he thought we were a pair of catamites," replied Hawkley bluntly. "That's against the law, in case you didn't know. We must leave at once—before he changes his mind and comes back to arrest us."

"But if he realizes that I'm a woman—"

"Then it will be all around London that the incorrigible Wild Rose dressed as a man and was found wandering alone in one of the seedy areas of the city," was the grim reply.

The memory of what could have happened to Rosamund roughened his voice, and reacting to that harshness she exclaimed, "*You* were here, and so were your friends."

"That's different," he retorted. "What I can do and what you can do aren't the same. I don't know what you're used to in Canada, but you're all abroad if you think this kind of behavior will answer in England."

It was too dark for him to see the narrowing of her eyes. "Really?" she murmured.

"You're a female, dash it. Don't you know that there are thatchgallows and slipgibbets around who'd kill you for less than a penny? And your clothes— Lord, you look like a dashed groom. If anyone saw you dressed like that, your reputation'd be ruined."

The tender lover of a moment ago had disappeared, leaving what she loathed most—the disdainful aristocrat who felt that birth and breeding made him better than the rest of mankind. Rosamund recalled the way in which Hawkley had tongue-lashed the constable into submission. Now he was daring to try the same tricks on her.

She said through clenched teeth, "I came here for a good reason. I am glad I came in spite of the—the press-gang."

But Hawkley was listening not to her words but to the quaver in her voice. He was recalling how one of those impressmen had dragged Rosamund down the alley. He wished he had killed the man.

"You're lucky I was near," he snapped. "Don't ever put yourself in such danger again."

"You don't even know why I was here," she protested, but he was too angry—and too frightened for her—to let her speak.

"There's no reason on earth for such behavior. How could you act like such a caper-witted hoyden?"

"You toplofty autocrat," shouted Rosamund, losing her temper. "How dare you lecture me?"

They stood under the streetlamp breathing hard and glaring at each other. In that moment, Rosamund hated Hawkley. She hated the fact that he had rescued her and had kissed her—and for one moment made her believe that he was human and full of tenderness. She hated herself for having been so sheep-brained as to kiss him back.

"I am going home," she said in her coldest voice. "I thank you for rescuing me, *my lord*. I am sorry I troubled you."

There was an odd sound as the Earl of Hawkley ground his teeth. He tried to speak but no adequate words would come to mind. Thoroughly frustrated he whirled on his heel and started to walk away, then stopped, aghast at what he was about to do. No matter what a vixen Rosamund St. Helm was, he couldn't leave a female alone and unprotected in the heart of London.

But Rosamund was already hailing a passing hansom. She told the startled driver where she wanted to go and climbed in. As Hawkley watched her, he was suddenly struck with remorse.

She had gone through enough horror to make any other female swoon dead away, and he had roared at her. "Wait," he called. "Come back, Rosamund!"

Half in and half out of the hackney, she turned toward Hawkley; he was a confused impression of burning eyes set in a white face.

"I am done listening to you, sir," she told him. "You can go to Jericho."

Then she slammed the door of the hackney shut and the hansom drove on. The earl stared after it for a few moments and then seized his curly beaver, threw it on the ground, and stamped on it.

"Oh, damnation," he roared. "Dash and blast that woman to everlasting perdition!"

As soon as she returned to the town house, Rosamund went to Lucy's room. She was afraid that she would be asleep, but there was a lamp burning, and Lucy was propped up in bed eating bonbons and writing in a notebook.

"I've been making a list of guests for the wedding," she said. Then, lifting her eyes, she saw Rosamund's attire. "Snakes," she gasped, "what's happened to you?"

Rosamund sat down beside Lucy's bed and explained where she had been and what she had seen. As she spoke, she saw Lucy's cheeks blanch. "Now you can see what kind of swine Lord Braden is," Rosamund concluded.

Lucy was silent for a long moment. Then she raised her head and met Rosamund's eyes. "Let's talk frankly, as two women of the world," she said. "Men ain't perfect, Rosa.

None o' them. Men have it easy in the world. They run after lightskirts or pinch the maids when they think their wives ain't looking. Or they gamble and get drunk and we have to clean up their mess."

She drew a deep breath. "There ain't no such thing as a marriage made in heaven except in books, dearie. And the pity of it is, a woman needs a man. We don't have any rights and we don't have any protection 'less we marry."

"But to marry someone like Braden— Lucy, he keeps a mistress. A young woman who no doubt toils so that he can have money to game with. They have a son."

Rosamund could see a silent war being waged in Lucy's unhappy countenance. Finally she heaved a deep sigh.

"All men sow wild oats," she said.

"Lucy!"

"Wild oats," Lucy repeated, adding grimly, "if you or I did any such thing, they'd call us sluts and adulteresses, but for men it's different. Even Sample had a fancy piece."

She looked up and squarely met Rosamund's astounded gaze. "She was a pretty young thing, 'most as young as Mona. He had her set up in a house in the next county, and he was allus going over there to see her."

"Didn't you tell him that you knew?" Rosamund took a deep breath.

"I told him it had to stop, and he told *me* he wasn't going to give her up. He said he'd allus treat me proper, but what he did for fun was his business. And if I left him—as I wanted to, dearie, you can make book on it—he said I'd leave with nothing but the clothes on my back. Not even my Mona, 'cause she belonged to her father." Lucy ran the back of her hand across her suddenly moist eyes. "Like I told you, Rosa—a woman don't have any rights."

Try as she would, Rosamund could think of nothing to

say. After a moment, Lucy went on. "When Sample died 'n' left me all that money, I swore I'd find a gentleman for my daughter. I'd rather she married a title and become Lady Someone instead of being plain Mrs. Nobody. There's *some* safety for her that way."

She paused. "I wanted a kind gentleman for my Mona, but none of them swells came up to scratch—except Lord Braden."

"But surely, after what I've told you, you won't allow him to marry Mona?" Rosamund pleaded.

"I've got to think it over," Lucy said miserably. "Maybe I can make an agreement with him. He needs brass, and I want the title. I could make him sign a paper saying that he'll get an allowance but Mona'll hold the purse strings."

"He'll break any promise he makes," Rosamund warned. "Lucy, you *cannot* want a title so badly."

But Lucy only repeated that she needed to think. Rosamund knew better than to argue, but her heart was heavy as she went to her room, where she washed and changed into her nightclothes. Then, much too upset to sleep, she settled down in a chair by the window with a book.

But the book's pages remained unturned. Lucy was right, Rosamund thought. Men could go and come as they pleased and caterwaul down the dark streets of London if that was their pleasure. All *she* had done was to try to find out what Hawkley would not tell her—and Hawkley had hectored her about her clothes and her harum-scarum ways.

"How dare he call me a caper-witted hoyden," Rosamund exclaimed. She slammed her book shut and glared out of the window as though the earl were there. "How dare he behave as though I were one of his servants . . ."

Her voice trailed off as, underneath the window, she glimpsed a dark figure enveloped in a cloak.

Hastily Rosamund blew out her candle and leaned closer to the window. There was no mistake. It was the same still, dark figure that had watched the town house some nights ago. But before she could reach for the bellpull, the door of the house opened and a second figure—also muffled in a cloak from head to toe—slipped out. As Rosamund watched, it scurried down the stairs toward the waiting man. Then both of them disappeared into the shadows.

Rosamund was not sure what to do. She had summoned the servants the last time, and the man had disappeared. Perhaps the servants were in league with the mysterious watcher in the shadows? Perhaps one of them or all of them were planning to rob the house? She had heard of such things happening before.

Then another thought assailed her. The Duke of Broon had made many unsavory references to Lucy's being a spy. That was ridiculous, of course, but His Grace of Broon was not the only one to be suspicious of Americans. Bleak or one of his minions might have seen the woman leave the house and started damaging rumors.

"This time I'll go by myself," she muttered. "I'll find out what is really happening."

Slipping on her shoes, Rosamund settled her cloak around her shoulders and left her room. It was cold in the hallway, and she shivered as she ran down the stairs. Then, taking a deep breath, she pulled open the front door and stepped outside.

For a moment she could see and hear nothing. Then she made out an agitated whispering. "I'll not do it," Anemone was protesting. "I don't care what happens to me."

Rosamund stifled a gasp of surprise. Mona conspiring with some unknown man? As she cautiously made her way down the stairs, she heard that personage plead, "You won't have to. I've got plans. We'll fool them all—trust in me—"

He broke off as Rosamund stepped into view. There was a stifled shriek, then a muffled oath. "All I need to do is call out and rouse the house," Rosamund warned.

"Don't do that—please, don't," Anemone entreated. She ran up to Rosamund and clasped her hands. "Rosa, it's Wilfred."

A slight young man with sandy hair and a ripple of mustache stepped into the dim light. Under the heavy hat that shadowed his face, his blue eyes were pleading.

"Beg to introduce myself," he said in a hurried, diffident voice. "Wilfred Dilber, ma'am . . . Assure you, your servant . . . Command me in anything."

Understanding washed over Rosamund. No wonder Anemone had looked so happy lately, she thought. "When did you come to London, Mr. Dilber?" she asked aloud.

"Ten days ago. Rosa, you won't betray us?" Anemone pleaded.

The young man coughed behind his hand. "Please be so kind . . . Allow us to tell our side of the story."

Rosamund nodded, and Wilfred Dilber drew himself up and launched into speech. "Not permitted to meet Anemo— Miss Sample . . . Had to resort to subterfuge. Didn't like it. Tried to find some way—any way—to convince Mrs. Sample to see me, listen to my suit."

Anemone clutched at Wilfred's hand. "Neither of us liked to lie to Mama," she said in a pleading voice. "But—but, oh, Rosa, I cannot *bear* the thought of marrying anyone else but Wilfred."

Here were no spies for America but two star-crossed lovers. Rosamund could not help smiling, and, seeing that softening, Wilfred Dilber begged, "You understand, don't you, ma'am? Anyone would— Miss Sample being married to some lord she doesn't love . . . Break both our hearts. Permit me to say . . . won't let anything like that happen to Anemone . . . Would die rather than cause her grief.''

Rosamund thought of Lord Braden, who undoubtedly would cause Anemone a great deal of grief, and listened carefully as Wilfred Dilber disjointedly poured out his heart. "Fact is . . . love her devotedly. Could make her a comfortable living—not princely—no title such as Lord Braden could give her."

Anemone turned fiercely to her cavalier. "I don't want princely," she said, "I want you. I have told Mama so. I have even told Lord Braden so."

The young man's eyes dilated. "Anemone," he said, breathing rapidly, "my precious love!"

"My dearest angel!"

Rosamund thought it time to interrupt. "I saw you both from my window, so others might have seen you, too," she warned. "You had better cut short this rendezvous, Mona."

Wilfred said darkly, "Don't want to keep it secret. Permit me to explain . . . Trying to talk to Mrs. Sample . . . she won't give me a hearing. Could you possibly—? Miss St. Helm, if you could but arrange an interview with the lady . . . eternally grateful."

Both young people stared hopefully at Rosamund, who remembered Lucy's cynical judgment on men in general. But from the way that Wilfred was gazing at Anemone, she could not believe that he would ever treat her the way Sample had treated Lucy.

"What will you do if Mrs. Sample won't listen to you?" she asked. "If you marry without your mama's consent, Mona, you may not inherit any of your late father's wealth."

"I don't care about the money," Anemone cried, and Wilfred nodded.

"Neither do I. Make decent money . . . grain business, you see. Money's not why I love Anemone anyway," he declared. Then he added, with simple dignity, "Want to take care of her—will, if I'm allowed . . . Hope Mrs. Sample will believe me. Please, Miss St. Helm, I entreat you . . . need your good offices."

Rosamund made her decision. "I shall try, but I can't promise it will do any good." As Anemone threw her arms around her neck, she added soberly, "Meanwhile, you must stop meeting in this clandestine way. It won't help your cause if Mrs. Sample finds that you've been party to this, Mr. Dilber."

Anemone followed Rosamund meekly back into the house. "Don't think me too forward for wanting to meet with Wilfred," she said as they regained her chamber. "I love him, Rosa. He is the kindest and most tender of men. He has saved some money, and he has a future in trade. We will be so happy together."

But Rosamund was more concerned with something else Anemone had said. "You said that you had told Lord Braden about Mr. Dilber," she said. "How did that come about?"

"Lord Braden was so sympathetic and kind one day when I was feeling sad, so I told him about my eternal love for Wilfred," Anemone explained innocently. "I thought that it would stop him from making an offer for me, but alas, I was wrong."

Far from withdrawing his suit Lord Braden had moved quickly to secure Mona's fortune. "I'll talk to Lucy in the morning," Rosamund promised.

But this was not to be. Exhausted by the night's efforts, Rosamund slept through the morning and awoke past two o'clock. Nancy brought her a cup of chocolate and said that Mrs. Sample and Miss Sample had lunched long ago.

"I told them you were tired, ma'am, but not from what," Nancy said. Then she added in a conspiratorial tone, "I just managed to nip those clothes back to Meadows before he found out."

She was obviously eager to hear details about her mistress's adventures, but Rosamund changed the subject. "Have the ladies gone out?" she asked.

Nancy shook her head. "Mrs. Sample is getting ready to receive Lord Braden. Himself is calling at three o'clock, I heard her say. Miss Sample has the headache and is lying down."

Rosamund set down her cup and got out of bed. "Help me dress," she said. "I have an urgent errand to run."

She now knew what had to be done. Rather than hope that she had convinced Lucy to refuse Lord Braden's offer, she would get him to cry off. To accomplish this, she needed to intercept Lord Braden *before* he saw Lucy. Rosamund dressed hastily, and, leaving the house, walked around the corner of the street and prowled about, keeping her eye out for Lord Braden. When he finally appeared, driving a landau, she hurried forward, waving.

"A moment, my lord," she cried when he halted the horses. "I must speak to you before you go to the house."

Lord Braden looked astonished. "Of course, Miss St. Helm. Your obedient servant in all things."

He would have stepped down to help her mount the landau, but she stepped up smartly and sat down beside him. "Drive on," she directed.

"Where to?"

"It does not signify. Anywhere will do. What I have to

say will not take very long." Rosamund took a deep breath and said bluntly, "I do not want you to marry Anemone."

She was conscious of his astonishment . . . and then his amusement. "My dear lady—"

"I am not your *dear* anything," she replied sharply. "I know about your household in the heart of London. I've seen your son and your . . . companion."

She saw his eyes narrow and saw the tightening of his mouth. Then he recovered and laughed. "I am at a loss to understand you," he said. "Are you saying that I am leg-shackled to a female and that I have a son? You must be feverish, Miss St. Helm."

With her eyes on Lord Braden, Rosamund explained. "I followed you last night . . . From the gaming place on St. James Street to Boar Square."

As she spoke, Braden's color receded until his face looked quiet gray. If any other woman had told him such things he would have laughed her out of countenance, but he had no doubt that the St. Helm vixen had done what she said. Fury and frustration choked him as he thought of all his carefully laid plans and of the debtors who had been snapping at his heels for a long time. Debtors who could have been satisfied by the fortune that was almost within his grasp.

Rosamund watched Lord Braden's face harden. "I don't mean to moralize," she said coldly. "What you do is your business, but Mona is not going to marry you. I want you to tell Lucy that you are not going to offer for her daughter."

Lord Braden thought once more of the creditors and of debtors' prison, then looked into Miss St. Helm's steady eyes. He decided that of the two possibilities, Rosamund was the easier to deal with.

"But I'm in love with Miss Sample and can't understand why you should tell such lies," Lord Braden said piously.

He added, "The man you followed could not possibly have been me. I dined at my club last night and left at about three in the morning."

"I don't believe you."

Her eyes were as steady as a duelist's, and her voice was crisp and assured. Inwardly Lord Braden swore. If he had his way, he would have liked to take a riding crop to this unwomanly female. But instead he smiled at her and spoke in his silkiest, most persuasive voice.

"Madam, you are most certainly mistaken. Like any man, I have—shall we say *erred* in matters of the flesh? But that is all water under the bridge. There comes a time when a man must marry and fill his nursery—"

"I would say you've already started filling yours."

There was no way that she was going to be cajoled into silence. Lord Braden abandoned his tactics and said, "It's your word against mine, Miss St. Helm. Would you put it to the test? In front of a magistrate if need be?"

About to shout Yes! Rosamund hesitated. She had just imagined what Hawkley would say if she did such a thing, not to mention her brother and his family . . .

Lord Braden misread her hesitation. With a smirk he said, "Now, I'm going to drive up to the Samples' town house. Far from crying off, I intend to go inside and meet Miss Sample and offer for her hand in marriage. Her mother is so enamored of a title that she'll snap up that offer as a fish snatches bait. And why not? We both want something that the other can provide. It's a bargain, you see."

He paused and lowered his voice to a confidential pitch. "That's the way of the world, my dear. Let us be friends . . ."

He was so sure of himself that he put his arm around her shoulders. Next moment he was reeling back as Rosamund

195

slapped him hard. She followed that slap with another box to his ears.

Then she jumped down from the landau and glared up at Lord Braden. "Very well," she grated, "I'll do as you suggest. We shall take it to the courts, sir."

She turned her back on him and began walking down the street toward Lucy's town house. As she did so, she heard the sound of wheels bowling behind her. They drew up sharply next to her, and she snapped over her shoulder, "There is no use trying to convince me. My mind is made up. I'm going to expose you for what you are, and everyone in London will be told of your unsavory reputation."

There was a choking sound from inside the conveyance. "A fine one *you* are to talk about reputation," said her brother's voice.

Chapter Eleven

Rosamund whipped around and saw poised above her the Viscount Craye's scowling visage. Whether its purplish color was caused by temper or the unaccustomed warmth of the afternoon, she could not tell.

"What are you doing here, Bevan?" Rosamund demanded.

The viscount rolled his eyes skyward as if to beg heaven to witness that he was being tried beyond his strength. "Doing it too brown, Rosa," he exclaimed. "You should know full well why. Your behavior's become a talk and a scandal and I'm taking you home."

"Are you indeed?"

A sharp cough from the interior of the barouche interrupted this exchange. Rosamund's eyes narrowed as she saw Lady Orme peering around the viscount. My lady's carefully powdered hair was dressed exquisitely around the same autocratic, bad-tempered face that Rosamund well remembered.

"How do you do, ma'am?" Rosamund said calmly.

"Unfeeling girl," quoth Lady Orme. "Little do you care what ruin has been brought to your family by your outrageous behavior. Cassandra has been prostrated. She has not been able to leave her bed for weeks."

"I'm sorry to hear it," exclaimed Rosamund in some concern. "Why didn't you write and tell me she was ill, Bevan?"

"Cassandra didn't want me to noise it about," the viscount explained. "Chicken pox, you know. Paltry thing to happen—not ton at all. She got 'em at the start of the Season, which is why we couldn't come to London as we wanted. We—"

"My daughter's illness," interrupted Lady Orme, "was exacerbated by the reports of your madcap behavior, Rosamund."

"Was it indeed?"

The viscount stirred uneasily at his sister's tone, but Lady Orme had no such compunctions. She swept on. "It was not enough that you chose to lodge with an American of low birth. It was not enough that you consorted with savages. No, you must insult the Duke and Duchess of Broon and scandalize all of London with your unspeakable behavior." She paused to draw breath, then added, "It is time you return to Kent before you completely disgrace the family."

"Thank you for your concern, but I assure you that I am happy where I am." Bowing slightly to Lady Orme, Rosamund began walking again.

"Rosa, by Gad, Rosa! You are the most provoking— Can't keep talking to you while hanging out of m' barouche." Rosamund walked faster. "Yes, I know, Mama-in-law. Oh, let me down, you fool," the viscount snapped at his coachman. "Rosa, wait. Wait, damn it all. Have to talk to you."

Panting and muttering, he caught up to her. "It's too bad of you. By Gad, Rosa . . . It shows a serious lack of family feeling, your carrying on this way."

"What way?" Rosamund demanded. "Are you speaking for yourself or for Lady Orme?"

There was a hissing sound from the following carriage, and glancing over his shoulder, the viscount saw Lady Orme glaring at them both. "N-not *all* Mama-in-law's idea," he said feebly. "There's been talk, Rosa, about your set-to with Broon and—and your other starts. Heard you was being called the Wild Rose." He saw Rosamund's eyes begin to smolder and added hastily, "I imagine not all of it's true, Rosa, but you know what society is like."

"Oh, yes," Rosamund murmured. "I know exactly what society is like. It will shield a rake and a coxcomb because he is a well-born *man*, but it will not allow a woman to be too forward. Now *that* is a crime . . . For a female to think for herself is unforgivable."

The viscount had begun to perspire. "Now, Rosa—" he began.

There was a rattle of carriage wheels behind them. "Craye," Lady Orme demanded, "have you made this ungrateful girl see the error of her ways?"

"No, he has not," Rosamund retorted.

"I say, Mama-in-law," the viscount suggested uneasily, "perhaps we had better talk about all of this someplace off the open road."

Ignoring him, Lady Orme leaned out of the barouche and fixed Rosamund with a withering gaze. "Oh, my dear child," she said in a voice that meant the exact opposite, "I grieve for you. Motherless as you are, headstrong like your father

199

before you— Truly, your conduct has been indefensible. No wonder Hawkley wrote to say that he washed his hands of you."

Rosamund felt as if she had been slapped in the face. She turned to her brother, asking, "Is this true?"

The viscount felt almost prickly with irritation. He recalled the commotion that had attended the arrival of Hawkley's missive, remembered Cassandra wailing about Rosamund disgracing the family, while Lady Orme castigated him for not controlling his sister.

As usual, he had been blamed for the whole sorry mess. The viscount glared at his sister and sputtered, "Yes, by Gad. Hawkley wrote about you. He said he'd done his best by you but that nothing could reclaim you to decency. Said he couldn't be responsible for such a hoyden."

Rosamund felt as though her heart had become too tight in her ribs. In another moment it must burst. She could not believe that Hawkley had shrugged her off as he might a soiled coat.

She and the earl had their differences, and yet there had been moments. They had laughed together. He had taken her to her first opera and given her the gift of music. They had worked in partnership to nurse a sick child. He had held her in his arms and called her his Wild Rose.

Perhaps he had only been taunting her. Rosamund felt tears sting her eyelids and knew that she could not cry in front of Lady Orme. With an effort she attended to what her brother was saying.

"I'm still the head of the house, by Gad, and I'll have no more of this, Rosa. D' you hear me? Cassandra's still poorly and can't be disturbed by your harum-scarum ways."

He cleared his throat and glanced sideways at his sister's white face. "M' wife feels lonely—y' know, isolated," he said in a milder tone. "Thought you'd want to come back and help her through her convalescence."

He was offering her a way of returning to Kent with some vestige of honor. He was trying to spare her from being hauled back in disgrace. But saving face did not matter. What mattered to Rosamund was the realization that Hawkley had written that letter to Bevan *before* he had kissed her last night.

When he saw her dressed in a man's clothes, he must have been convinced that she was nothing more than an adventuress used to easy kisses. Rosamund's cheeks burned, and the realities of the world ebbed away, leaving only one thought: She wanted to be as far from Hawkley as she could.

She looked up at her brother's worried, sheeplike countenance and then at Lady Orme. "Very well," she said abruptly, "I will return to Kent with you. But I must tell Lucy about my decision, and I must have time to pack. When do you wish to leave?"

Looking vastly relieved, the viscount said that they would leave London tomorrow at first light. They were, he added, staying over the night at the Silver George. "I'll go with you now and explain matters to this . . . er . . . to Mrs. Sample," he offered.

Since nothing would induce Lady Orme to exchange words with a lowborn American, she waited in the barouche while her son-in-law escorted his sister into the Samples' rented town house. Here they were met by Bleak, who looked down his nose at the flushed little viscount and announced in his most dampening tones that Madam was not at home.

"And Miss Anemone, where is she?" Rosamund demanded, whereupon Bleak said that Miss had retired to her bed with the headache. Sure that the headache had been the result of too many tears, Rosamund tasted more bitterness.

Before she left London, she promised herself, she would try once more to talk to Lucy.

"I cannot leave without seeing my hostess," she told her brother. "I'll be ready to leave in the morning. Is that satisfactory?"

The viscount felt unhappy. Wrong-minded Rosa might have been, but he misliked the pale, set cast of her face. "We'll dine together tonight," he offered in a conciliatory tone. "Capital food they serve at the Silver George, Rosa. We'll dine and—and talk."

Rosamund was too dispirited to make any objections, and after having told her he would come to fetch her to dine at eight, the viscount went away. The sound of the door closing after her brother only reminded Rosamund that Hawkley had effectively slammed the door on her.

"He had no right," she whispered to herself. "Why write to Bevan? Why not simply tell *me*?"

She tried to whip up anger to stiffen her spine, but as she summoned Nancy and told her that they were leaving for Kent, she was conscious only of a heaviness of heart. Nancy, who had sighted Lady Orme waiting in the barouche outside the door, was full of indignation for her mistress.

"Saints alive, ma'am," she protested. "It's bad luck entirely—and the Season only just starting. Miss Anemone will miss you something terrible when you go home."

But Kent was not "home" and never had been. Home was Canada. Rosamund tried to conjure up soothing memories of that beloved place and instead found herself imagining a tall, broad-shouldered man with smiling brown eyes.

It had hurt her to leave Canada, but she had managed to survive. Now once again she was being forced to leave something that she had come to love. No, Rosamund amended with bitter honesty. Not something. Some*one*.

"I am an idiot," she said aloud.

Nancy looked at her mistress in surprise, but Rosamund did not even note that look. Truth was truth, she thought bleakly. Hawkley had often infuriated her, but he had also made her happier than she had ever been. And in his arms she had found a world that was far more wondrous than Canada.

But she must forget him now—and she would. Rosamund shook her thoughts away and asked, "Where did Lucy go, Nancy?"

The abigail did not know. "But," she added, "there's been strange goings-on entirely, Miss Rosa. First Lord Braden came to call, but Miss Anemone was still feeling poorly, so he left after a short talk with Mrs. Sample. Then, Mrs. Sample came out of the Gold Room looking ready to cry and said she couldn't stay in the house a second longer. Herself and Mrs. Dewinter went off somewhere together. Maybe Miss Anemone'd know where."

Not wanting to awaken Anemone with bad news, Rosamund decided to pack her clothes and wait for Lucy. But though her clothes were soon packed and ready and the afternoon lengthened into sunset, then finally into twilight, Lucy did not return. Finally, knowing she could not put off the moment longer, Rosamund steeled herself and went to tap on Anemone's door.

There was no answer, so she pushed open the door and saw that the room was empty. The bed was neatly made, but everything else spoke of haste and confusion. Anemone's dressing table was disordered and her hat lay near the bed as though it had been impetuously discarded. As Rosamund automatically bent down to pick it up, she noticed a scrap of paper lying on the floor.

She picked it up and read:

If Mr. Dilber will come to 18 River Place, a friend who does not want Lord Braden to marry Miss Sample will tell you certain damaging facts about his lordship's character.

As she read, Rosamund felt mounting horror. She had recognized the bold, fanciful writing as Lord Braden's own.

She ran across the room and, jerking on the bellpull, summoned Anemone's abigail. "Do you know who brought this note?" she asked.

The wide-eyed girl at first denied that she knew anything about a note—but when pressed began to sniffle and said that Miss Mona had made her promise not to speak a word. "A young gentleman brought it, miss," she said. "Madam was already out when 'e came, an' 'e asked me to bring it up to Miss Mona. She went down ter 'im and then 'e went away alone."

Wilfred Dilber had received the note from Lord Braden, taken it at face value, and come to give Anemone courage. Then he had gone off to try and prove that his rival was unfit to marry Anemone.

"And where did Miss Mona go?" she asked.

Weeping and insisting that she had meant no harm, the abigail confessed, "Miss Mona was that worried, ma'am. She begged the gentleman to take 'er with 'im, but 'e wouldn't 'ear of it. After 'e left, she told me to get 'er a 'ansom and made me swear to say she was resting wi' the 'eadache. I don't know where she went, really I don't."

But Rosamund did. Though she was not sure where 18 River Place might be, there was no doubt that Anemone and Wilfred were walking into Lord Braden's trap.

It was drizzling and chilly, and though it was still only seven o'clock, the thick fog creeping in from the river made it difficult to see. The hansom cab rattled and bounced on the uneven terrain before creaking to a halt.

"Is *this* where you want ter go, miss?" the cabbie asked doubtfully.

Rosamund's heart sank as she looked about her. River Place had turned out to be an especially vile area of London. She could smell the river's damp odor mingling with several other unpleasant aromas. When she looked about her, the dwellings that hugged the water had a sinister look.

As Rosamund hesitated, a gang of ragged street urchins closed around the hansom and shrilly demanded money.

"Gerrout of it, you lot!" the cabbie snarled. He laid about him with his whip and the urchins ran away, shaking their fists and sticking out their tongues as they ran. "Shall I drive you back ter town, miss?" the jarvey then asked.

Swallowing the lump in her throat, Rosamund shook her head. "I must meet my friends," she said.

But where was Number 18? As she looked at the fog-shrouded tangle of tumbledown shacks and warehouses nearby, Rosamund's heart sank still further. She now wished that she had told someone where she was going. But, she reminded herself, Nancy would only have worried, and Lucy had still been out, and Bevan would have been too timid to help. The only man she could have counted on was Hawkley, and as matters stood she could hardly turn to *him* for help.

Even at such a time, Rosamund felt a prickle of misery. Then she drew herself together, felt in her reticule for her bone-handled knife, and resolutely descended from the hansom. "Please wait for me here," she told the jarvey. "I will not be long."

Her voice shook with nerves, and as she started to walk forward to the warehouse ahead of her, something soft squirmed and squealed underfoot. "Steady," she told herself. "It's only a rat. You've faced much worse than a rat in Canada."

But Canada had been broad and clean and smelled of wind and wilderness. Rosamund's resolve nearly faltered as a gust of malodorous wind whipped fog around her. Perhaps she should retrace her steps and alert the law—

A door banged somewhere, and a voice, rough with drink, demanded, " 'Oo's out there? 'At you, Muggins?"

Rosamund held her breath and hoped that the fog was too dense for anyone to see her or the hansom down the street. Her luck apparently held because another rough voice answered, "Aye, it's me. 'Ave you got our lovebirds wrapped up snug?"

Lovebirds—then Anemone and Wilfred *were* here. Rosamund strained her eyes and saw two hulking shapes through a break in the fog. They were standing in front of what looked to be a warehouse, and the one called Muggins was saying, "I don't like it, Nash. It's a 'anging offense, what we're doing."

" 'Anging, nofink," replied the other tartly. "We 'ands over the flash cove and 'is mort, and we gets our silver feeders and 'op the twig. *'E'll* soon be 'ere to tell us what the lay is. Now, go in and watch 'em. I've bleeding done me watch."

Rosamund flattened herself still further as a burly man stalked past her and disappeared into the fog. The one called Muggins now swaggered toward the warehouse, went in, and closed the door behind him.

Stealthily Rosamund approached the door. It was warped and did not shut properly, and by applying her eye to a crack, Rosamund could see into the room. There, in a bleak, dirty room full of boxes and bales, she could see Anemone and Dilber sitting on the floor with their backs to each other. Both were bound hand and foot and they were also gagged. Anemone's dress was torn and her hair was disheveled; it looked as if she had struggled with her captors. Dilber's eye was swollen shut and there was a nasty gash on his forehead.

The man who was guarding the prisoners was a big, hulking creature with a flat face and cruel, hard little eyes. He hooted with laughter when Dilber strained at his bonds.

"No use trying to get loose," he jeered. "Only way yer going to leave this place is by the river."

Anemone began to struggle, too. Tears were running down her cheeks and into her gag, and Rosamund wished with all her heart that she had a pistol. She would have shot the villain Muggins without a qualm.

If she could create a diversion before the other villain came back, perhaps Muggins would leave his post long enough for her to rescue the prisoners. Rosamund looked about her and spied some boxes and barrels that were stacked some distance away. She backtracked and heaved one of the boxes over.

Boxes and barrels collapsed in domino fashion, and the noise brought Muggins running to investigate. "That you, Nash?" he yelled.

Receiving no answer, he stood irresolute for a moment and then lurched down the steps toward the noise. At the same time, Rosamund sped through the door and into the room.

"It's all right," she whispered as the prisoners stared mutely at her. "I'll soon have you free."

With her knife she cut Anemone's bonds and then Wilfred's. Anemone began to cry. "Hush," Rosamund whispered. "You must be brave, Mona. We must get away before Muggins and his friend return. Can you stand up?"

Anemone tried, but she had been tied up too long and her

legs gave way under her. "Lean on me, dearest," Dilber said, panting.

In spite of his brave words, he looked quite green and appeared ready to faint. "I will help Mona," Rosamund told him. Then, as she supported her friend toward the door, she added, "I have a hansom waiting for us not too far away, but we must hurry."

Anemone was shaking so hard that her teeth chattered. "Oh, R-Rosa," she stammered, "it was all s-so hideous. Wilfred received a note to co-come and meet someone here. We hoped what he learned w-would prevent me from m-marrying Lord Braden. Wilfred didn't know I was following him until we both were tr-trapped by those brutes."

Praying that those brutes were still far off, Rosamund cautiously opened the door. There was no sign of Muggins or Nash, so she led the way outside and down the stairs. "It's only until the end of the street," she whispered. "Be brave, Mona. We'll soon be out of this."

As she spoke, they became completely enshrouded with mist. On the river a foghorn hooted mournfully, and the river rats squeaked underfoot. Anemone was trembling violently as they reached the place where Rosamund had left the hansom.

"Where is the hansom?" Wilfred asked. "I see nothing here . . . Mist's heavy . . . Anemone at the end of her strength."

Rosamund felt faint herself. "Perhaps the driver is waiting further up the road—" she began.

"If you're looking for that hired hack, it's gone. I sent the jarvey away saying that he wasn't needed now that I was here."

Anemone screamed as Lord Braden strolled out of the fog. He looked jaunty and pleased with himself and was dressed as if he were going to a party, in buff pantaloons, a brocaded waistcoat, and a fawn-colored coat with silver buttons. He swept off his curly beaver to the ladies, saying, "Miss St. Helm, Miss Sample, your most obedient servant."

"Run!" Rosamund cried. She drew her knife and faced Lord Braden, but Anemone was at the end of her strength. She collapsed in the filthy street and began to cry. Wilfred Dilber hastened toward her but was intercepted by Muggins, who with Nash had followed Lord Braden onto the scene. As Muggins twisted Dilber's arms behind his back, Lord Braden drew a pistol from inside his jacket and motioned to Rosamund to drop her knife.

When she had reluctantly complied, he picked up the knife and pocketed it. "I regret the use of force, but you leave me no choice."

Furious words sprang to Rosamund's lips, but she bit them back with an effort. Temper would not serve now.

"I'm sorry that you ladies walked into a trap that was meant only for Dilber," Lord Braden was saying. "Curiosity killed the cat, as they say."

"What—what are you going to do with us?" Dilber said, panting.

"First, let's get back to the warehouse." Lord Braden snapped an order at his attendant villains, who dragged their resisting prisoners back to their prison. "Now, isn't it better to be out of the fog?"

Rosamund could no longer keep silent. "There is no 'better' about it," she cried. "You are a kidnapper, sir! I hope you will hang for it—you and your brace of villains."

Lord Braden's henchmen looked somewhat discomfited, but his lordship only laughed. "Strong words for a lady, Miss St. Helm—but then you are not really a lady, are you?" He cocked his head, taking her measure. "You boxed my ears yesterday, and I have a debt to pay to you. But enough of that for the moment."

He turned to Wilfred Dilber. "To answer your question, you are about to become a patriot."

"What? What're you talking about?"

Lord Braden smiled, showing his beautiful white teeth. "You are going to join the King's Navy and fight the Americans," he said.

"Can't mean— Not saying I'm to be impressed into the navy?" Dilber said, gasping.

Rosamund had heard about the poor wretches who were kidnapped and forced to serve in the Royal Navy. Starvation, sickness, and harsh discipline awaited Wilfred Dilber. If he did not die from these, sea battles with the Americans would finish him off.

Anemone began to weep, but Lord Braden merely stood there smiling. Loathing him, Rosamund said, "I understand now why you sent Mr. Dilber that note. Once Mona told you about him, you knew that he would do everything in his power to stop you from marrying her. By having him impressed into the navy, you are going to remove him from your path."

"How clever you are," he replied pleasantly. "After Dilber is handed over to the press-gang, I'm going to fly across the border with my sweetheart, Anemone."

"I'll never go anywhere with you," Anemone sobbed. "I'll die first."

Lord Braden showed his teeth again. "I doubt it. Young ladies talk about dying, but in reality death is painful and final. Believe me, it's far better to become Lady Braden as your dear mama planned—before Miss St. Helm began to meddle in matters that didn't concern her."

Then Lucy had refused his suit! Even at such a time, Rosamund felt a sense of triumph.

"I'll never go anywhere with you." Anemone clenched her small hands and raised her voice to a shout. "Never, never, never! I will make a scene. I'll run away from you—"

"If you don't do as I say, your lover dies here, now," Lord Braden interrupted. He drew out his pistol again, held it to Dilber's head, and cocked it. "Well, my dear? Do I shoot him—or will you swear to behave yourself till we tie the knot? No starts, no screams, no attempts to escape?"

"Anemone, don't do it," Wilfred cried.

Lord Braden cuffed him across the mouth. "I mean what I say. Promise, or I shoot Dilber—and Miss St. Helm as well."

"Villain!" Rosamund shouted.

Anemone looked from Rosamund to Wilfred and began to cry. "I'll do anything you like," she said, sobbing. "Only don't hurt Wilfred and Rosa."

"Your wish is my command. If he doesn't drown or get blown to pieces by Americans, Dilber will return to England eventually. Tie him up, Nash. Tie Miss St. Helm, too. And you'd better gag them both while you're at it."

He came close to Rosamund and smiled down at her. "What a beautiful creature you are, with that mane of black hair and those eyes. No wonder Hawkley was mad for you. You put me in mind of a wild mare, one that I would enjoy taming—and riding." His lip curled as he said coaxingly, "Come, wouldn't you like to be Lady Braden? After all, you have a fortune of your own, and I may be disposed to take you rather than this insipid little creature."

Rosamund spat in his face. She had the satisfaction of seeing him go white with rage for an instant before he raised his hand and slapped her across the mouth.

"Bitch," he said in a voice that was sheared of every grace and affectation. "I'll make you sorry for that."

Wilfred writhed in his bonds as he shouted, "You—you cur. Filthy brute . . . I'll kill you, you bloody swine!"

"You are wasting your time." It took all of Rosamund's courage to speak steadily, but her voice was clear and full of scorn. "His kind never fight cleanly. They crawl out from under rocks like maggots. Like rats, they hunt in packs. Braden is below contempt."

He seemed ready to hit her again but instead turned and looked out of the window. "Tongue-valiant," he said, jeering at her, "but a gag will take care of that." As this command was ruthlessly carried out, he added, "You should not have interfered, sweet Rosamund. As soon as the King's Navy comes for Dilber, Anemone and I will be on our way."

Chapter Twelve

Hawkley frowned down at the silver card tray in the hall of his Mount Street town house. Among the many cards of those who had called while he was out was that of Bevan, Viscount Craye.

"Confound that fellow," he muttered.

Hawkley had just returned from an afternoon with his sister and the Marquess Hare. Though he ordinarily enjoyed their company, today he had felt restive and irritable. Hare had droned on interminably about some idiotic curricle race he had won while his sister, usually so charming and amusing, had seemed like an empty-headed rattle.

Old bores prosed on about the war, Hawkley gloomed, while young bores nattered on about hunting and betting on horses and on their shooting prowess. Gaming at Boodles's, late suppers at the Piazza Coffee House, sparring at Jackson's

Saloon—diversions that had pleased him well in the past—now all seemed pointless and uninteresting.

And, of course, he'd had to endure all of it with a smile. After Rosamund's conduct at the Countess Standen's, he had needed to mend fences with his friends. The worst of it was that when Nicholas had made some joke about the Wild Rose today, Hawkley had wanted to strangle him.

"I wish I'd been home when Craye came to call," he growled. "I'd have given him some words with no bark on him."

He stalked up the stairs and into the study. Perhaps because there was no fire lit in the grate, the room felt somber and cold even in May. But then there had been a fire at his sister's establishment, and it had felt cheerless there, too.

He had no idea why he felt so flat. Each day began and ended without surprises or disasters. There was nothing to enrage him or make him feel desperate. Life was all he could wish for again.

There was a diffident cough at the door, and the earl glanced up to see that his secretary had entered the room with some envelopes in his hand. "What's that you have there?" he demanded.

"The mail, m'lud, and a letter from Her Ladyship, the dowager countess." Noting that the earl's countenance remained as bleak as winter weather, Beamler added hastily, "And there has been word from Hawkley Manor, m'lud. Mr. Wagonner has initiated repairs. The tenant farmers are satisfied."

This was important. With an effort, Hawkley forced himself to attend to what his secretary was saying. "So Wagonner's taken hold," he said. "Thought he would. How's his wife?"

Wagonner, Beamler thought, was not the only one who

had taken hold. Aloud, he said, "Much better, m'lud. If I might make so bold, it is your forbearance and compassion that saved the day. If it had not been for the specialist you suggested, Mrs. Wagonner might not have survived. And in any case they could not have afforded the doctor if you had not given him the money."

Into Hawkley's mind came the memory of a small cottage and Rosamund singing a lullaby to a sick child. "Man was in service to my family for years," he said stiffly. "Why shouldn't I frank him with a little blunt?"

He took his mother's letter as he spoke and read it swiftly. In her fond note the dowager countess hoped that he was well, asked after his sister, then added that the roses were in bloom. Was it not time to bring dear Rosamund back to Fairhaven Manor?

Hawkley folded the letter and put it into his pocket. "What else is there in the mail, Beamler?" he asked.

"A letter from Mrs. Sample, m'lud. It came by messenger early this afternoon."

Beamler saw his employer's frown and judged it prudent to say nothing more. He had been well aware of the earl's moods of late and guessed the cause. The earl had ceased to smile when he fell out with Miss St. Helm.

None but the most pudding-headed could have failed to note that the earl had seemed a different man since coming to London. He had been considerate to everyone around him and had floored his valet by inquiring solicitously about his bad tooth. The earl had then actually sent Inchley to an expensive London dentist. He had also been sympathetic when Beamler's son fell ill and insisted that his secretary return home to Sussex at once with gifts for the child. And when the new boots boy ruined his favorite pair of boots, Hawkley had only shrugged his shoulders and enjoined more care in the future.

No one belowstairs could understand the unnatural benignity in which the earl seemed to live. Mrs. Hoose, the housekeeper, suspected that the earl had been converted to religion, but Beamler knew that it was all tied up with Miss St. Helm. The unconventional lady with the amethyst eyes had captured my lord's heart.

Even now, though the earl was obviously in a taking, he did not roar or fume or put his underlings in a quake. Instead he stood tapping Mrs. Sample's letter on his hand with a look in his eye that made Beamler ache for him.

"Is there anything more you require, m'lud?" he asked gently.

"Craye has come to take his sister back to Kent," the earl said. "He came because I wrote to him and told him I'd washed my hands of the plaguey female. I was right to do so."

The secretary bowed. It was the closest thing he could do without openly disagreeing with His Lordship.

"What else was I supposed to do?" Hawkley went on forcefully. "Made everyone uncomfortable—no, be damned to that—she was making *me* dashed uncomfortable. She turned everything upside down." He shook his head. "Now, she's going back to Kent, and good riddance to her."

And yet he felt unutterably miserable. It was as if some mainspring in his existence had snapped and caused the universe to come tumbling down around his ears. He could not get Rosamund St. Helm out of his mind, no matter how hard he tried. . . . Hawkley turned abruptly and began to stride out of the room.

"Perhaps, sir, if you read Mrs. Sample's letter . . ." Beamler ventured to say.

Hawkley turned sharply and saw such concern and sympathy in his secretary's eyes that the rebuke on his lips died unspoken. Rosamund, he recalled, had once told him that he should listen more to his servants.

"Dash and blast that woman," he said, sighing. "Hand the letter over."

He read the letter as his secretary exited and felt Lucy's directness come through the cramped, badly spelled script. She began by observing that she had not seen Hawkley for several days and added that she was unhappy about the rift between them. She concluded that it was bad for neighbors to nourish a grudge. "Best to let the cat out of the bag and hear it meow," wrote Lucy.

The cat in question had consigned him to the devil the last time they had met. Hawkley vividly recalled Rosamund with her dark curls spilling out from under her horrible cap. She had put on a man's clothes and gone into one of the seediest districts in London—had gone alone because she was Anemone Sample's friend.

And now she was being taken home in disgrace. The earl looked at Lucy's letter a second time and felt a dull ache under his breastbone. "At least," he said slowly, "I should say good-bye."

A moment later he was shouting for his curricle, and shortly thereafter he arrived at the Samples' town house. Disregarding the unfamiliar barouche that was waiting in front, he strode up to the door. "Is Miss St. Helm at home?" he demanded when Bleak manifested himself.

Before the butler had a chance to answer, a surprised voice exclaimed, "Julian! By Gad, it's you."

Viscount Craye was standing in the staircase hall. He was wearing a riding cloak over his round shoulders and an anxious frown that gave way to a smile as Hawkley mounted the stairs. "By Gad, it's good to see you. Called in to see you earlier—missed you. I owe you an apology, Julian."

At this juncture Lucy bounced out onto the staircase hall, calling, "That you, Rosa? Oh . . . it's you. I hoped you was Rosa."

Hawkley disregarded this less than cordial welcome. "Where is Miss St. Helm?" he asked.

"Demmed if we know," was the viscount's answer. "Chit's off someplace. Shows no sign of family feeling, by Gad. I specifically told her that we was to dine together tonight. Mama-in-law's much put out."

Hawkley noted for the first time that a tall, aristocratic lady was standing in the doorway of the drawing room. Her narrow, disapproving face was familiar, and the earl recalled Craye's mother-in-law, whom he had met at the viscount's wedding.

"Nothing Rosamund does can surprise *me*," declared the lady. "She has already set the countryside on its ears with her harum-scarum ways. 'Wild Rose' indeed. The girl is the outside of enough."

Lucy regarded Lady Orme with cordial dislike. "I don't know anything about any harum-scarum ways," she retorted. "Rosa must have her own reasons for being out tonight, and it's not for us to pass judgment till we know what's what."

As Lady Orme haughtily lifted her quizzing glass to her eyes, Hawkley was suddenly reminded of the way the Duchess of Broon had studied Rosamund.

"Rosa's a lovely, good-hearted girl," Lucy continued, "and I won't listen to her being abused in my house. Snakes, if that's how you go on about her, it's no wonder she don't want to go back to Kent with you."

Ignoring the fact that Lady Orme had begun to turn a

purplish hue, Lucy turned back to Hawkley. "You and Rosa went about together these past weeks, my lord," she said. "Don't you know where she might be?"

Hawkley had been racking his brains for an answer. All he could remember was their last meeting. The impressmen, the talk of Lord Braden, and their final argument. A sense of unaccountable dread filled him and he demanded, "Do you know if she ever met Braden?"

Lucy's face expressed both distaste and deep regret. "If you're asking did she tell me about his lordship, the answer's yes. I sent him packing today when he come to ask for Mona." A deep sigh shook her. "Imagine me turning a lord away. I was so upset I had to go out right afterward. Me and Mrs. Dewinter went shopping. Calms the nerves, that does."

That lady, who had been hovering nervously in the background, suggested that perhaps Miss Anemone might know Miss St. Helm's whereabouts. "She is still abed," she twittered. "If you wish, I shall awaken her and ask."

While Mrs. Dewinter hurried up the stairs, Craye shook his head and announced that Rosamund was given to such starts and would be all right. "Independent-minded, you know," he added. "Has a mind of her own."

"I know it only too well," Hawkley agreed wryly.

Lady Orme interposed, "I must apologize to you, my lord earl, on behalf of the family. I am persuaded that she was a sore trial and a burden to you."

"No such thing," Hawkley retorted, and then checked himself. He had been on the point of telling the old harridan that he regretted not one instant of the time he had spent with Rosamund.

There was a knock on the door. "Rosa!" Lucy exclaimed in relief. "Thank God she's home—"

She broke off as Chief Storm Cloud stalked through the

door. Without removing hat or cloak, he pushed past Bleak and bounded lightly up the stairs. "Know where woman is," he declared.

"Where?" Hawkley demanded.

Before the Mohawk could answer, Lady Orme demanded to know who This Person was. Storm Cloud looked Lady Orme over, apparently did not care for what he saw, and dismissed her with one of his grunts.

"Saw her in hansom that pass me near river," he told Hawkley. "I go walk there sometimes, but it's bad place for woman, so I send Flying Crow and Silver Beaver to follow hansom and report back to me here."

He was interrupted by a shriek on the stairs. "Oh, Mrs. Sample, we are undone," wailed Mrs. Dewinter. "Miss Anemone is not in her room. She has vanished!"

Lucy gasped and turned pale. "Oh, by Gad . . . She's going to faint," the viscount exclaimed.

But Lucy was made of sterner stuff. "Ain't going to do any such thing," she announced. "I want my cloak, and I want the closed carriage brought around. I'll bet you a dollar that my daughter and Rosa are together. Maybe they're in trouble."

"Rosamund was in hansom alone," Storm Cloud maintained.

"Well, *really*!" gasped Lady Orme. "How dare this savage person refer to the sister of a peer in so familiar a manner?"

She broke off as the door was hurled open again and Flying Crow and Silver Beaver came pelting up the stairs. Though dressed in English clothes, the two had painted white circles around their eyes and yellow bands on their cheeks—and looked so savage that Lady Orme actually took several steps backward before collecting herself enough to stop and glare at them.

The braves spoke swiftly in their own tongue, and Hawkley gripped Storm Cloud's arm. "What is it? What're they saying?"

"Say that Rosamund go into big house by water—not come out. Bad-looking men go in, too." Storm Cloud started for the stairs, adding, "I go there now."

"I'm going with you," declared Hawkley. Storm Cloud gave him a white-toothed grin and a companionable nod. "Ride with me in my curricle, Chief."

"And I'm coming too, by Gad," cried the viscount. He trotted down the stairs, seized his umbrella from the stand in the vestibule, and waved it like a rapier. "She's my sister, after all."

Lucy was already ordering the footmen to arm themselves with staves and to follow her. "And I," announced Lady Orme ominously, "will come as well. Someone must keep a semblance of decency in this situation. Craye, do not attempt to dissuade me; my duty is plain. I am going to see this disgraceful affair to the end!"

She started to sail down the stairs but then caught sight of Bleak, who was looking scornfully after Lucy. The fact that an underling dared to show emotions of any kind was the last straw.

"Sirrah, my cloak!" Lady Orme snarled in such a terrible voice that Bleak started.

"My cloak," went on her ladyship imperiously. "What is the matter with you? Is your hearing impaired?"

Under my lady's basilisk stare, Bleak became nervous. As he presented Lady Orme's cloak, his hand trembled and he dropped the garment.

Lady Orme was delighted to have found someone on whom

221

to vent her spleen. "Incompetence," she snarled. "Your stupidity is inexcusable. Do you dare call yourself a butler? You are not good enough to be an underfootman." She started down the stairs and then turned to administer the coup de grace. "You are not even fit to serve an *American.*"

Bleak's dignity collapsed. All his hauteur gone, he looked as if he was about to cry. Delighted that she had diminished the upstart underling to rubble, Lady Orme took her son-in-law's arm and sailed after the others.

It was not, Rosamund thought, that she was really afraid of dying.

Death had come for many people dear to her, and besides, Tall Reed had explained that death was but another facet of life. When his time came, that wise old man had added, he would face the moment with a smile on his lips.

Rosamund did not feel like smiling. It was grossly unfair to have to die while a counter coxcomb like Lord Braden triumphed. No matter what he had said, Rosamund was sure that Lord Braden planned to kill her since she was privy to his plans.

Slumped in a chair beside Lord Braden, Anemone was weeping silently. Wilfred, gagged and bound like Rosamund, was staring at Mona and trying to convey his feelings. At least, Rosamund thought, with an ache in her heart, they'd enjoyed love for a little while.

And I, she thought, will never be able to tell Hawkley how I feel. He will never know that I love him.

If only she had told Hawkley about Lord Braden's trap, he would have helped her, she knew. Her pride had held her back. It was too late now, for Lord Braden was raising his head to listen.

"Footsteps," he said. "The navy is coming for our friend Dilber."

As he spoke, Muggins strode in to announce, "T' impressmen are 'ere."

A dozen river rats of the most disreputable kind had followed Muggins into the room. Lord Braden pointed out Dilber. "There's your man," he said.

Anemone ran to Wilfred and clung to him, but Lord Braden commanded her to stand aside. Terrified that he would carry out his threat to shoot the others, Mona obeyed. Piteously she wept and wrung her hands as the ruffians hoised the trussed Wilfred and bore him to the door.

"Say good-bye, young fellow," one of the press-gang said jeeringly. "You won't be seeing yer sweetheart agin. But don't worry . . . yer won't be lonely. We got us a fine haul for the King's Navy tonight."

When the impressmen had gone, Lord Braden took some money from his coat pocket and paid Nash and Muggins. In a voice pitched so that the sobbing Anemone could not hear, he ordered, "As soon as we're gone, throw the woman into the river. Weigh her down with rocks so that her body won't be found."

"Mind if we 'ave some fun with 'er first?" Muggins asked. He and Nash leered at her in a way that made Rosamund's skin crawl.

Lord Braden touched his cheek where Rosamund had slapped him yesterday. "Just make sure you kill her afterward."

He turned to Anemone and held out his arm. "Well, my dear—" he was beginning, when he was interrupted by a commotion outside. "Wot in 'ell's that?" Nash wondered aloud.

His words ended in a shriek as Hawkley lunged through

the door. Behind him, knife in hand, came Chief Storm Cloud.

"Coward and squab," announced the Mohawk. "I take your scalp."

There was the sound of a pistol shot, and simultaneously the lamp went out. The warehouse rang with howls, oaths, and the crashing of boxes and furniture.

The darkness reeled dizzily around Rosamund as eager hands tore aside her gag and slit her bonds. "You're not hurt? Those bastards didn't—? Answer me, Rosamund!"

He was here. Against all odds, Hawkley had come. "All right," she croaked. Then, drawing air into her lungs, she managed to gasp, "The press-gang have taken Mr. Dilber, Julian. Twelve of them—"

There was the sound of howls and whoops outside as well as yells and challenges in English. "Whomever you're talking about, they won't get far," said the earl.

He lit a match and relit the lamp, and Rosamund could see Muggins and Nash lying sprawled unconscious on the ground. There was no sign of Storm Cloud or anyone else.

"Mona," Rosamund cried. "Braden has taken Mona!"

"Stay here." Hawkley let go of Rosamund and bounded out of the house. Rosamund followed at his heels.

They erupted into foggy darkness. Here a battle was raging between the Mohawks and Lucy's footmen on one side and the press-gang on the other. Flying Crow was sitting on a prone ruffian's chest and pounding him. Lucy, standing on the box of her carriage, laid about her with a buggy whip. Rosamund could also see the portly figure of her brother standing on the sidelines together with Lady Orme.

Suddenly one of the press-gang broke away and grasping Lady Orme around the neck pressed a knife to her throat.

"Gerrout of 'ere or the old trout gets scragged," he threatened.

Lady Orme made terrified sounds as her captor began to edge away from the fight. Silver Beaver started forward, but the river rat shouted, "I mean what I say. Stay back—"

He squawked as he tripped over the umbrella extended by the Viscount Craye. As he fell, Silver Beaver lunged forward and caught the man by the throat.

"Oh, well done," crowed the viscount. "By Gad, got the blackguard. Er . . . are you all right, Mama-in-law?"

Lady Orme looked about ready to faint. For once she was bereft of speech and could only cling to the viscount's arm for support.

"Dangerous moment, that. By Gad, lucky I had my umbrella with me. Oh, I say, Julian, I see you've rescued m' sister."

"Rosa!" Lucy screamed. "Rosa, is Mona with you?"

Before Rosamund could do more than shake her head, Storm Cloud came running swiftly through the darkness. "Coward got away," he announced grimly. "Must follow!"

Rosamund's heart sank as she realized that Braden had escaped with Anemone as hostage. The closed carriage was not swift enough to overtake him. She turned to see what Hawkley was going to do and saw him making for his curricle.

Storm Cloud started to follow the earl, but Rosamund was quicker. She ran after him, calling, "Take me with you. I know what he plans to do."

Disregarding his emphatic refusal, Rosamund climbed into the curricle beside him. "Hurry," she pleaded.

The earl was about to say that nothing would induce him to take Rosamund on a mad and dangerous chase through the worst parts of London when Lady Orme intervened.

"Rosamund!" croaked her scandalized ladyship. "How can you act in such a brazen, coming way? No wonder you have horrified polite society. Get down from the earl's curricle *at once*."

Hawkley and Rosamund looked at each other. It was a fleeting but eloquent moment. Then Hawkley whipped up his grays and the curricle leaped forward.

As they careened together through the noisome darkness, Rosamund shouted, "How did you know where to find us?"

"Storm Cloud was walking by the river, saw you pass by in the hansom, and had you followed," the earl yelled back. "You were caper-witted to come after Braden alone. Must be short a sheet myself, taking you with me now. *Why* didn't you tell me you were going after Braden?"

"How could I when you had written to my brother saying that you had washed your hands of me?" she shouted back.

He turned to look at her. Her hair streamed like a coal black banner behind her, her eyes blazed with concern for Anemone. She was magnificent, Hawkley decided, and his heart expanded until it seemed as though it must crack his ribs.

"You said you knew what Braden's plan was," he bellowed at her. She told him. "A flight to the border—not original, but the only thing he could do under the circumstances. Who's Wilfred Dilber, anyway?"

"He is— Oh, do be careful," Rosamund cried as Hawkley guided the curricle past a hairpin curve. "It will never do to smash up your curricle when Mona needs us to save her."

Hawkley threw back his head and roared with laughter. "Any other woman would be fainting," he exclaimed.

And any other man would have been lecturing her on her unfeminine conduct. In spite of her anxiety for Anemone, in spite of the terrors and dangers of the night, Rosamund felt free—and happier than she had ever been before. But this sense of joy was short-lived as Hawkley pointed with his whip.

A landau loomed ahead of them, traveling fast. Grimly Hawkley set himself to overtake it. He was an accomplished whipster, but here was a severe challenge. To catch a desperate man on a foggy night in one of the most foul, narrow streets in London was no easy task.

He feather-edged his curricle around a narrow turn, and Rosamund said encouragingly, "You are gaining on him. We are much closer now."

Closer . . . closer still . . . And now they were forcing Lord Braden's carriage to the side of the road. Next moment, it had crashed against a wall.

Rosamund dismounted and flew toward the upended carriage, calling, "Julian, he has a pistol. Mona, oh, Mona, I'm here. Let go of her, you villain!"

Lord Braden, who had been attempting to drag Anemone out of the carriage, saw Rosamund advancing and drew a pistol from his belt. "Stand back," he warned.

It was the last thing he said before Hawkley closed with him. The pistol flew into the air, and Lord Braden collapsed onto the ground.

Rosamund, who was holding Anemone in a tight embrace, looked up to exclaim, "Oh, well *done*, Julian!"

On the heels of her triumphant cry came the sound of shouts and hoofbeats, and Lucy's carriage careened into view. Chief Storm Cloud jumped down from the still-moving carriage and ran forward, accusing, "I get here too late. You already kill him."

Hawkley smiled grimly. "He's very much alive." Then, as Storm Cloud advanced menacingly, he added, "No, Chief. This *gentleman* has a great deal of explaining to do."

"We make him talk," promised Storm Cloud.

Meanwhile, with fervent yells of "Anemone!" Wilfred Dilber was racing toward Anemone. Anemone freed herself from Rosamund's arms and ran toward him.

"Angel!"

"Beloved!"

"My baby!" Lucy trundled up to the entwined lovers and embraced them both, and next moment all three were clinging to one another and weeping with joy.

Rosamund sighed in deep satisfaction. "So," she murmured. "All's well that ends well."

"Not quite yet."

Hawkley was looking at Lord Braden, who was now sitting up and groaning. Lucy, with her arms tight about her daughter, snapped, "Tar and feather the bastard."

"Better yet, hang him," snarled Lady Orme.

"Give him to us," Storm Cloud said softly. "We know what to do."

As Silver Beaver and Flying Crow nodded, Lord Braden was seen to turn quite gray. "Hawkley," he quavered, "I demand that you protect me. You're an Englishman—"

The earl interrupted sternly, "You've forfeited any rights. Guilty of kidnapping and attempted murder. Mrs. Sample's footman has gone for the constables, but if you don't make an immediate confession, I'll hand you over to my Mohawk friends."

With his eyes on the Mohawks' eager faces, Lord Braden began to talk. He confessed to everything. He explained that because of enormous gambling debts, he had been in desperate need of cash. He had decided to marry Anemone for her money, and when Lucy had refused his offer, he decided to elope with Anemone.

But even before this, Lord Braden confessed, he had plotted to eliminate Anemone's sweetheart. Having arranged for Dilber to be kidnapped into the navy, he had sent the note to come to River Place. The timing was right, the plan was under way, and with Dilber out of the way, he had anticipated no problem in carrying Anemone off. But then Miss St. Helm had meddled once more.

Lord Braden shot a look of hatred at Rosamund, and Hawkley could hardly contain himself. He wished that he had broken the cur's neck when he'd had the chance.

Storm Cloud said hopefully, "He confessed. We get him now?"

With great reluctance, the earl shook his head. "I'm afraid not, Chief. We have to obey the law."

As he spoke, constables converged upon the scene and arrested Lord Braden. He surrendered with obvious relief and was heard to plead, as he was led away, that he be put in prison, where he could be safe.

There was a small silence. Then Anemone turned to Lucy. "Ma," she whispered, "I'm sorry I lied to you, but I love Wilfred. I don't want to marry anyone else."

"And so you won't," Lucy exclaimed. "I was a durn fool to think I wanted that skunk Braden for you just because he was a lord." She held out a hand to Wilfred. "Shake hands and say there ain't any hard feelings, young feller, and then let's go home and talk about you and Mona. Anyone who'd fight for my baby like you did tonight is all right by me."

The viscount offered Lady Orme his arm. "Lots of things happening tonight, by Gad," he said. "Exhausting. Best to go back to the inn and rest, Mama-in-law."

He turned to Rosamund. "I hope you're packed and ready, Rosa. London's a terrible city. The sooner I'm back in Kent the sooner I'll like it."

"Rosamund doesn't have to go back to Kent."

Everyone turned to look at Storm Cloud, who ignored them all and addressed Rosamund in dignified if fractured English. "No need to go back to brother's house," he repeated. "You fine woman. Come home to Canada with me, be my wife."

There was an absolute silence—during which Rosamund racked her suddenly numb brains for something to say. How could she refuse this offer without hurting Storm Cloud's feelings? But before she could marshal her thoughts, Hawkley had stepped to her side and put his arm around her.

"I'm very sorry, Chief," he said firmly, "but Miss St. Helm has already agreed to be *my* wife."

Rosamund gasped. Lady Orme's eyes dilated. Viscount Craye dropped his quizzing glass. Lucy shouted, "Really, Rosa? Well, if that don't beat all. At least *one* of you girls caught a lord."

But, of course, she was not going to marry Hawkley.

Rosamund stood by the dying fire in Lucy's drawing room and stared into the embers kindled against the evening chill. They stared back like wolves' eyes.

Hawkley had lied to save Storm Cloud's feelings. He had also come to her aid and had put paid to Lord Braden. She was grateful to him, and she would tell him so. And then she would go back home to Kent.

"It's high time," she murmured.

"Talking to yourself, now?"

Hawkley had come into the room. Apparently it had begun to rain, for raindrops shone on the shoulders of his coat and his damp hair glittered like bronze in the firelight. Rosamund felt the almost irresistible urge to run her fingers through that crisp, dark hair.

She put her hands behind her back and tried for a matter-

230

of-fact tone. "It's hard to believe it is all over," she said. "I never would have believed that a man could be so wicked."

"I should have told you the whole truth about Braden," Hawkley said, "but I'd given my word to keep silent. A lady's reputation was at stake."

"But if Lord Braden speaks of it now—"

"He's no fool." The earl came across to the fire to stand beside Rosamund and spread his hands to the blaze. "He knows the lady's husband is a very powerful man and can affect the outcome of his trial."

He rubbed his hands together as he resumed. "After our meeting at Boar Square, I went to see the lady in question. She gave me permission to reveal her secret to save Anemone from marrying Braden. There's no need for any disclosure now, so all I'll tell you is that when she met Braden, this lady was already a married woman. He filled her head with nonsense and persuaded her to run off with him, but he never really cared about her. Money was what he wanted."

Hawkley's eyes hardened as he recalled how he and the lady's brother had driven through a night and a day to stop them before they reached the border. "By then she was hopelessly compromised," he told Rosamund. "If her husband had found out, there'd have been the devil to pay."

"You should have shot the scoundrel," Rosamund exclaimed.

"I wanted to, believe me, but my friend knew that the scandal'd ruin his sister. He paid Braden off, instead, and the swine left for the Continent promising silence."

"And since no one else knew what he had done, he was received when he came back to England." Rosamund regarded the fire wrathfully. "Shooting is much too good for him."

"Chief Storm Cloud would agree with you." Hawkley's

stern face relaxed into a grin. "I escorted him and his braves back to their lodgings and stayed to have a brandy with them to toast our union."

She looked up quickly at that. "About that—" she began.

He interrupted her. "Storm Cloud made it plain that if he hadn't liked me, he'd have fought me for your hand and removed my scalp. I don't doubt it, either," he added as an afterthought. "The chief was quite impressive today against the river rats."

Then he looked at her and smiled. "But I would have fought him anyway," he told her. "I would have fought him for you."

Rosamund caught her breath at the sweetness of the earl's smile. "That is moonshine," she managed to say sternly. "Thank you for helping me, but you need not lie any further."

"Am I lying, Rosamund?"

He got up and stood so close to her that she felt breathless. "Aren't you?" she whispered.

For answer he put his arms around her and drew her so tightly against him that she felt as if he were imprinted against her body. His lips met hers in a kiss that was as elemental as the flames on the hearth.

"Am I lying?" he whispered against her lips.

"Yes—no—I don't know," she cried. He kissed her again. "When we last met, you said that I was a caper-witted hoyden."

"And you told me to go to Jericho. Those tender words are still ringing in my ears."

Rosamund winced. "It does not sound as if we would suit, Julian."

"Nonsense, we'll suit very well. We'll wrangle and fly

into a passion and kiss like this and make up. Oh, my love, marry me."

"But I'd bring disgrace on you. Your sister and your friends will be horrified if you marry the Wild Rose."

"To hell with my friends. I'm marrying you, not them." Hawkley paused before adding, "You see how you've changed me."

"Changed you?" she murmured, thinking that the firelight made his eyes glow and dance. "How have I changed you?"

"Too much for me to be happy without you in my life. Too deeply not to see that the things that I thought were important are really as empty as shadows. How can you fight shy and desert me now?"

Rosamund felt herself sinking fast, but she made one more attempt to rally. "I will never come up to scratch, Julian. As Lady Orme says, I am incorrigible."

He laughed at that. "Did you notice how meekly my lady took your brother's arm tonight? She's come to a different opinion of him since he saved her life. As to your being incorrigible, I'd rather have you as you are than anyone in the world. But there is one thing."

She watched him grow serious, almost stern as he went on. "It wasn't till this evening when Storm Cloud made his proposal that I realized just how impossible it must be for you to live in England. Too narrow for you, too full of prigs and fools. Why should *you* be forced to change your life when you're perfect just as you are? Why shouldn't you live where you're happiest?" He drew a deep breath. "After we're married, we'll go to live in Canada."

"To live in— But what of your estate and the title? What of—what of England?"

"None of that matters."

Rosamund felt as though her heart were soaring. She looked at the earl with shining eyes and told him softly, "It's not necessary, Julian."

"Yes, it is." Sternly he added, "I won't have you be homesick."

"You didn't let me finish. It's not necessary because I haven't been homesick for Canada for a very long time now."

"Truly?" Still holding her, he drew a little apart and looked intently down into her face. "Be honest with me, Rosamund. I want you to be happy."

It seemed to Rosamund that the night had unaccountably disappeared and that they were standing together in a meadow bright with dawn. Larks sang, dew glistened like pearls, and the sun rose into a cloudless sky.

"As long as I am with you," she told him joyously, "I will be happy. *You* are my home, Julian. And together we will show the world how happily a Wild Rose can bloom in an English garden."